D1565409

American Indian Literature
and Critical Studies Series

Gerald Vizenor and Louis Owens, General Editors

SURVIVOR'S MEDICINE

SURVIVOR'S MEDICINE

Short Stories

by E. Donald Two-Rivers

UNIVERSITY OF OKLAHOMA PRESS : NORMAN

This is a work of fiction. Names, characters, places, and incidents are either the product of the author's imagination or are used fictitiously, and any resemblance to actual events, locales, or persons, living or dead, is entirely coincidental.

Library of Congress Cataloging-in-Publication Data

Two-Rivers, E. Donald, 1945–
    Survivor's medicine: short stories / by E. Donald Two-Rivers.
        p.   cm. — (American Indian literature and critical studies series; v. 29)
    ISBN 0-8061-3092-X (cloth: alk. paper)
    1. Indians of North America—Social life and customs—Fiction.
2. United States—Ethnic relations—Fiction.   I. Title.
II. Series.
PS3570.W6S8   1998
813'.54—dc21   98-16758
                                                                                        CIP

Survivor's Medicine: Short Stories is Volume 29 in the American Indian Literature and Critical Studies Series.

The paper in this book meets the guidelines for permanence and durability of the Committee on Production Guidelines for Book Longevity of the Council on Library Resources, Inc. ∞

1 2 3 4 5 6 7 8 9 10

Dedicated to my people,
the Seine River Band of Ojibwe Indians of
Ontario, Canada, and to the
American Indian community in Chicago.

CONTENTS

ACKNOWLEDGMENTS

I'd like to extend my gratitude to the following people who gave me help, support, motivation, and love during the creation of this work:

Jacquelyn Kilpatrick, professor of Indian Studies at Governor's State University, who planted a seed and nourished it. She gave me encouragement and introduced me to Gerald Vizenor and Louis Owens.

My wife, the beautiful and talented Beverly Moeser, who believed in me enough to stick with me in this effort. Her love took me where I needed to be when I needed to be there. Much more than that a man cannot ask of a woman. Many thanks also to my eight wonderful children.

Michael M. Egan III, Tom Lenane, professor of speech and theater at Truman College, Terry Straus, professor of anthropology at the University of Chicago, Craig Howe, director of the Newberry Library, Ann Howe, Fred Harris of Joliet Junior College, and Bob Bolek, my fishing buddy and best friend. Thanks to all of these people for having faith in me.

Finally, I'd like to thank Truman College, truly a community college, for providing support and resources.

To all, a big thank-you. Megwitch, my friends and loved ones.

SURVIVOR'S
MEDICINE

"OH WAH! SUCH A SHINOB!"

"You know what?" she said "You'll always want to dance late at night in a dark kitchen."

"You think so?" I asked.

"Yeah, because that's what I taught you."

"Well, I like dancing with you, but I don't think I'd like dancing with a girl."

"Oh, you will, son. You definitely will." She laughed and I laughed with her, like mothers and sons sometimes do. It was a special moment in that dark kitchen. She filled my life with those moments. No matter how rough life got, my mom always managed to be a happy and smiling woman for us kids. She and her friends were all like that.

They were always teasing. Teasing each other, teasing their kids, teasing other women, and any man that happened to be around. Oh, how they loved to tease men, those five women—my mom and her friends. They'd talk about a man like he was a dog. Because of the way they talked about men, I used to run and hide whenever she'd tell me to act like a man. Why would I want to do that? The last thing I wanted was for her and her friends to be talking about me that way. On a serious note, though, my mother's style was to stand proud. She was among the women who depend on their own strength to carry them through. Women with red dresses and dancing shoes and kids. Hypnotic pow-wow women who laugh easily. Indian women who fall in love deeply and often. Women who know their own beauty and all that they can do. Mothers of the Anishanaabe Nation.

Oh, there were quiet moments too, when Mom would be sad and, perhaps, lonely. On those nights she'd send us to bed early and stay up late listening to her music. I'd lie in bed listening as she played her Hank Williams records over and over on the crank-up gramophone. She was a Hank Williams fan, all right. I'd hear her dancing by herself as she hummed along with the music. The kitchen floor creaked as she danced round and round in a world of her own. One night I startled her when I got up to pee. She didn't notice me until I spoke up.

"What are you doing, Mom?" I asked.

"Dancing." She smiled her sweetest Indian smile at me.

"With whom?" I asked.

"With whom?" she said, echoing me. "With a handsome young Indian man. That's with whom." She grabbed me and we danced with only the moonlight illuminating the room. I thought she was so beautiful. She brushed the hair out of my eyes and smiled the smile I knew had put many a man in dreamland. Hank Williams played on and on and we danced on and on as well.

I can recall a time in Sapawe when she and a couple of other Indian women sat under a birch tree beading, laughing, and, of course, gossiping. It was late in the summer, just before ricing time. She had put my little brother in his tickanogin and hung it from a tree branch. The wind rocked the tree gently. His eyes were heavy with contentment. That image burned itself into my mind as a fine definition of Indian: not the stoic Indian on a horse with fierce eyes and weapons and definitely not the Last Ride Indian, either. I've always hated that image of the vanishing race. It was my mom and her friends who made me dislike that story—and they were right.

Mom's friends were Indian women much like herself. There was "three-man" Deena, a half-breed named Toni whose French husband beat her a lot, and then Hilda, whom no man dared to beat lest he lose his family jewels while asleep. She too was a Hank Williams fan. "If that pretty-singing cowboy would come up here fishing," she'd say, "the only worm he'd need would be the one in his cowboy jeans." They'd all laugh that high-pitched laugh of Indian women. The kind that comes from a life of hardship. The kind that serves to release tension. The kind that starts deep inside a hardy soul. Then there was Verna's mother. A small woman with a big heart and the cutest flirting ways.

These women were good role models. They assumed their traditional role as leaders and made decisions that affected more than a dozen big-eyed, black-haired, brown-faced children. Everything they did, they did with a courage and a style that got things done. They did tasks as a group and were always laughing, teasing, or listening to Hank Williams's music on my mother's wind-up Gramophone. That Gramophone was truly her most prized possession and I was fascinated with it. I can't begin to count how many times I got slapped upside my head for messing with that machine.

The women would sit under that birch tree and sew countless items that were all dazzling to look at. There were jingle dresses and buckskin vests with flowered woodland Indian designs that made you stand proud. Sometimes they'd grab one of us kids and make us model for them. They were all artists in their own right and they knew it. They'd have you stand this way and that so they could view their creations. "Oh wah! Such a shinob!" they'd exclaim. Sometimes you'd think they were talking about you, but you'd be wrong. They were talking about their work or themselves. No matter though, the payoff was pure delight. They'd get a good laugh, then reward you with a hug and a kiss and maybe a chunk of bannock with strawberry preserves, made by my mom. Mighty good eating for a hungry little shinob.

Between them they had lots of kids. I guess we were raised in the traditional manner because they'd let us run free. With so many kids, of course, there were small tragedies. Someone would fall, a knee would bleed. Sometimes we'd play with too much enthusiasm and our combined creative energies would overwhelm us and fists would fly for real. We were mischievous children, excited by adventure and living in a paradise of granite and pine. No playground I have ever seen in urban life can match the gift Mother Earth gives to children blessed enough to have the freedom to enjoy it. Exploring the world around us certainly had its ups and downs, but a scraped knee or such was always worth it in the long run.

We were curious children and sometimes that got us into trouble. Once we found a bear cub off by itself and we started yelling and acting just like the cowboys we'd seen in movies. My mother and her friends went into a panic. They actually were screaming as they grabbed us. I could see my mom was really scared and so I offered no argument. They had all been raised on stories about bears and Anishanaabe people and I can tell you this much, those stones weren't about Smokey the Bear or Bambi. My mom cried as she smacked me with a red willow switch. She cried as she made me promise never to do that again. But I knew I would if I ever got the chance—and so did she.

Shortly after that incident, things changed: I was pushed out of the wigwam, so to speak, and into another world. I suppose it wasn't long after that I started combing my hair and buttoning up my shirt. I was entering a different world where every male relative had something to teach me about life, where concentration was demanded, where being a man meant doing a thing right and with just the right amount of respect. The survival instincts my mom had taught me were being reinforced with skills given me by my dad—and this was good. There were those moments, however, when I wished I was still a little boy who knew or cared about nothing but how much fun the world was, how warm the sun felt, or how good a glass of Kool Aid tasted. Of course, in those days we called Kool Aid "freshie," and if you remember that then you've dated yourself and you ain't no spring chicken. Not by a long shot.

Oh yeah, I remember my mom all right. I remember her with flour on her hands and dress. A woman who could throw a hook upside your head no matter how you dodged, no matter how you bobbed and weaved. It was always a hook thrown with love and you knew it so you forgave her as easily as she forgave you. I remember her cooking while singing along with Ole Hank. I remember all that laughing, teasing, and dancing. I remember her smiling at her image in the mirror—red dress and dancing shoes, on her way to the Saturday night Hoot and Holler Club. She turned this way and that way, inspecting herself. "Oh wah!" she'd say. "Such a shinob!" Forty-two years later, I remember Mom and say to myself, Such a Shinob, indeed!

JASON HIGH-FLYING

When it rained in Sapawe, mushrooms grew.
—Jason High-Flying (1887–1975)

He was dying and he knew it. It was happening just as he expected. He wasn't afraid. Although he did have a few minor regrets, he was essentially satisfied that he'd lived his life pretty much the way he wanted. He didn't fight death, he gave in to the process as a natural occurrence. Between waves of pain, he smiled at the irony of his situation. He was psychologically prepared to die. He found it odd that he felt more prepared for this than he had for any event in his entire life. He wondered, was this life, then? Had he spent eighty-eight years preparing to die? Maybe so, but I sure as hell lived, he reflected, as he turned his attention to the twelve-year-old boy who stood there, staring uncomfortably down at him.

The boy was small for his age—he looked maybe ten at tops. He wore a striped shirt and blue jeans. The kind with an elastic waistband. He hated those pants.

"You were named after me, boy. Do you know what that means?" the old man whispered feebly.

"Don't talk, Grandpa. They said you should relax," the boy answered.

Young Jason High-Flying was thinking hard about his grandfather. He understood the old man was about to die. He looked down at his scuffed running shoes, curled his toes, and squeezed his eyes real tight to keep from crying.

"I want you to be a good boy and help out your grand-mother. She's going to need you to be strong because my time is up. I'm checking out. I'm dying, my son."

"No you ain't. You're gonna get better, Grandpa. Here, take some medicine," Jason pleaded with the old man. He poured the thick liquid into a spoon. His eyes darted from the door to the window and back again in an attempt not to look at his grandfather. His voice was high-pitched with fear. "It'll make you feel better."

"I don't want anymore of that stuff," the old man whispered. "It's white man's medicine. Doesn't help me in the least."

"But grandpa, I don't want you to die. I love you."

"Look at me, Jason. Turn your head and look at me." He waited as the boy slowly turned his head. He saw the fear.

"I know you love me and I love you too, but it's time for me to leave this world." He coughed. His frail body shook as pain teared his every fiber. So, he thought, this is what it's like to die.

The young Indian boy watched his elder. Thoughts rushed through his mind. He saw the old Indian man sink back into the pillow. He reached down and straightened the blanket. The old man looked pathetic; he was sick, cranky, irritable, and dying ever so painfully. He'd always been a healthy man but when his health went, it went quickly. Jason never had the opportunity to adjust to that. It seemed so unfair: one day the old man was healthy, happy, and laughing, the next, he was lying in this bed, dying.

Jason looked down at the old man again and noticed the old man's eyes. Once crystal-clear with understanding, they were now clouded over by the searing pain that scorched his body. The old man returned his gaze and held out his hand. The boy took it in his own hand. He remembered those hands. They were skillful hands that had built canoes, beautiful snowshoes, and fine cabins. He remembered them as authoritative hands that could fix a bike or mete out punishment when necessary—which was on a rare occasion—or tenderly caress a scraped elbow. Jason sensed a flood of panic coming on. He wondered, what am I going to do without him? He's always been the one that knew everything. He was always there with an answer when I needed one. And now he's going to be gone. What am I going to do?

He noticed his hands were shaking. He felt too stiff with tension to move. His neck hurt and he knew it was from the tension. He glanced in the mirror and saw that his face had turned a little white. Tears were spilling over the rims of his eyes, which were red with grief. He wanted to be brave, but inside he hurt. He thought his heart would explode inside his chest. His nerves were dancing—not a pretty dance, but one that jangled his ability to think. It felt like an earthquake, he though. It was an earthquake and he had no place to run. Why am I thinking like this? Got to stop!

The room was shrouded in silence. Only the old man's slow breathing sliced through it. The old wind-up Big Ben clock that had sat on the dresser his entire life had stopped several months ago. Like some kind of omen. It was shortly after that the old man got sick, Jason recalled. He knew in his heart there was no connection, but still, he couldn't help but wonder. For a second, Jason hated that clock. He wanted to grab it and throw it against the wall, smash it into a hundred pieces. It sat there on the shelf like an ornament, its spring sprung, lifeless. Maybe if it worked again his grandfather would get better. He knew it was wishful thinking, but he took a step toward it.

The old man coughed again. Jason stopped, stood still. His hand reached out involuntarily to stroke the old man's hair. Jason shuddered when one finger, then two, and finally his whole hand touched the dying man. He shut his eyes and felt the damp skin on the old man's forehead. His silver-gray hair was matted against his frail skull. The old man opened his eyes and whispered the boy's name. Young Jason leaned closer to hear the old man's words that never came.

He looked at his head. The old man's eyes had sunken some and beads of sweat had gathered at his hairline. His brown skin sagged just below his ears. When the old man had grown sick the skin on his face had lost much of its luster. His skin had continued to wither until it now clung, wax-like and pale, to a skeleton that had once provided him with a more robust and energetic frame. The boy let his fingertips linger on his elder's jaw. He felt the muscles twitch a bit and heard his grandfather sigh weakly.

The old man knew the end was very near and yet he felt good. Better than he had during the last two years when the pain had stolen his life, gradually sucked away his vitality, pleasure by pleasure, organ by organ. First his legs and then his heart, but he smiled to himself because he'd managed to keep his senses. He'd known what was happening at all times and for that he was thankful. His one fear was that he'd become a vegetable. At least he'd avoided that. He'd decided when he would die and felt as if he was actually ahead of the game. A few regrets, he thought to himself. The boy, he thought, I hope I did good with the boy. And the novel I started and had done all the research for. That was one thing he regretted not finishing. But what's to be done, he thought, as another wave of pain hit his tired body.

Jason watched his grandfather's gnarled knuckles clench into feeble fists as pain smashed against his body. The old man groaned. Young Jason's own hands trembled as he tightened them into balls of rage. Why, God? Why now? Why can't you let him live? What kind of God are you anyway? I hate you, God. He clenched his teeth and eyes to keep from yelling or crying. He felt ravaged to his heart by this pain. He became aware that his throat was hurting again. He felt an attack of guilt flush through him. His grandfather had spent years teaching him to respect and appreciate the work of the Great Spirit. Even now, he smelled the acrid odor of the sage and cedar that burned in the room. Spirituality permeated the room.

The boy looked into the small, cracked mirror that sat on the table next to the bed. He smiled to himself as he recalled the image of himself and the old man sitting beside the lake as his elder talked to him about life. The old guy always had a way of making things crystal clear and easy to understand. He was an excellent storyteller. He looked down at his elder now as he lay there. He was always full of steam, the boy thought. Laughing and teasing in a quiet voice as they walked through the woods. He had always been ready and willing to take the boy on camping trips or just paddling in the canoe all day and sleeping wherever they landed. The old guy was always raring to go and so when the sickness first started the boy noticed it right away. He noticed how his grandfather had grown weak and devitalized. When the old man started coughing every morning and spitting up blood, the boy knew something was wrong. Both he and his grandmother had started worrying over the old man, but he had insisted he was okay.

"Leave me alone," he had protested. "You're treating me like a baby."

"But Grandmother told me to make sure you take your medicine. She said you needed it," Jason had replied.

"What I need is a good stiff shot of whiskey. Be a good boy and go get it for me, would you?"

"She said she threw it away, Grandpa. That's what she told me."

"She wouldn't do that. I know her. Go look in the cabinet under the sink."

"Well, I can't get it for you. Open up your mouth. Here's your medicine."

He could remember that day clear as a bell. He stood looking at his elder. His thoughts darted frantically between life and death. His emotions leaped from fear to love and then hopped to pride. This was his grandfather, the man who was respected by everyone around him. The man who had carried him on his shoulders, who had taught him to ride a bike and set a snare. This was the man who had taught him about life, and now he was dying.

The old man could barely hear anything going on around him. He couldn't focus his eyes, but he knew the boy was there with him and that gave him comfort. They'd always been able to communicate. He gritted his teeth as another wave of pain washed over him.

Tears ran freely now down the brown face of the boy. He experienced a sensation of intense pride that his elder uttered no cry of pain. Like his grandfather, young Jason bore his pain and sorrow in silence. He wished he could stop the old man's pain. He wished he could stop the tears that slipped from his own eyes. He silently prayed for some delay—a little time, a minute more, just one minute more—but he knew, he understood somewhere deep down inside of him that it couldn't be. He recalled some words the old man had said to him.

"Break the chains of your thought and you break the chains of your body, too." Young Jason wondered if death was like breaking some kind of chain, then he just wished it was all over and the old man could relax. He realized with a start that he was ready for the old man's death.

The old man heard the others enter. He heard his wife's soft sobbing and wanted to hug her. What a great woman, he thought. She made life good, she put up with me. Then he heard his son—his first born, the one who is all business. He heard the boy's mother, his daughter-in-law, whom he'd come to love as his own daughter. He remembered his son—her husband, the boy's father—who had been killed in a Chicago bar fight. He was the carefree one, the wild one, he recalled. He lived life too hard and too fast. He wasn't bad, just too damned happy-go-lucky.

With an effort that came from deep inside, the old man forced his eyes open. The image of his family floated before him. He smiled happily. His wife leaned down and kissed him gently. They all heard him sigh. In her hand, she held a water glass half filled with her husband's favorite whiskey. She turned and looked at Jason, a smile on her face.

"Give this to the ornery old bastard," she said as she handed him the whiskey. She smiled again. "You know this is what he wants." Her chin quivered slightly and she continued. "Life was good with him. I loved him all the way."

Jason nodded at his grandmother, hugged her, then turned to place the glass at his grandfather's lips. The boy was sure his grandfather was smiling as he opened his mouth. Jason slowly gave him the whiskey. He swallowed deeply. His body shook ever so slightly. The young boy heard his labored breathing—a quiet wheezing. His body shook again as the shock of the whiskey hit. Jason heard the weak, sighing cough, and then the twelve-year-old Indian boy heard silence. An absolute quiet filled the room. He sensed the end had come. He knew his grandfather was gone.

Another flood of tears ran down young Jason's cheeks as he put his arm around his grandmother and joined her in a soft chant. The rest of the family joined in and old man Jason High-Flying went to the next plane of existence, a happy man. Young Jason was about to pass into another phase of his life as well. He walked over to the shelf, picked up the clock, and studied it for a long time. Then he put it down gently and went outside to get some fresh air. The cold air felt good.

Old Jason High-Flying died early one January morning in 1975. It was a cold, crisp morning and the eastern sky glowed with a warm red hue. Daylight was sliding across the lake as it always did. Jason watched it getting lighter as he stood outside the cabin. Dawn's purple shadows seemed to linger a moment longer than usual. Jason noticed the shadows and thought to himself, what now?

He felt alone. The silence around him seemed to amplify his sense of loneliness. Then he heard a bird singing. It was welcoming in the new day, as it had always done. He knew he'd miss the old man but life would go on. He smiled to himself because he realized he had to piss.

HAROLD BALL

As you can well imagine, living in Chicago you get to meet a lot of characters. Like this guy I met named Harold who struck me as kind of odd. I saw the man go through changes and I hope he became a better person because of them. Well, to tell you the truth, I know the bastard did. There's a few things about Harold I need to tell you up front. The first is that Harold Ball felt cheated by life, plain and simple.

He wasn't a big guy, but he looked solid. He didn't have a sense of rhythm but that never did make any difference to the people who cared about him. Nevertheless, he liked to point that out. He was also probably the most intolerant black person I or anybody else will ever meet—at least that's what he'd tell you. He's something of a legend on the North Side because he once talked a despondent Arab out of committing suicide on his bus. Of course Harold claimed it was because he didn't want to have to go to court to testify. The city gave him some kind of medal for it. Harold said he threw it away. His wife said he has it hanging on his mirror in their bedroom. I'll bet his wife was telling the truth. Finally, he was so full of contradictions it was hard to figure out sometimes if you liked the son-of-a-bitch or hated him. Sometimes I just wanted to stay away from him, but that was hard to do because he showed up at the oddest of times. The man's favorite word was *hate*—at least to hear him tell it. He claimed he wasn't biased because he hated everybody the same.

Harold drove a bus for his living. He claimed to hate his job. He hated noisy teenagers, especially black girls and Mexicans. Didn't love his wife but didn't hate her. He hated the things she had done. Her friends all felt sorry for her because she was married to Harold. He hated most of them. He hated the *Chicago Sun-Times* because of its conservative writing, yet he read it every day without fail. He also hated the *Chicago Tribune* because of the way it was folded. He read it every day as well. You'll notice a lot of CTA (Chicago Transit Authority) bus drivers do that. They like to stay informed, I guess. There they'll be, kicked back and reading a paper while your mother is waiting for a goddamned bus on the corner with the wind blowing and goofy-looking dudes driving by blowing their horns at her. Yeah, Harold claimed to hate both rags but he read them like the Bible. He even read the ads. But that was typical of Harold—contradictions seemed to be a part of his life.

He wouldn't go to church. In fact, he proudly informed everyone who would listen that he hadn't been in one since he'd gotten married. He once said he thought his wife was having an affair with her church's preacher. Harold was drunk when he said it so no one paid him much mind. I met his wife twice. He was a lucky bastard to have her, as far as most of his friends were concerned.

Harold's bus route was the 151 Sheridan, second shift. He hadn't missed a day in fifteen years. He was a working man and prided himself on that fact. He'd driven that route for fifteen years, four-thirty to twelve, every day. Rain, shine, or snow, he drove that route and he knew every bump and pothole. Harold was sitting with Oliver, another bus driver, in a restaurant at Foster and Sheridan, waiting to take over his bus. He knew he would hate tonight's traffic.

"So Jesse Jackson says that 'poor people are not black or brown, they are white, they are female, and two-thirds are children.' Ain't that something?" said Oliver, as he read the newspaper spread out on the table. It was the start of their shift.

"He be bullshittin' too," Harold answered dryly.

"It says it right here," Oliver answered, pointing at the newspaper.

"I read it, I know what it says. But he ain't said shit. What makes him so righteous? Out there always talking about this and that. I don't like no peoples like that."

"It's the message brother, not the messenger. The message is good. The dude's right on track."

"Anyway, who the hell made him the spokesman for every nigger in this country? He did, that's who! Where's he live at anyway?" Harold asked. "I bet in some fancy suburb. He ain't never ridden on my bus."

Oliver ignored him.

"I really liked the part about what he calls the higher realm. He be talking right on, man. Character, brother! That's what we need to be looking for. We need to be looking past the goddamned color of skin and be seeing into each other's hearts. We need to see each other's character. Hell, when I was in Nam and the shit was coming down, do you think I cared about color or culture? Hell, when Charlie got to laying down his law on us, I couldn't give a damn about the color of the soldier next to me as long as he had on the same uniform. At that point, I'll tell you, when you be in a war, peoples just forgets about color. We was all Americans together. The other shit was forgotten about. I didn't care where the next guy was from. Didn't mean shit to me—or him either. I had a white guy save my ass once. That's why I don't pay no mind to that racial shit. Mostly idle talk. When things get really bad, then the real deal comes down. I'm here to tell you, race don't mean shit then." Oliver got up to get another cup of coffee.

"Take the receipt. She'll give you a free refill," Harold reminded his friend. As Oliver walked away Harold peered down Sheridan Road to the south. He was looking for the bus whose driver he would relieve. I hope she's running late, he thought. She needs to be written up. I don't know why no woman wants to be driving no bus. She should be home tending to her babies. As Oliver sat back down, Harold told him how he felt about woman bus drivers in general and the day driver in particular.

"Oh shit, man. You sound like some kind of caveman grunting around when you talk like that. This is 1997, boy. Wake up and smell the coffee. You got to admit she holds her own. She don't take no shit. Not even from you. You got to admire that."

"I don't got to do nothing but pay taxes and die. Don't be telling me what I got to do. I think she's one of them there bulldaggers the way she be so anti-man."

"Oh, man!" Oliver laughed. "She's got three kids."

"Why ain't she got no man?"

"She got a man. Remember that Oriental fellow? Don't you remember last year at the Christmas party? That was her man," Oliver explained.

"That ain't saying nothing about her. Not really. Look how she be the rest of the time," Harold countered.

"They got three beautiful kids together. He's a machinist somewhere. I think he said Elk Grove Village up north. Hell bro, he makes his. They be doing pretty good. They're trying anyway."

"Then how come she be so damned uppity with men?"

"You mean with you, right?" Oliver said as he stirred his coffee.

"Okay, then, tell me why she got to marry a Chink? She should be married to a nigger. Isn't that what she is?"

"I don't know about you sometime. Hell, this is 1997."

"So what it's 1997? Why don't she marry her own kind?"

"You know she's half-Indian too. I heard her tell you that one time," Oliver said.

"I don't believe that." Harold reached in his shirt pocket and continued. "Why would anyone want to be saying they be Indian? White man done took care of his ass. Why hell, them there Indians ought to just stay on the reservations and admit they be lucky to be alive. They all be a bunch of drunks."

"Don't even go there," Oliver warned. "My momma is half-Indian."

"Why all these niggers be saying they be part-Indian?"

"Jesus Christ, man, you are really a work of art. I'm going to bring you a book by this dude William Katz. It's called *Black Indians*. It tells a part of history that you never going to learn in school. Hell, you probably got some Indian in you too. Most people in this country do. It's just not mentioned in the history books."

"Here comes my bus. I got to go." Harold began gathering up his gear.

"See you at Laurie's for a quick one, okay? I'm buying."

"Maybe. I don't know. Yeah, okay. I'll be there." Oliver shook his head and laughed.

Harold's first run went without incident. Mostly working folks wanting to get their square asses home, he thought to himself as he pulled the bus up to a stop sign. Now he was heading south, his second time around. The riders had all changed. They were mostly young people heading out for the evening. A lot of them were students heading to night school.

As he drove, he recalled the words in the *Sun-Times* article that reported Jackson's speech at an all white school, about young black males and jails. "They come out of jail sicker and slicker and conditioned to recycle their pain," he had said.

Recycle their pain is right. Recycle it right back on other poor folks, Harold thought. There's more black-on-black crime in this city than needs to be, but according to Jackson it's the poor white women who are victimized the most. Then how come there's so much black-on-black crime? I be willing to bet most of those black-assed criminals ain't never robbed a white person. Harold smiled to himself at the thought. Those bad-assed niggers be robbing their own kind. It don't take no social scientist to figure these things out. Screw them, he thought, they ought to be locked up. Harold had a lot of misgivings about life, and crime was one area where he had definite concerns. His feelings about these guys, which he realized were partially irrational, were based on the fact that he had once been the victim of an armed robbery carried out by some young guys, one black and the others white. Recalling that humiliating night, he pulled the bus over roughly at Sheridan and Argyle where a young couple with two small children waved him down. The bus rocked as he screeched to a halt.

"Get on if you're getting on," he called out loudly. Look like Spanish to me, he thought. Both of them walked onto the bus with a child in their arms. They walked past the fare box and neither of them paid.

"Hey!" Harold called out sharply. "You got to pay." Wonder who the hell he thinks he is? Showing off for his woman. Harold didn't have a lot of patience when it came to what he referred to as "them foreigners." "They just take American jobs," he always said. Here we got nearly a million niggers ain't working and these folks come marching in here willing to work for near nothing. They be coming in here from Mexico, Poland, and even from Ireland. No wonder the Honky wants to hire him, he thought as he looked into the rearview mirror. The young man was putting his wife and kids into a seat.

"Hey, you! Amigo, you didn't pay. Ain't no one rides for free on my bus."

The young man looked up and nodded to Harold. Harold glared and pointed at the fare box. The young man looked at Harold intently, embarrassed by the implication. He stuck up his index finger to indicate he'd be right there. That son-of-a-bitch, Harold thought as his blood pressure went up two notches. He tapped on the fare box impatiently.

He glanced at a young, professional-looking black woman who had a pile of books on her lap. She'd gotten on at Berwyn and Sheridan. Harold knew she was heading for Truman College. She looked at Harold. Her large brown eyes snapped away sharply. Harold let his gaze slide down her body as he admired her Coke-bottle figure. She noticed him, snapped her legs tightly together, and looked out the window. What's wrong with her? Thinks she's hot shit, Harold concluded as he glanced back at the young man who was making his way to the front of the bus to pay.

"Ain't no one rides for free, Amigo!"

"I'm not your Amigo there, pal. I wasn't trying to ride for free. I was merely making sure my family was okay." The young man checked Harold with his flawless English. It made Harold look at him more closely.

The first thing Harold noticed was his shoes. They were Stacey Adams. He noticed that because they were his favorite brand. Then he saw the expensive black silk shirt and slightly faded, black Levi's jeans. Harold noticed that the young man wore a faded—or bleached—Levi's jacket with beadwork on it. He had long black hair neatly braided into a ponytail. Harold noticed a blue-and-white bone choker around the man's neck. He was digging in his pocket for the fare. Their eyes met and Harold glared at him defiantly. He didn't understand it, but he was going through some kind of emotional change. So I was wrong—he ain't no Mexican. But the sucker sure is an arrogant fellow. The young man returned his glare. Not blinking or yielding, he stared straight back into Harold's eyes. Harold blinked and looked away to check the road. The young man smiled.

"Rough night?" he asked in a soft but confident voice.

"And it's still early." Harold grunted by way of an answer. He looked at the young man who was smiling sympathetically. Harold felt less threatened—or whatever it was that he'd formerly been feeling.

"Yeah, I bet it's tough out here. I don't think I could deal with it myself."

At that moment, Harold noticed a car half a block away. He instinctively focused his attention on his driving. Probably going to pull out. Got to watch the son-of-a-bitch. People always in such a rush to get nowhere. His instincts proved correct. The car shot across the lane, heading in the opposite direction. Harold touched the brake and he tensed, ready to swerve if necessary. "Asshole," he said as he held the bus under control, avoiding hitting the car broadside.

"Nice driving," the young man commented.

"Thanks. I got to be on my toes all the time out here," Harold answered.

"Got to be tiring."

"Oh man, if you only knew," Harold laughed, almost bitterly. The young Indian man finished paying the fair and returned to his family. Harold watched them in his rearview mirror. The man's two-year-old son climbed on his lap, excited about the sights.

"Look at that! Look at that!" the child exclaimed. The little boy reminded Harold of his own kids, now fully grown and out of the house. He smiled as he thought of his kids. They didn't turn out half bad, he thought, as a feeling of contentment began to spread through his body. At Wilson, the pretty young woman pulled the stop cord.

"Have a nice night," Harold remarked as she stepped off the bus. She didn't reply or acknowledge him in any way. Screw you too, Harold said softly to himself. He pulled into traffic and forgot about the stuck-up woman.

At Sheridan and Montrose a small crowd of riders waited. It had just started to rain lightly. Not much more than a slight drizzle, but Harold knew what it would do to traffic. People just can't drive in rain or snow, he thought. He pulled the bus over with a jerk. Three young teenage girls, one black and two white, boarded. They were talking and laughing. Harold stiffened. He glanced in the rearview mirror and noticed several of the riders shifting uncomfortably. He shut the door and pulled away a little quicker than he had intended to. He didn't like teenagers like these ones. They ought to be in their houses doing their homework, he thought. Probably going to the Century Mall at Clark and Diversey to look at boys and who knows what else. As the bus jerked into the traffic, the girls let out a scream and one of them swore.

"Shit!" she said, "Can't you drive a little more careful?"

"What did you say?" Harold asked.

"Nothing!" she answered curtly.

"You keep on using foul language and I'll put you off this bus. You understand, young lady?"

The girls made their way toward the back of the bus. Harold cursed at the way they were dressed. Damned pants could fit me, he thought. They dress like a bunch of bums. A young girl should try to look pretty and sophisticated. Those baggy pants with the butt hanging below her knees look totally silly. The belt line was below her hips, revealing a pair of boxer underpants with spots on them. Harold looked back again to see if he was really seeing what he thought he was seeing. Those are boys' underwear she got on. What the hell is that all about? And that hair, he thought, got so much gel in it. Must be two gallons of axle grease on that head. The girls sat down and immediately began chattering and snapping their bubble gum. One of them started making funny faces at the Indian baby. The baby squealed with delight and cooed. Harold cursed under his breath and thought about telling them to leave the other riders alone. The Indian parents were smiling and began talking with the girls. The girl reached over and the woman handed her the baby. She began tickling it. Everyone was smiling. As he drove, Harold watched the scene. He wondered how come they were all so friendly.

Marine Drive was all torn up so Harold had to make a scheduled detour down Pine Grove to Addison, then over to

Broadway as far south as Belmont. It added an extra fifteen minutes to his trip but he didn't mind because he got to see the sights on that street. What a bunch of liberal freaks, he thought as he expertly wheeled the bus through the congested traffic. At Broadway and Belmont two gay men got on his bus. They made him feel uncomfortable. Oliver often teased him and said gays made Harold uncomfortable because he was a latent homosexual. A closet queen, Oliver had said. Harold sometimes had questions about Oliver himself. Like with the Oriental guy, the husband of his day driver. As far as Harold was concerned, Oliver was just too damned accepting of others. A bleeding liberal of some sort.

Harold wondered how the hell Oliver could be so supportive of the couple when just a few years ago he'd served in Viet Nam and was paid to kill guys that looked just like him. When he asked Oliver about it, the friendly-natured bus driver had laughed.

"Ain't nobody wanted to be in the war. We was all in the same boat. It wasn't my war. I got drafted." That answer hadn't satisfied Harold. It seemed too pat and shallow.

"Would you let us know when we get to the water tower?" one of the gay guys asked.

"It'll be on the right. You can't miss it."

"Well, sir, we're strangers here."

You ain't kidding, Harold thought, stranger than hell if you ask me.

"Well?" the gay guy asked.

"Well, what?" Harold shot back. His body stiffened and he gripped the steering wheel tighter.

"I want you to announce when we get to the water tower. It's your job, isn't it?"

"My job is to drive this bus. I'm not a tour guide. Would you take a seat?"

"God, what an attitude! You should take a course in public relations. You don't have to bite my head off."

"Just take a seat or I'll have to ask you to leave this bus," Harold responded somewhat impatiently. Then in a low voice, he added, "Goddamned faggot."

"What did you say? What did you just call me?"

"I didn't call you nothing. Now take a seat."

"You called my friend a faggot," the second guy spoke up. "You are not allowed to say stuff like that."

"Would you please take a seat?" Harold had lowered his voice. Several of the riders were leaning forward to hear the exchange.

The second gay guy stood up. "I'm calling the bus company about you. What's your badge number? Get the name off his tag," he said to his friend.

"I'm going to have to ask you to leave this bus," Harold said as he pulled over at Sheridan and Diversey.

"I am not going anywhere. I paid and you insulted me by calling me a derogatory name," the first gay man said.

"You don't get off this bus, I'll kick your ass." Harold hadn't meant to threaten him, but it slipped out. He was getting enraged.

"And how do you think you're going to do that?" the guy asked with a laugh.

Harold looked closely at him. A well-built guy, he didn't flinch.

"Look, old man, you know and I know you can't kick my ass, so why don't you just drive the bus and I'll forget this whole ugly affair."

Harold glared at the guy. He didn't budge. Harold felt an agonized pang pass through him. Son-of-a-bitch, he thought. He's right, I probably can't kick his ass.

"Well, if you'll take a seat I'll drive."

"I'll do that as soon as you apologize."

Goddamned militant faggot. "Okay, okay. I'm sorry. I'll tell you when we get to the water tower. You get off at Chicago Avenue."

The gay guy stood his ground a minute more. His friend was urging him to sit down.

"Come on, just let it slide. He's an old guy."

"Like I'm getting sick of this shit. I have rights too."

Harold heard the two talking but was not able to respond even though they were calling him an old fart and several other things he didn't particularly care to hear. His mind was racing about a thousand miles an hour as he tried to concentrate on his driving.

He recalled a time he'd gone to the lake early in the morning to think. Some young guys walked up to him and asked for a cigarette. There were three of them. Harold handed one guy his pack and the guy put it in his pocket.

"Hey dude, what's up with you?" Harold asked.

"What do you mean?" the young guy said with a cocky grin on his face.

"You got my cigarettes in your pocket."

"You gave them to me. Made a donation to my cause. Right?"

Harold looked at the three of them. Petty-ass punks. They're going to take my cigarettes? No way! Harold considered grabbing the guy by the throat. He hesitated for a moment and the leader laughed.

"Old man, I wouldn't even think about it. You'll get your ass kicked. Why don't you just get on out of this park?" The smirk on his face irritated Harold. "I said get on out of this park before we decide to take everything you got."

Harold noted that one of the guys had edged over to the left where he picked up a good-sized stick. It was about the size of a baseball bat. The other guy moved to the right and took off his belt.

"So, what are you going to do old man?" the punk with the cigarettes asked.

Harold started backing away. The guy with the stick started to advance. The one who had removed his belt stepped further to the right and moved toward Harold. The leader stood his ground and smirked at Harold.

"You better get on out of here before we hurt you bad, old man. Get your old ass on out of here."

"You just going to take my cigarettes?" Harold asked.

"That's right, old man. I done took them."

Harold put up his hands and started to walk away. The punk grinned and relaxed. The other two, his sidekicks, stopped their advance toward Harold.

"Yeah, old man. Get out of here like he said," the one holding the stick recommended.

Harold walked away. Inside he was steaming and his face felt flushed. What is this? he wondered. This is the first time I've ever been victimized. What is it? Am I getting soft? Why didn't I just grab that punk and beat the shit out of him. It's what I would have done in the past. I must be getting old. My age must be showing.

Suddenly Harold slammed on the brakes and pulled hard on the steering wheel of the bus.

"Shit!" he said as he just missed a car that had turned sharply in front of him. "Goddamned assholes."

"Hey, why don't you take it easy? Don't you know how to drive?" It was the gay guy.

Harold turned and looked long and hard at the guy. He returned Harold's glare with his own.

"Okay. You want to try me, punk?" Harold said as he stood up and stepped away from the driver's seat. "Come on then."

"What are you doing, old man? You're going to get yourself beat into a heart attack, that's what." Both of the gay guys stood up threateningly.

Suddenly the young girl who had been holding the baby spoke up. "Sit down you sissies. He's an elder. Ain't you learned no respect for elders?" She got up and walked toward the front of the bus.

The young Indian man had handed his child over to his wife. The baby slept on the seat. He also stood up and walked to the front of the bus. "Come on guys, take it easy. We don't need this, do we?"

"I can handle this." Harold said.

"But you don't have to, guy. Does he, fellows?" he asked as he turned to the two gay men.

"Well, he should learn some respect. We paid to ride. Look how he's driving."

"Hey, it's not his fault traffic is so heavy, now is it, guys? Why don't you just sit back down and relax? Okay?"

The gay guy stared at the Indian for a long time, trying to decide what to do. When he made up his mind he spoke.

"No. No, it's not okay. Come on Jerry." He said to his friend, "Let's just catch a cab. I've had enough of these ethnics. See how they stick together. Grease balls."

"Look, guys, this isn't about color. Why you have to bring up ethnics is beyond me," the young Indian said.

"The hell it isn't!" one of the gay guys responded.

He turned to the young girl and said, "Bitch!"

"Faggot!" she shot back as she snapped her bubble gum.

Several of the riders started to laugh.

"Tell him, honey," someone spoke up.

"That's not necessary," the young Indian guy said to the girl.

"Well, he started it," she replied, but turned to go back to her seat.

"Come on, Jerry, I've had enough of this. Let's catch a cab. Let me off of this bus."

Harold opened the door and the two gay guys got off. Both cussed at Harold as they jumped down from the bus.

"You okay?" the Indian asked Harold.

"You could have whipped the both of them if you had to." It was the young girl. She looked out the window and stuck up her finger at the two men. They returned her gesture, plus some. Another night, Harold sighed.

"Yeah. I'm all right. I'll be okay." He turned to the other riders and offered his apology. No one said anything as Harold sat back down and put the bus in gear. Harold noticed that his hands were shaking. His knees felt weak. Two more months and I can retire, he thought. He and his friends were planning a big party at Laurie's on Broadway and Foster. A lot of bus drivers hung out there.

Once I retire, I'm getting my ass out of Chicago, I can tell you that much. I hate it here. Harold stopped for a moment and rethought his last thought. No I don't. All these years I thought I did, but really I don't. In fact, I kind of like it. He remembered the words in the article about Jesse Jackson's speech to a bunch of white kids. Too bad they couldn't have had this experience that we all just went through. You know, maybe Jackson's got a point, Harold thought to himself, maybe he's got a point. Character. That's where it's at. The Indian got character and that young white girl too. If that ain't character, I don't know what is, he thought. Respect your elders. Now that's character, he thought, despite the baggy pants and her daddy's underwear. Even those two gay guys. They was willing to stand up for what they believed in and get their gay asses whipped if they had to or, maybe, whip some old foolish ass. The last thought made Harold just a bit uncomfortable, but he dismissed it with a smile. They had character as well. Hell, everybody got character. We just need to see it, that's all. This whole city's full of people with character. Just got to be looking for it.

He started whistling. He looked into the rearview mirror at his customers. A bunch of nice people, he thought to himself. The three girls were gabbing excitedly and snapping their gum as they eyed young boys walking down Michigan Avenue. The Indian held his baby and rocked him gently. His other child, the two-year-old, sat on his mother's lap and looked out the window.

"Look at that! Look at that! Mommy, what's that?"

"It's life, boy!" Harold whispered in answer to the child's innocent question. He decided then and there to invite everyone on the bus to his retirement party. They might even come, he thought to himself.

I remember Harold's retirement party. Everyone was there. For an old guy who claimed to hate everyone, he sure turned out a good crowd. The small bar was full of people from every race. It was a multicultural event, the kind that some social scientist might spend big bucks to create, and it was all about old Harold.

Oliver and the woman bus driver were laughing about a time when Harold had gone off on her about some nearly forgotten incident. The Arab guy whom Harold had saved was uncovering a large tray of dolmas, which are rice and hamburger wrapped in olive leaves or something, that his wife had made. A Mexican with a CTA uniform was helping out the bar maid. I was sitting at the bar with my date telling her about how Harold always bitched about everything I ever wrote and said I was a dreamer. Harold, well, Harold was at the other end of the bar being all sentimental and slobbery. His wife and the preacher were cutting a cake with a bus on top of it. The three young girls and the Indian couple were sitting at a table laughing about the time Harold had stood down the mean-assed gay guys. I listened to the sound of everyone recounting their experiences with old Harold. It was a happy sound. I looked over at him. He was hugging Oliver and handing him an envelope.

"What's this?" Oliver asked.

"It's that there newspaper article that changed my life." Harold answered. "Let me read it to everyone."

"Listen up everyone." Oliver yelled, " Old Harold's going to read something to us." Well, Harold started reading but he never got to finish because when he got to his favorite part, he started crying. The joint was absolutely silent. The only sound that could be heard was the traffic on the street. Oliver took the article and finished the part that Harold couldn't. He read out loud. "—A higher realm, and that's character." Harold blew his nose noisily and someone started singing,

"For he's a jolly good fellow, for he's a jolly good fellow." I looked over at Harold and the son-of-a-bitch was grinning and crying at the same time. His wife had her arm around him. For he's a jolly good fellow all right, I thought to myself, as I wiped a tear from my eye. My date leaned over and whispered a promise I won't repeat here, but for all you guys, sometimes it's good to let the opposite sex see your softer side. Harold leaned over and kissed his wife, then looked at me and winked. That's the last time I seen him but when I do see him again and I show him this story, I bet he'll say he hates it. But I know what he'll do: he'll fold it away and put it in his wallet. That's Harold, the retired 151 Sheridan CTA bus driver for ya.

THE HORSE BARN
AND LITTLE LADY JANE

I don't know what made her the maddest, the fact that I landed on my feet or that her hand landed in a steaming pile of fresh horse shit, but that little Indian girl Verna sure was mad, and what's more, she stayed that way. I guess she had placed too much trust in me and I messed it all up. She found that very hard to forgive. If you know Indian females, then you know what kind of hell they can put you through. Those snapping eyes and rude little remarks can cut your feet out from under you when you least expect it. Well, that's how Verna got with me.

Verna was a cute little brown-eyed, black-haired Indian girl. As children growing up in Sapawe, Ontario, we hung out together. I guess she could be called my first sweetheart. I don't remember much about her parents except that sometimes on the weekends they would drink a lot. They would fight—and I mean in public. That's how I first got to know her real well. It was a long time ago, but as close as I can remember, it went like this:

One day, I was walking home from school and I saw a group of kids surrounding this one girl. They were teasing her about her parents because another of their family fights had gone public. As I got closer, I could see that she was virtually helpless against these kids. She was crying and begging them to leave her alone. My heart went out to her right there and then. So I intervened. I ran them off and she looked at me with these big tears in her eyes. She seemed so grateful. She thanked me in our language and that small act cemented our friendship.

It's not that I was being this nice guy or anything like that, but in this case, I would have fought that entire group of kids to make them leave her alone. Usually, I was as bad as the worst of them. I teased a lot, but not about something like that. I knew from personal experience how embarrassing those kinds of situations could be. Sometimes my own parents fought when they drank and once my mother went to jail for five days because she busted her man's head. But he was choking her, for Christ's sake. He had her on the floor and was choking the crap out of her. All of us kids were totally freaked out. We were screaming for him to stop but he wouldn't. He was going to kill her right in front of our eyes. She reached up over her head and grabbed a stick of firewood and slammed it into his skull. It was like Mike Tyson had punched him. He was out like a light and we kids were cheering. I always felt that he was the one who should have gone to jail, but he was white, the cops were white, and my mom was a full-blood Indian and proud of it too. It doesn't take a rocket scientist to figure out the dynamics of that situation.

Spousal abuse was dealt with differently in those days. Women didn't get much of a fair break. Sapawe, in that sense, was a man's world. In fact, my mother had a girlfriend who was abused on a regular basis. I remember her getting her collarbone broke by her man. We found her hiding in our chicken pen. I have never been able to forget the image of her in that chicken coop. I doubt I ever will and I've been around a whole lot since then. She was crouched down and crying, her face was black-and-blue, and she was terrified. I started to cry when I saw her. She stayed with us for a couple of weeks but she went back to him eventually, only to meet with more of the same. Anyway, everybody in town knew what Mom had done and I took some teasing, just like this pretty little girl did. I could sympathize with her, which is why I chose to get involved.

I walked Verna home to make sure no one else would mess with her. As a reward for my act of chivalry, she became my buddy. It got to the point where she would bring me treats in her little lunch box. Of course that didn't go unnoticed by my group of friends nor the other bunch of juvenile thugs who called Sapawe home. I naturally took heat because of it but by then not much could bother me. At any rate, I had something I could use against every one of those kids. Pretty soon the sight of her and me together just became part of the town scenery. In my mind, we had become a team. With her, though, it was different: she thought of us as boy-friend and girlfriend. In her mind, we were going steady or something. It got just slightly embarrassing, but she was pretty and so I tolerated it, maybe even encouraged it. She did a lot of things for me, including playing the cowboys I would kill seven or eight times over in our little make-believe world. Being an Indian kid, you knew it was the cowboys who died.

Movies were a rare thing in Sapawe. There was no theater, so Mr. Sanchez, who owned the only restaurant and was a real social guy, used to get movies and had a projector he would set up. He'd charge a small fee and the whole town would show up to watch. It was a social event, a chance for the folks to get together and visit. He'd sell popcorn and pop. It was a great time for us kids. We'd run around and play as kids do. Whatever the story was about, we would spend the next several days playing it out. The richness of our imagi-nations would unfold as we elaborated on the storyline, adding new possibilities as we explored the what if's.

Sapawe was a fascinating town for a kid to grow up in. There were thousands of places to play. Horses were used in those days to pull logs in the bush and they were stabled in a fair-sized barn. The barn was a great place where we could build forts out of bales of hay and play games for hours. The horses seemed to enjoy the company too. Some weird things happened in that old barn. Once, Grant fell out of the rafters.

Another time, I caught my younger brother kissing this little Polish girl in the barn. You know we teased him about that. And Gary nearly got kicked by a horse he liked to tease.

Another interesting thing about that barn was the horses themselves. Each of those horses had its own character that made it unique in our minds. There was Old Joe, a horse I thought was the ugliest and yet the smartest horse I ever met, and I've met quiet a few of them—although I will confess that I've met more horse's asses than I have horses. (That was just an afterthought and has nothing to do with Verna landing in that pile of fresh horse shit.) Anyway, Old Joe always looked at me with an evil eye, even when I was feeding him. I knew in my heart that he knew that I had said he was ugly. I figured he'd try to get even with me at some point, so I stayed out of his kicking range. I just did not trust that horse. Other kids kissed their favorite horses and brought them treats but you'd never catch me kissing that ugly son-of-a-bitch. I just gave Old Joe a healthy bucket of oats and hay.

As I said, we would go see these movies, then for several days afterward, we would replay the story line. That week we had just seen a Tarzan movie. Suddenly the old horse barn became a hot, steamy jungle. We had a rope tied to the rafters we could swing on. Fresh hay had been delivered, so we were able to swing from pile to pile across the gap. Verna watched as I did it several times. I tried to get her to try but she was afraid. In our little fantasy, this tribe of Africans were after Tarzan and Jane.

I was Tarzan and Verna, of course, was Jane. The gap was a big river filled with snakes and alligators waiting for a victim. We had to get to the other side. She was afraid and of course I wasn't about to leave her. In my child's mind, Tarzan never would have deserted a woman in need. So I had no choice but to do like I was sure Tarzan would have done. I swooped her up in my arm, grabbed the rope and, over her very vocal protests when she realized what I was about to do, swung out over the river. I let out a Tarzan yell, she screamed, and off we went. For a brief second it was wonderful. I was really Tarzan and she was Jane—but only for a second. I could feel my hand slipping. No matter how hard I tried, I couldn't hold on, and suddenly the truth was staring me in the face. We were falling and there seemed to be nothing I could do to stop it. Then human nature took over. Survival instincts, being what they are, assumed control. I let go of her and concentrated on landing without getting killed.

To this day, I swear I don't know why she didn't do something to break her fall. In retrospect, I see it was probably a good thing; because of the way she landed, she didn't get hurt. She screamed as she plummeted toward the old horse-barn floor. She landed in the sitting position. Her little derriere hit the floor with a thud. A puff of dust shot out from under her butt cheeks. To make matters worst, I landed on my feet. The very second she hit the floor, she reached out her left hand to try to maintain her balance—and that's when it happened!

Old Joe, besides being an ugly horse, used to let out these turds that were just awful things to step on. They stunk worse than any of the other horses' manure and they were much more watery. The old horse must have had some kind of stomach problem or something because he always made a mess. Verna's delicate little hand landed right in a pile of his manure that couldn't have been more than ten minutes old. To this day, I wouldn't wish that on anybody in the world. Aside from being a mess, it was also extremely embarrassing, particularly for a pretty little girl. At that moment, that wasn't what I was most concerned about. I was worried about her being hurt. I reached down to help her up and she automatically reached up with her right hand. That was fine, but then when she moved her left hand, we both noticed where it was. I let go of her right hand and she landed right back where she was except that this time her whole forearm slid into the pile. There was no way in the world I could keep from laughing!

I could plainly see she wasn't hurt, at least not physically. I thought the situation was hilarious, but she of course considered it a disaster. She started wailing and I realized I had to do something—anything—to lessen her humiliation. I mean this was the girl for whom I was willing to face several bullies. Of course I was concerned for her, but I just couldn't stop laughing. Being somewhat of a quick-witted boy, I whipped off my tee shirt and handed it to her so she could wipe her arm off. She accepted.

I tried my best to comfort her and was actually getting someplace. I apologized and promised that I would never do anything so stupid again. Finally, I got her to the point where instead of this steady screech, she was at least sobbing and could actually talk. I had even managed to stop laughing. What I was trying to do was find a way she could live with what had happened. Besides, the week had been a bad one for me. All my mother would need to hear was that I had done something as stupid as this. I was well on my way to a whipping or, worse yet, being grounded. It was that kind of pressure that made me say what I did.

"It's not all that bad."

"Yes it is."

"At least you didn't get hurt."

"But I got all stinky."

"You know that stuff makes things grow," I suggested.

"So, what has that got to do with me?" she asked.

"Well, think about it. Maybe it'll make your things grow real big."

"What are you talking about?" she questioned. A certain edge had creeped into her voice. Her body stiffened just a little. A man of the world would have automatically recognized the warning signs but I was a little boy just beginning to live life and they escaped me. I did, however, sense that somehow I had entered into territory that maybe I shouldn't have, but I was in too far. I wanted to show her what I thought would be the bright side of things.

"You know, your titties."

She looked at me like she couldn't believe what I'd said and then started wailing again. She called me everything but an Indian—and I mean in both English and Ojibwa. She threatened to tell my mother and everyone else with any authority. At this point, I didn't know what to do or say. That power that females have over males came into play. I almost felt helpless.

I looked over at Old Joe and he had this stupid-looking expression on his face. I swear that old nag was grinning, like he had finally gotten his revenge. I swore at him for good measure. The horse just looked at me, raised his tail, and farted. At first I thought that Verna would see the humor of the situation, but no, not her. She started crying again and Old Joe went back to chewing on the hay. A lesson was learned right there. I got dumped by a girl for the first time in my life. It was a little disheartening, but I got over it soon enough.

Verna found a new hero and a new boyfriend and I got to tease her for several years about the incident. The mere mention of horse shit and I could turn that girl's face red. I always felt like somewhere in that incident was a message for me about the need to sharpen my social skills but what I know for sure is that women can be hard to figure out sometimes. I also learned that's part of their mystique. I don't play Tarzan anymore, or at least not that much. I can remember one time I did, when I was high on LSD, but that's another story.

IDENTITY CRISIS

In his head, Jed Big-Otter heard a drum and some Indians singing, but it was only in his head. It always was. Especially when he thought about his father. He'd spent his whole life wishing for his father and his brother.

The only thing he could remember clearly about his dad is that he liked to sing Indian songs. The other thing he remembered was the day the county came to remove him and his brother from his father's house because a neighbor had said he was abusive to them. Nothing could have been further from the truth. Jed could recall the horrified look on his father's face when the sheriff and a caseworker had come to take his children away from him. At the time, Jed was five-and-a-half years old.

The image always came in singular short flashes, like in a bad dream. Always the dream left him sweating yet chilled. He recalled that his father's eyes had been pleading at first, then anger had swollen up from deep inside him. In the struggle that followed his father was shot. Jed remembered crying and reaching for his dad who writhed in pain on the ground. He could still picture the blood and mud that immediately caked his father's head. His father's eyes were the last thing he saw that day as the police car sped away.

There was no pile of photos, letters, or old video tapes, no tangible mementos to remind him, but he never forgot that look in his dad's eyes. Jed never saw his dad again. He had been sent to an orphanage, then to a series of foster homes where he never did fit in. Always they were the homes of white people who treated him as an oddity. But Jed never did forget his father's singing.

What happened to him over the next decade and a half reflected the common experience of many Indians. He was deprived of his culture by the government's actions. Over the next nineteen years the only thing Indian that Jed Big-Otter experienced was on TV and in movies. Inside, he felt a longing that he could never describe. It just gnawed away at him and left him feeling empty and he didn't know why. The questions he had about himself seemed enough to break up the sky sometimes. He couldn't shake that nagging feeling. No matter what he did it just wouldn't go away.

He looked around the Arrowhead Bar and watched some dust particles dance in the shafts of morning sunlight. The place stunk and, as far as he was concerned, it stunk bad, like old smoke and stale beer, the kind of odor that only a certified winehead could appreciate. He sat on a stool right where the bar turned. He had a good view of everyone in the joint, and that's what he wanted: to be able to see. It didn't help him any though, because when they came in, they came through both back and front doors. He had nowhere to go.

Everyone in the bar heard the roar of motorcycles thunder to a stop out front. They could hear the sound of kickstands being set, then footsteps and chains rattling and cussing and vulgar laughing. No one moved when they walked in; the bar was completely quiet. Jed wondered if he was tripping or something, but only for a moment, because he knew that what was circling the room was very real. An aura of evil seemed to have appeared and everyone within its reach could feel its influence. He listened to the silence and pretty soon was able to hear people breathing, very quietly and intently. It was as if they were all afraid that if they breathed too freely they would draw attention to themselves. Every-one in the room knew it wasn't a good idea to get Wild Willie's attention. In fact, it could be fatal. Rumors abounded about the man's pure meanness. Then he heard footsteps through the stink and labored breathing. Boots—heavy work-boots! he thought. The sound was close. Time seemed to suspend itself at that very moment. He felt the blood rush to his ears and face. They were here for him and he knew it.

A heavyset woman sitting several seats away caught her breath when she saw the man walk in. Her eyes opened wide for a moment, then a curtain of fear slipped over her pupils. Jed looked into the cracked and smoke-stained mirror that lined the crumbling wall behind the bar. He saw the man's image against the open door. He couldn't see his face or any depth. What he saw was a shape, black and flat. The image reminded him of a figure cut from cardboard: .a harsh silhouette framed by the doorway and illuminated by the bright morning sunlight. He reached onto the bar and picked up his gin and tonic. He took a quick swallow. So this is him, Jed thought. It's finally going to happen.

"You be the dude out looking for me?" Jed could not remember where or when he'd heard a voice that echoed so much rage. It was a raspy voice, quiet and slow, with a shadow of violence. He spoke with the unhurried tone of a man sure of himself. His words were jagged with a rage that seemed to leap to the tip of each vowel like it wanted to jump out and choke you. The kind of voice that made you take a second, very close look at the man speaking.

A woman who had entered from the back door walked slowly around the bar. She wore leather and high-heeled boots. Her hips swayed invitingly with each step. Her blonde hair was piled on the top of her head. She looked out through eyes that were painted and somewhat pained, but a pain that reflected violence. This was one bad momma. Her breasts strained against a too-small tee shirt—strained to be free, to feel the kiss of the wind, Jed thought, or maybe some-one's hands. She walked slowly toward him and past. He didn't turn. Suddenly there was a loud bang and a flash of light. He thought he must have been shot. His ears were ringing.

"What the hell?" he blurted out. She had fired a twenty-two pistol at the ceiling, about a foot from his right ear.

"Just to get everyone's attention," she remarked with a giggle.

He heard the other man's laugh. It was a cruel laugh. Jed's eyes were burning. The heavyset woman who sat down at the bar gasped, then farted in fear. Jed Big-Otter felt like he'd been locked into a room of scalding-hot air. The sound of Indians chanting began slowly and quietly in his ears again. He could hear the sound of a drum and the chanting began to pick up speed. Was the chanting coming from within the man's voice? he wondered. Some kind of ancestral knowledge?

The man came a step closer. Jed could see nothing but his eyes. He blinked and the man began talking. The chanting grew louder and somewhere a flute began to wail. Jed knew, of course, that the music existed only in his head. The eyes of the two men met then locked. In the other man's eyes, Jed perceived a ferocity that threatened to leap out at anyone caught looking at them. The man began to talk again. Jed saw his mouth and tongue move, making a thick, wet sound. He could feel the soggy, cool air from the air conditioner brush against his forehead. His eyes began to hurt from the effort he was making to focus on the man's features. He blinked again and rubbed his eyes quickly. His back felt strained from sitting half-turned on the bar stool. In spite of his discomfort, Jed did not feel fear. This man, this wretched, cruel man, could not scare him. Somehow they both sensed that.

"I asked if you're the dude been looking for me?"

Jed forced himself to focus on the eyes glaring at him. Yes, he thought, they're the same eyes. He took a closer look to make sure and saw the darting silver slivers that seemed to light up the backs of the man's eyes. The chanting sound that Jed had been hearing slowly died out. The room grew totally silent as all ears strained to hear his answer. Jed nodded.

"Why? What do you want?"

Jed sat there. He couldn't answer. Oh, it had all been clear in his mind. He knew what he wanted to say but the words wouldn't come out. He had pictured what it would be like when they finally met, but this man standing in front of him, threatening, hostile, and dangerous, was not part of that picture. Suddenly the man grabbed Jed by the throat.

"Didn't you hear me?" he hissed.

So we finally meet, Jed thought, as he reached up and poked a finger into the man's bulging left eye. The man hollered and pressed his hands against the stinging eye.

"Son-of-a-bitch!" he screamed. "Why'd you do that?"

Jed jumped to his feet, ready to fight off the assault he was sure was about to come. He felt a jab of pain shoot through his left side. Someone had punched him in the kidney. At the same time he heard the smashing of broken glass as it shattered over his head. He fell to the floor. His arms were pinned down and someone kicked him in the groin. He moaned and curled his body for protection.

"Should we kill the son-of-a-bitch?" someone hollered.

"No! Let him up." It was the man's voice. "I want to talk to this bastard."

Jed Big-Otter was pulled roughly to his feet. He was having trouble breathing and pain seared through his brain. He wanted to scream out in agony but gritted his teeth instead. He braced himself for the assault. It never came.

"Bring him outside," the man ordered, then turned quickly and walked away. Jed was dragged out the door. The woman with the big breasts was told to stay inside and make sure no one called the police. Everyone in the bar—including her—thought that Jed would be killed.

"Why the hell did you do that to me?"

"'Cause it's the only way to make you stop choking me," Jed answered. When he was a boy, his dad had taught him that trick.

"Ain't nobody done that to me since my little brother—" The man stopped and looked closely at Jed.

"Who the hell are you anyway? Why are you looking for me?" The man stood motionless, hands at his sides. Jed stared at his hands. They were large and calloused. Just like his dad's hands except these hands had a meanness to them. Move your hands, Jed thought. As though he had heard Jed's thoughts the man put his hands on his hips. His action had a quality of ceremonial violence. Not that he had made any threatening gestures, it was just that his movements had a fluidity to them that implied the capacity for violence—extreme violence. It's because the world's tossed a lot of pain the guy's way, Jed concluded.

"Well? Who the hell are you?" Jed heard the voice, speaking to him, cold and hard, but he couldn't answer, not for a long, slow minute. He was filled with doubt, with an urgent, terrible doubt.

"What the hell do you want?" the man asked.

"I don't mean you no harm. I just want to find my big brother. His name was Billy Big-Otter. We got separated when we was boys by the county police and welfare workers. I thought you were him. Are you Billy?"

"You want us to bust this sucker's arms?" one of the thugs asked.

"Yeah, let us do him," the other pleaded.

"Get the hell away from him. Both of you. Go wait in the bar," the man answered. The two thugs complained bitterly but turned and reentered the bar. Jed and the man stood there staring at each other. The big-busted woman looked out the bar window, saying nothing. She seemed surprised when the smaller man lifted his pant leg and pointed to his right shin. She saw the man's face contort. She watched him shake his head, then run his fingers through his thinning hair. Watched as some of the meanness seemed to evaporate.

"Hey Betsy, that punk thinks Willy be his bro," one of the thugs said to her as they walked into the bar. She didn't reply but watched her man intently through the window.

She couldn't hear what her man was saying but she knew he was talking. She'd been with him for fifteen years, through good times and bad, and she knew him like a book. She could see that what was going on outside was having a major effect on him. His tired body seemed to perk up somehow. She watched hate melt from his face to be replaced by a huge smile. Son-of-a-bitch, she thought, what's next—a picnic in the park? She turned to the bartender.

"Hey, mother-fucker, give me a double shot of some good whiskey. Top shelf and hurry it up. I think my family's growing. I ain't sure I'm ready for all that."

She viciously kicked one of the thugs and turned back to the window.

She wasn't altogether surprised when Billy threw himself upon the smaller man. Just like Billy, she thought, my big, tough Billy. She saw the tears that streamed down his hardened face. She smiled as he hugged the smaller man to his chest. She knew he was moaning and crying. She took a swallow of the whiskey, lit a cigarette, and wondered what she would do if her man gave it all up and went straight. She had known about his little brother Jed. Billy had told her the story. She watched them hug and begin to laugh and dance and knew it was good. She knew that all three of their lives would change. She cussed quietly to herself and turned toward the door to go join the two Big-Otter boys. Son-of-a-bitch, she thought.

JOE WALKS-BEAR COMES HOME

"Cool? You think the guy dresses cool? He's an old geezer," the young man said to Suzanna when they first saw Joe Walks-Bear in the town park. He was sitting, looking around.

"He may be a geezer, but I think he looks so cool. He's very handsome," she replied.

"He just got out of prison. Everyone in this town knows he's a killer. You stay away from him."

"That was thirty years ago, " Suzanna answered. "And besides, I understand there were some serious questions about whether he was guilty."

"Who told you that? That crazy uncle of yours? That's why he was run out of this town," the young man said.

Her muscles tightened for a second, but she wasn't in the mood to argue with her boyfriend. She glanced over to where Joe Walks-Bear sat. He was looking down as if he were watching a bug. He looked to her as though he were in deep thought. She liked the way he dressed. He wore gray slacks, a three-quarter length leather coat—a Carbretta and a damned fine one at that. And he had on these pointed shoes just like her father's. Her dad would grin and say these shoes had more class than any Reebok gum-rubber gym shoe, that they were from the old school when people still had the class to tell a quality item.

"Well I'm telling you, Suzanna, you stay away from him. I don't want to be digging you out of some ditch."

"Why would you say something like that? You're so judgmental. You're not even giving him a chance," the young woman commented.

"I don't know why he even bothered to come back here anyway. I would have gone somewhere else. Someplace people don't know me. Where I would be welcome. He's not welcome in this town. I can tell you that much. Ain't nobody wants a killer walking around loose."

Suzanna ignored his comment. "Can you even begin to imagine what it must feel like to him to be home after so long? I bet he's really happy."

The young man glanced over to where the ex-convict sat. "He don't look any too happy to me. He's stupid to come back here. A dumb-ass Indian."

Suzanna looked sharply at her boyfriend. For several weeks now she'd been agonizing over how to break up with him. He was insensitive and self-centered. She couldn't tolerate that in others and felt that it would be better if they just remained as friends—not lovers like he wanted. She knew that within a week they would go their separate ways.

Joe Walks-Bear had been locked up for thirty years. Much of that time he had spent in solitary confinement. What a bitch, he thought. Thirty years of my life for something I didn't do. What a bitch! He held up his hands and looked at them. They aren't like they should be, he thought. They were too soft for a man his age. There were no scars on them. His fingernails had never been grimy from the grease of a day's work. That had been taken from him thirty years ago. So much had been taken. He shut his eyes and leaned back against the park bench. It came to him then, like it always did, unexpectedly. The store, the sting of the bullet hitting him, the police, the trial, the judge pronouncing the sentence, then nothing, just this mind-bashing silence from everybody who had ever been in his world. In his mind, he saw it as a rapid sequence of events, a series of tragic intensified recollections. They took it all from this Indian, he thought to himself. They took it all. His legs began to tremble.

Suzanna and Joe met a week later. He was walking down by the community pond when she came up behind him on her ten-speed bike. She startled him and stopped to apologize for scaring him. She liked the way he smiled. She got off the bike and began to walk beside him. At first he seemed a little uncomfortable, but she was determined to talk to him. She smiled as she introduced herself.

"Hi. My name is Suzanna."

"Hello, Suzanna. That's a nice bike."

"You like riding bikes?"

"It's been a long time since I rode one."

"Would you like to ride mine? Go ahead, try it."

"No, no. I'd better not." He hesitated as he looked her in the eyes. "Do you know who I am?"

"I know what your name is."

"You do? Why?"

"Well, this is a small town and we don't get many strangers here."

"I'm not a stranger. I was born here. I left here when I was about your age. How old are you?"

"I'm nineteen."

"I left before you were born. Didn't think I'd ever see this town again."

"I heard all about you from my friend. People are talking. In fact, my mother knew you in school."

"Really?" He hesitated again, looked at her closely, then continued. "You know what? You are the first person that's said more than two words to me."

He was soft-spoken and didn't talk a lot. His sentences were short and clipped. It seemed to her that he picked his words carefully. She liked that. Suzanna was attracted to him immediately. She glanced sideways at him. She thought he was checking out her legs. For a moment she felt flattered but then she realized he was studying her bike.

"What you looking at?"

"I was just noticing the way you're built." Suzanna caught the mortified look that leaped to his face. He blushed, embarrassed.

"I'm sorry," he stammered, then paused as if he were trying to collect his thoughts. "I mean the bike."

They both laughed. Suzanna was happy to see him relaxing a bit. She trusted him. He didn't feel like a killer to her. In fact, he reminded her of a young boy. As much as she tried to fight it off, she felt a certain excitement in knowing she could attract his attention—that she could foster an intimacy between them so easily. She realized he was truly embarrassed by what he had just said. Suzanna was not a raging feminist but she was acutely aware of the roles women were forced to take in society. Yet she also found a certain pleasure in teasing men and observing their reactions.

"These bikes sure have changed since I was a kid. Like everything else around here."

"You sure you don't want to try riding it?"

"You really wouldn't mind?"

"Not at all."

He studied the thin tires of the red ten-speed for a minute. "Why are the tires so skinny?" he asked.

"Oh, go ahead. Take a spin around the pond. I'll sit right here and wait. I need a breather anyway."

"How far did you ride?"

"Six or seven miles. I do that everyday. It's good for your health."

"You sure you don't mind?" he asked a second time. He didn't sound like a killer to her, but she realized with a smile that she wouldn't know how a killer was supposed to sound anyway. There's something about this guy that excites me, she thought.

She gave him the bike. He took the handlebars carefully with one hand. She noticed that his leather jacket was draped over his other arm.

"Here. Give me that jacket."

He handed the jacket to Suzanna. It was heavy. She heard something rattle in the pocket. It made a metallic sound. For a moment she wondered if he had a gun in the pocket, but then she dismissed the idea. Just because the guy is fresh out of prison, does that mean he'd be carrying a gun? she thought to herself, then felt a flush of embarrassment surge through her body.

"I'll go sit on the side of this hill."

"I don't know if I can still do this," he said, laughing nervously.

"You never forget how."

He swung his leg over the crossbar and pushed off. The bike teetered for a moment, then he got it under control. He turned it onto the grass. He rode in a tight circle, laughing as he did so.

"Why is the seat so high?"

"It cuts the wind resistance," she replied.

"It makes me feel like I'm going to fall forward on my face," he said with a laugh.

It was an infectious laugh and Suzanna laughed with him. He sounded happy and so Suzanna was surprised when he said, "I didn't do it, you know."

"Didn't do what?"

"I didn't kill that store owner."

"I believe you."

"Good," he said as he steered the bike onto the sidewalk that circled the small pond. She watched him peddle away, then noticed that a bed of flowers had recently been planted near where she sat. Well, at least the Park District Commissioner is keeping his election promises, she thought. She decided that this would be their special garden. Thirty minutes later the two of them were walking side by side, talking.

"So anyways, as I was saying, I was over at this girl's house. Her mother was cooking dinner for the three of us.

Boiled potatoes and pork chops. My favorite. Her mom needed some salt so she asked me to run to the small grocery store to get some. That's when it happened." He stopped talking as he walked along. She watched him shake his head as though to clear away a bad memory.

"You don't have to talk about it. If it's too painful . . ."

"No, no. I need to. Now more than ever."

"Let's sit over here in the shade awhile."

"Good idea. You know what I got?" he asked as he began to dig around in his coat pocket.

"No, what have you got?" she asked with a laugh.

He liked the sound of her laughter. It was young and sounded so alive. It was easy to listen to and to join in with.

"Peaches. I bought a can of peaches," he answered with a big grin.

"You have a can of peaches? So that's why your coat was so heavy."

"I've always liked them. How about you?"

"I don't mind them."

He pulled out the peaches and a can opener. Then he pulled out a spoon.

"I used to crave them in prison. You never really know how much you like something until you can't get it. You want some?" he asked as he began opening the can. "It's the first can I got since I've been home. I was going to make it into a little celebration. I'd be honored if you'd join me."

"I'm the one who should be honored," she answered and meant it. The intimacy of the moment caught her by surprise and made it somehow more exciting for her.

After they finished eating, Joe sat quietly looking out over the water. A family of ducks had caught his attention. He watched them swim around the pond then disappear into a patch of cattails on the far side. He turned halfway toward Suzanna. She leaned against the trunk of a tree as he began to tell her the story.

"I ran into the grocery store, like I'd done a thousand times before, but this time it was different, much different. Everything was weird. It was quiet, but man, there was tension in the air. I knew immediately that something was wrong. Everything was too quiet. You know what I mean?"

Joe stopped talking, picked up a small twig, and studied it. Suzanna sat up, and Joe resumed his story.

"There were three people at the counter, two teenage girls and a guy. The guy was maybe twenty years old. He had a gun pointed at the old man behind the counter. He turned halfway around to look at me and that's when all hell broke loose. In that instant the old man grabbed a gun from somewhere under the counter and started shooting. For an old man he moved real fast."

Joe stopped talking again, studied the twig, then tossed it aside. A bird in a nearby tree began singing, and Joe continued.

"You know it's like it all happened yesterday. One of the girls screamed. I heard the young guy cuss and felt something hit me. It felt like a bee sting at first, but the force of it knocked me backward. I knew I'd been shot. I mean I felt the bullet hit. As I fell I could hear everything. The girl kept screaming and the old guy just moaned. Then I heard a crash and I was out like a light."

Joe hesitated again and rubbed his right hand across his eyes.

"The old man has been shot twice. Once in the chest and once in the face. He was dead as hell. I was shot in the shoulder. I woke up in the hospital with a cop sitting next to me. They had me handcuffed to the damned bed. It was uncomfortable and my shoulder was hurting something terrible. I asked the cop what was going on. He didn't even bother to answer. Three days later I was transferred to Cook County jail and that was it. They had a dead man, a weapon, and me. They didn't even listen to what I told them."

He stopped talking and lit a cigarette. Suzanna noticed his hand was shaking. She reached out and touched it. She saw his body tense as he pulled away. For five minutes they sat, saying nothing.

The park was peaceful. Some children were playing tag over by the swings. Their chattering and yelling added warmth to the atmosphere. Suzanna lay on her back with her eyes shut. It was mid-afternoon—the time of the day for sighing. That second when everything is just right and silence slices through time. A slight wind rustled the leaves of a nearby tree and the moment was lost to the past.

"What happened then?" Suzanna asked.

"They told me I was charged with one count of murder and one count of armed robbery. After that things just went from bad to worse. The trial was a joke. The first five years in the joint were pure hell. Not hearing from anybody made things rough. I never got a letter—not one letter. The whole thing was like a bad dream."

She liked the sound of his voice—it seemed to suggest another meaning for what he was saying. She sensed a tenderness trying to break through the brittle surface of his words. Suzanna found herself responding to them on an emotional level. She wanted to be friends with this man, she thought, maybe more. She wanted to help him.

"I used to stand in the middle of the prison yard and look up. The wall was high and bleak. I'm telling you, Suzanna, there ain't nothing could depress a person like the sight of that wall on a rainy day."

She liked the way he used her name, the intimacy it made her feel. She wondered if he knew the impact he was having on her as she listened to him.

"The water would run down it and it felt like your life running down into the ground. Oh, that place can do some things to your head and your soul—especially your soul! I liked looking at the clouds, though. They were free and I used to imagine myself riding on them. I'd shut my eyes and look down on the world. But you know what? All I could ever see was this town. The high school football field. Ain't that the damnedest thing?"

Suzanna looked at Joe. His face was quiet, like his hands. Suddenly Suzanna knew she wanted those hands to touch her in the ways she had never let anyone touch her before. Joe noticed her studying his face. He saw her expression change, read her body language, and could tell what was going on inside her. And somehow it made her afraid. Their eyes met and she felt an attraction for him like she'd never felt for anyone else. His skin looked soft and much younger than forty-seven years old, the age he had given her. She felt attracted to him like a magnet to steel. Her hands reached out involuntarily and touched him. He jumped back. His muscles had tightened and he found it hard to breathe. She resisted the urge to reach out to him again, to tell him it was okay.

"I had hope, all the way up to when those big doors slammed shut behind me. I hoped some witness would step forward or that they'd arrest the right people. You know, I even hoped that one of them would at least help me out by making an anonymous call, but no. Not a single word from anyone. I even fantasized that a call would come from the government telling them that a mistake had been made and that I was free to go. Like I said, I never heard a word from anybody—not a single word. I tell you, Suzanna, when those doors slammed shut they snapped off the sunlight and my life became a shadow."

"But you're a free man now. You can do whatever you want."

"Am I really free?" he asked. "I don't even know what it feels like. I know that I'm feeling really good but I want to ease myself into this world. The only places I've gone so far is here to this park and to the small grocery store."

Suzanna said nothing as she watched him slip off into thought. A few minutes later, she asked him why he looked so young, why his skin looked so smooth. He laughed and told her that it was because he had hardly ever gone outside while he was in prison.

"Who was the girl whose house you were at before the robbery occurred?"

"That was Brenda McFarley."

"Didn't she write to you?"

"Not once."

"Did she testify at your hearing?"

"They told me her health was bad. She always was kind of fragile. I guess that's what I was attracted to in the first place."

"Well, I don't understand why your lawyer didn't do something. I would think her testimony would have helped your case."

"I didn't really have a lawyer. I had a public defender. I only got to talk to him for about twenty minutes."

Suzanna was stunned. She knew there were cases of injustice like this but this one was close to home. She remembered that her uncle had been a lawyer in the area, but had left in protest against the way justice was abused and influence used by county officials. He had lodged formal complaints at the state level. There had been an investigation and an insignificant traffic judge had taken the blame. She recalled hearing that the guy had been put on probation for a few years. The message was clear: this is the way things are and they shouldn't be messed with.

Of course Suzanna didn't believe that—not for a moment. Especially now that she had met Joe Walks-Bear. She resolved to call her lawyer uncle who was now living in Chicago and teaching criminal justice at the University of Illinois. She also wondered why this Brenda McFarley hadn't written to him, especially since they had been boyfriend and girlfriend. Maybe her parents had forbidden her to write. It all seemed odd to Suzanna. She decided to find the whereabouts of this Brenda.

Suzanna looked at her watch and realized she had to rush off to a literature class at the community college. She invited Joe to join her that evening for a movie at the college film and video festival. He was reluctant at first, but she finally convinced him to come. They made arrangements to meet for dinner then go see an old classic movie that was the feature that evening. They would meet at seven at a local restaurant near campus.

"Don't be late now. I don't like waiting," she told him.

"I'll be there at exactly five to seven. Oh yeah! Let me ask you something. Do I have to dress up?"

"That's up to you. It's not really necessary but if you feel like it, it's fine," she answered. "So we have a date?"

"I guess we do, don't we? It's my first in so long, Suzanna. I'm going to be nervous."

"You, nervous? You'll be all right," she reassured him.

"I'm going to dress up. I mean it's a date, right?"

Suzanna laughed sweetly. "I'll be waiting."

Her smile made Joe catch his breath. What a beautiful woman, he thought to himself. She waved good-bye, hopped on her bike, and pedaled away. Joe reached into his pocket and pulled out a handful of money. He counted it quickly then headed downtown to purchase a suit for that evening. He whistled a tune that matched the happy rhythm of his gait. I'm actually going on a date. Imagine that! At my age, I'm going on a date with a woman young enough to be my daughter. Not bad for an old Indian, he laughed quietly to himself.

Suzanna went to the local library after her last class to search through the back issues of the town's newspaper. She looked at several old copies but didn't find anything. More in-depth research would be needed, perhaps with Joe's assistance. She thought about their plans for the evening and moaned, for there was so much to do.

But as she considered what she would wear for their date, she found herself feeling just a little giddy. It was, after all, a formal date and she wanted to look good for him. She would wear something sophisticated, she decided. Then she wondered what they would talk about.

Their backgrounds were so different. Their life experiences hardly coincided at all. What we do have in common, she thought, is that we're both of Indian descent. He was a full-blood Ojibwa from Canada and she was Irish and Oneida from Wisconsin. Of course, she hadn't been raised on the reservation. Her father, a half-breed, had maintained contact with his Wisconsin relatives but his life revolved around this town. He had worked hard to develop friendships that placed him high on the town's social ladder. People will talk, but so what?, she thought. I don't care what they think or say.

She pulled her sports car into the parking lot, checked her make-up, then walked into the restaurant and was totally astonished. Joe Walks-Bear had changed his image from the leather-coated DeNiro style to a look of suave coolness in a single afternoon. He didn't notice her at first as he sat at the bar sipping on a Coke. Holy Christ, she said to herself. He looks like he just jumped off a page of *GQ*. He had on a soft brown sport coat with a subtle pattern of large checks and pale trousers. Every detail of his outfit was coordinated. He wore the clothing well, she noted, as if he'd just stepped out of a tailor shop. His long hair was pulled back into a tight ponytail, braided and wrapped with leather thongs. The effect pleased Suzanna. Very handsome, she said softly. She was glad she had invited him out for the evening.

He noticed her as she was checking herself in the mirror. Her short, stylish black dress looked good on her. It was accented by a string of pearls that hung around her neck, a family heirloom from her grandmother. Her purse matched her black high heels and her short-cropped auburn hair framed her small face, giving her an angelic look. Joe whistled silently as he admired her. He noted with pleasure how various heads had turned as she walked into the bar. The number of observers increased as she joined him.

"My, my! Joe Walks-Bear, you look—dapper, that's the word. You look really nice."

"Thank you," he murmured as he pulled out a chair for her to sit on. He smiled shyly. "It's not too much, is it?"

"No, no. The women all have their eyes on you," she said as she looked around the room.

"They must be looking at you with envy. You're absolutely beautiful tonight."

She blushed slightly. Joe noticed the color creep into her face. "I'm sorry. I didn't mean to embarrass you."

"You didn't."

Just then the headwaiter walked over to inform them that their table was ready. As they moved toward the table, Suzanna noticed heads turning. Joe was an intriguing man and his clothes only added to the effect. The two of them made small talk as they ate. Suzanna was impressed by his grasp of world events. She wondered how he came to know so much. With a proud smile, he told her that he read a lot in prison, especially when he started getting short.

"Short? What do you mean by short?" she asked.

He laughed and told her that it was prison talk. It meant his release date was getting closer. Current events, he told her, became more important to him then. Throughout dinner they talked and laughed as Joe relaxed more and more. To a curious observer—and there were many of them, Suzanna noted—they looked like a professor and his pet student. In a college town it was a rather familiar sight: younger women with older men. There was always speculation about the nature of these relationships— and judgment. Suzanna knew they looked good together and flushed with pride as she leaned closer to Joe, captivated by his smile and his stories. His eyes had lost some of the hard glint she had noticed when they first met. Now they sparkled as he talked.

"I might just enroll in some courses at the community college."

"It couldn't hurt."

"Make my parole officer happy."

"You're on parole?" she asked him, surprised.

"For the rest of my life," he answered.

"Why?"

"I had a fifteen-to-life sentence."

"And you served thirty years."

"Not quite. I did twenty-nine years, eight months, and ten days," he corrected her, then added with a grin, "and fourteen hours."

Suzanna said nothing as she felt a sadness creep over her. She wanted to reach out and touch him but recalled how he'd withdrawn earlier that day when she did.

"I'll tell you this much. The fourteen hours was the longest."

Joe noted the change in her bearing. He glanced around the room and realized that he liked the luxurious atmosphere. Sure as hell is a far cry from the prison mess hall, he thought.

"This place is really nice. It's got class. Here I am in a classy joint with a classy lady. This calls for a drink. How about an after-dinner drink?" he asked.

"A glass of wine would be nice," she replied as her eyes followed his around the room. The restaurant did have a relaxing atmosphere, she said to herself. It's even kind of seductive, she thought, then blushed, this time, at the frankness of her own thoughts. Since her early teens she had been pursued by men. Suddenly she realized that the roles had been reversed and now she was the one pursuing a man. Subtle as her pursuit was, there was no denying it.

Suzanna entered this new state of affairs easily. Joe, on the other hand, was unsure of what was happening. These were new emotions and feelings to him. If this is freedom, he thought, then I like it. For so long he hadn't enjoyed the luxury of feeling completely at ease. In prison one had to always be on guard. To do otherwise could be fatal. Now he began to feel much more relaxed than he'd ever felt before.

More than once he resisted the temptation to lean across the table and kiss her. Her lips looked so soft, her cheeks glowed, and her neck was arched toward him. Joe noticed the curious looks of nearby diners and leaned back timidly in the plush chair.

Suddenly the tranquility was shattered by a piercing scream. A heavyset woman stood there, staring at Joe. Her eyes bulged and her breathing came in halting gasps. "Is that you?" she exclaimed. She stared at Joe as she backed away. She held her hands about six inches from her face as though to block out his image. Suzanna saw the signs of recognition becoming visible on her friend's face. They started around his eyes, then the muscles in his jaw twitched several times. Joe licked his lips as he pulled at his tie. He too was having a difficult time breathing. "Brenda?"

"They told me you were dead. That you hung yourself." Brenda's hands moved in a circular motion as if they were searching for something—a shred of a memory perhaps.

"What did she say?" Suzanna asked.

"Joe, is that really you? I wrote you every day but the letters kept coming back." Brenda stopped talking. She stared for a long time, then began to sob softly. Joe tried to approach her but she backed away from him.

"Are you all right?" he asked.

"They told me you were dead. Committed suicide. That's what they told me. How can I believe you're here, still alive?" She held her face in her hands for a while, then walked out of the restaurant and got into a long, black limousine. Joe didn't move but sat there staring at the door.

Everyone in the restaurant had stopped eating and was staring at them. Suzanna could hear Joe's name being whispered at several tables. An elderly couple stood up, glared contemptuously at Joe, and left in a huff. They were followed by a family at a nearby table. As they walked by, the woman hissed, "Killer Indians and their little whores shouldn't be allowed around decent folks."

Suzanna was mortified. Joe sat very still. He looked down at the table. His hands began to make small circles with some water that had splashed onto the polished wood of the table. He said nothing. The manager of the restaurant came over to their table. He looked apologetically at Suzanna.

"I'm sorry, Miss, but I have to ask you and your friend to leave this establishment. I'm losing customers. Tell him that I'm sorry."

"Tell him yourself," she snapped.

"I don't want to have to call the police, but he has to leave. His presence is upsetting my customers. I'm running a business. We need our customers. He has to leave. I'm sorry to inconvenience you, Miss, but Mr. Walks-Bear cannot stay."

"You're sorry to inconvenience me? What about him? Why don't you apologize to him?" She was getting very angry.

"Look, Miss, I'm trying to be nice about this, but you must remember that he's a convicted killer and besides, Indians don't ordinarily frequent this place. It makes my customers uncomfortable."

"They weren't uncomfortable before they knew who he was," she fumed.

"Well, just get him out of here."

It wasn't a sudden movement nor was it necessarily a violent movement. Joe just reached his hand up, took hold of the front of the man's shirt, and pulled his head down to the table. The manager's face turned ashen white. He tried to resist but his effort was fruitless. Suzanna swore later that she heard him pass gas.

Joe's voice was just louder than a whisper. He brought his own face close to that of the other man's. "I didn't mean to start any trouble but if you don't look at me when you talk to me, I'll break your goddamned neck."

"I'm sorry, Mr. Walks-Bear, b-b-but my customers are all leaving," the manager stammered.

"Another thing. Don't you ever talk down at me. If you have something to say to me or about me, you'd better be man enough to say it directly to my face. You understand?"

The manager nodded his head stupidly. His face had turned red and he was trying to loosen his collar.

"You call the cops and I'll be back to give you a good reason to. I'll leave your joint because I don't like the way it smells in here, especially around you. You smell like a coward. Are you scared?"

The man nodded yes.

"Good, because what I feel like doing to you should scare you."

"Let the man go, Joe. He ain't worth the bother. He's a weasel."

Suzanna, Joe, and the manager all turned to find the man who had spoken. His voice was compelling in a quiet way, yet firm. It didn't sound as if it belonged to the man standing by Joe's side, smiling. He was a big man, easily six feet tall and two hundred and thirty pounds of hard muscle. The first thing Suzanna noticed was his hands: they were gigantic, meaty, red, and calloused. Working hands at the end of hairy arms as big as small tree trunks. His shirt was open at the collar, exposing a barrel chest and a neck ruddy from the bite of sun and wind. His hair was thinning and receding. He looked tough from head to toe except for his eyes. They were soft, gentle, and fluid. His voice was gentle as well. It was a voice you trusted, that made you feel at ease. Suzanna saw Joe responding to the man's urging: his facial muscles relaxed and his eyes softened. She was relieved. She knew everything would be all right now that this man was in command of the situation.

"Let him go. Okay, pal? Just let him go." The man smiled and touched Joe's arm. "Screw this asshole. He ain't nothing. Let him go."

Joe released the manager, who scurried away, visibly shaken.

"Who are you?" Joe asked.

"I saw the whole thing. It wasn't your fault. Running into her must've been tough—on both of you. You know, Joe, she has really been sick. She was in a mental hospital for a while because of a nervous breakdown. She just got married a few years ago."

"Who are you?" Joe repeated his question.

The man smiled and extended his hand. "Vince. Vince Mascetto"

Joe took the man's hand.

"Mascetto? Mascetto. I remember that name from somewhere."

"Hell, yeah. You should remember it. You son-of-a-gun, you broke my school record in baseball."

Suzanna watched as recognition flooded Joe's face and eyes. "Oh yeah! I remember now. The school baseball team. You were a big shot on the team."

"Until you came along." Turning to Suzanna, he laughed and offered his hand. "Vince Mascetto. I held the school record for bases stolen, but this young Indian buck came along and broke it. By a dozen or so, wasn't it?"

"It was by eight," Joe said.

"And that was only in his junior year. It still stands, Joe. Did you know that? You know, I saw you in that Naperville game."

"Naperville game?" Joe thought out loud.

"The one where you stole home base and won the game. I remember like it was yesterday," the man said.

"Yeah, I remember that game too now," Joe said, looking back over the years.

Suzanna smiled at Joe. "So you were a baseball champ? I'm impressed."

"Hey, Joe, why don't you and your lady friend join my wife, Joyce, and me for a drink. We'd be honored."

"I'm sorry, Vince, but they asked us to leave," Suzanna informed him.

"Well, if you ain't good enough for this dive, then neither are we. I know a better place than this."

"Joe?" Suzanna looked at Joe. "It's up to you."

"Come on, Joe. I know a real nice joint where we can let our hair down and have us a blast. Hey, we can talk sports." Turning to his wife, he practically yelled across the room, "Hey Joyce! Come on over here and meet the best damned base runner in this county."

Joyce came over and joined the group. She smiled at Suzanna as they were introduced. Suzanna immediately liked her down-to-earth manner. She was warm and outgoing and with her husband made the rest of the evening enjoyable for both Suzanna and Joe. Vince invited Joe to join him and some other men at the local park where they coached a Little League baseball team.

"Hey, we also have a league that plays on Thursday nights. It's a bunch of us older guys. Keeps us on our toes. People call it the Ben Gay League, but not to our faces. They know better because we still can whip most of them any day of the week—even in overtime," Vince said with a laugh. "We could use another player. Did you play any ball in there?" he asked.

The following Saturday, Joe and Suzanna spent the entire day in the local library researching Joe's trial. Very little had been written about it except that he had been given a life sentence for the murder of the grocery store owner. Reading the article left Joe feeling empty. They had said so little. Memories came back to Joe in a burst of powerful images. Suddenly Joe jumped up and said, "He saw it! I remember that him and another guy were working in an alley across from the grocery store. I seen them as I ran to the store! They were there, Suzanna. I seen them."

"Who? What are you talking about? Who did you see?" She asked.

"Vince. He was working in an alley right there. He must've heard the shots. He must've seen something. He had to—him and another guy were digging a ditch right there. There's no way they couldn't have heard or seen something."

"Are you sure?"

"I remember it clear as day now."

"Why didn't he step forward or something?" Suzanna asked.

"I don't know. But he seems like a really nice guy."

"What should we do?"

"I want to have a talk with him, I'll tell you that much."

"I'm sure you do, Joe, but maybe we should talk with my uncle before we do anything. There's something fishy here."

"Who's your uncle?"

"He teaches law at the University of Illinois—downtown Chicago. I think he could give us some good advice. Can you remember who the other guy was who was working with Vince?'"

Joe shook his head. "He was in the ditch, but I remember Vince real clearly. He looked straight at me as I ran by. I think he even nodded his head to me." Joe shut his eyes in an effort to remember. "Yeah, I think he did. I can see it."

"We should talk to Brenda McFarley too, to find out what she knows. She's got to remember something."

"The way she freaked out when she saw me was really weird. I wonder who told her I had killed myself. She must have been trying to find something out. "

"She said all her letters had been returned to her. So she did try to reach you. We really need to talk to her, but maybe we should talk to my uncle first."

"Maybe you're right. Do you think that you can set it up?"

"I'm sure I can," she told him, then added, "We have to be really careful what we say to people."

Their appointment to talk with Suzanna's uncle was set for the following weekend at the university. They would meet him at the annual powwow sponsored by the Indian students. When Suzanna told Joe, he was very excited.

"My uncle said he'd talk to some other people who might be interested in your case."

"Do you realize how long it's been since I went to a powwow?"

"It should be fun. Can you dance, Joe?"

"I used to be pretty good. Of course, I've probably forgot how."

"It's like riding a bike: you never forget."

"Hey, it's really good that we're meeting at a powwow." Joe turned to Suzanna, placed his hands on her shoulder, and looked her in the eyes. "Suzanna, I want you to know how much I appreciate what you're doing for me."

Suddenly everything where they sat talking in the park, grew still—or so it seemed to Suzanna. She was acutely aware of how close Joe was. She could smell the cologne he was wearing. The scent of pine mingled with summer wind. It was pleasant and relaxing. She could feel the August heat, comfortable, not stiflingly humid. In the distance she heard the sound of an ice-cream truck playing a familiar jingle. She became aware of the warmth on her shoulders where his hands rested gently. The wind tousled his hair slightly. She reached up and pushed it back in place.

As she did, Joe closed his eyes and stopped breathing for a second. The sound of a small boy blowing a whistle tickled his ears. The proximity of Suzanna tickled his other senses. He searched his mind for something appropriate to say but he couldn't come up with anything. Her hand moved ever so gently to the back of his head. She saw Joe shudder; she hesitated, then continued rubbing his neck in small, tight circles. He sighed and smiled. She felt in charge, more in charge than she'd ever been before. Her face moved closer to his. Their lips touched gently. He didn't resist. She let her lips explore his and was pleasantly surprised by their softness. She felt his hands move from her shoulders to the small of her back. The tips of his fingers moved in a circular motion. She pressed her breasts against his chest. She felt how the movement of his hands grew faster and more urgent. Her tongue pressed against his lips, his teeth. She tasted the 7-Up he had been drinking a moment before. She pressed with her tongue a little harder. Her nipples stiffened against his chest, his mouth opened. Their tongues danced a gentle dance of exploration, increasing in anticipation, then bursting into a frenzied rush of desire. Suzanna's emotions spun around as she moaned softly. Then Joe pulled away.

"Let's get some ice cream," he said.

"What's wrong?"

"Nothing. I just want some ice cream."

Suzanna was flabbergasted. As they walked through the playground she didn't speak. Neither did Joe at first.

"I'm sorry about that what just happened. I guess I just freaked."

"I was out of line, Joe. I'm sorry. I didn't mean to do that."

"I'm glad you did."

"You are?" The surprise was evident in her voice. "Why'd you pull away then?"

"I don't know why, Suzanna, but look, the damned ice-cream truck just pulled away too."

"What luck! That's twice I missed out." They laughed but both of them knew their relationship had moved to another level.

During the week Joe went about getting IDs, doing some job-hunting, and enrolling in an adult education class at the local community college. He liked the campus and the atmosphere there. It made him feel young, adventurous, and curious. His classes would start in a month but he went ahead and bought books and other things he would need. He was looking forward to going with Suzanna to the powwow at the university the following Saturday.

Joe found his old checkbook and was surprised to see that he had saved nearly two thousand dollars before he went to prison. He went to the bank to see if he could withdraw some of the money. He was nervous as he approached the teller because it had been so long since he had been in a bank, but it felt good to be able to do whatever he wanted. Prison had taught him to hope for the best but expect the worst. The Indian was thinking that his mother or some other family member had probably withdrawn the money long ago, but much to his surprise they hadn't touched a dime. Joe was shocked when the clerk at the bank informed him that because of compound interest his account now totaled more than fifteen thousand dollars. That was more than what he ever could have hoped for. He withdrew enough to cover his expenses for a couple of weeks and to get something to wear to the powwow. He was going to make it a special day.

Suzanna and Joe went to hear a poetry reading at the university multicultural center that Friday evening. A friend of Suzanna's was the featured poet. He became fascinated with Joe's story and promised to write a poem about him. Later, as they drove in the country, Joe told Suzanna he had written a collection of poems while he was in the joint.

"Will you let me read them?"

"I don't think they're that good, but I'll show them to you if you want me to."

"I'd like that, Joe."

"Man, it's really nice out here, ain't it? I love these pine trees."

Suzanna looked around as she drove. It is really nice, she thought. It's secluded, private—a good place to take a walk and have a chance to talk. She steered the car onto a small gravel road and parked. Suzanna estimated that they had about an hour or two of light before night settled in. "Want to take a short hike?" she asked Joe.

"I used to come up here when I was a little boy. When I was a teenager too."

"Have you ever been to the top of that hill?"

"Sure I have."

"Want to race to the top?" she asked.

"What do I get if I win?"

"How about me?" Suzanna held her breath. She hadn't meant to be so forward but the words had slipped out. She waited for his answer.

"What if you win?" he laughed. "Do you get me?"

"I guess those are the rules. That way no one loses. "

"On four. One, two, three, and four!"

They ran up the hillside, laughing as they did. Joe immediately took the lead. About halfway to the top Suzanna caught up to him. He tried to maintain his lead but she was in much better shape. As she passed him she slapped him on the rear end. "Come on old man. I'll be waiting at the top of the hill." She looked back at him, laughing. "Your ass is mine."

When Joe reached the top of the hill she sat there grinning, smugly chewing on a piece of grass. "I won."

"You sure did."

"That means you're mine."

"I guess I could think of worse things."

"You have to do what I say. Anything I say."

"Does that make me a love slave?"

"It sure does, Joe Walks-Bear. And I'm a mean master."

"So what is it my mean master wants me to do?" he asked bowing playfully.

"The first thing you can do is sit and catch your breath. You need to run more, you know."

"You mean you want me to run? I thought you said I was a love slave."

Suzanna laughed softly. "Oh we'll get to that part sooner than you think."

"So what's next?"

"Kiss me."

He kissed her gently on the cheek.

"Not like that. Like this." She pulled him to her and planted a kiss on his lips. The same passion she had experienced before rushed forth. This time Joe did not pull away but returned her kiss with a fury that, for a moment, scared them both. They pulled apart. "Wow! What got into you?"

"I don't know," he answered.

"Well, that was some kind of kiss. Almost like I was getting thirty years of—. I'm sorry. I didn't mean to bring that up."

"Don't sweat it. Suzanna, I want to tell you something, but promise me you won't laugh."

"I promise."

"I've never been with a woman. So I might be kind of shy, or awkward."

"You mean you've never been with a woman since you were locked up?"

"No. I mean I've never been with any woman, ever. I was seventeen when I got locked up. I hadn't slept with anybody. I'm a virgin, Suzanna. A goddamned forty-seven-year-old virgin."

"A virgin? Oh my god, I hadn't even thought of that. There's nothing wrong with it, Joe. I've only been with two guys before and both of them were young."

Joe took her into his arms and kissed her again. This time they didn't stop. As their passion grew they ripped the clothes from each other's bodies. Suzanna met Joe's every thrust with one of her own. Joe shut his eyes, experiencing the end of thirty years of frustration, thirty years of imagining this moment. Never had he experienced such a feeling of ecstasy. It left his mind swirling. He gave himself to her—not only his sexual being but his mind and yes, he thought, his soul. He put them all into his lovemaking as a way of worshipping the young woman whose every fiber, whose every nerve ending reached up to grasp what he offered. In a matter of minutes both were spent. They lay in each other's arms gasping and laughing.

"Not so bad for a forty-seven-year-old virgin. I'm lucky you aren't ninety." Suzanna kissed Joe tenderly. "God that was good, Joe. It's never been like this for me."

"It was even better than what I'd dreamed."

After making love again, this time more slowly but with the same urgent need, they walked back down the hill. Suzanna teased Joe and he responded with kisses. They walked with their arms around each other's waists. The bliss they were feeling burst as they cleared the trees.

"Oh shit! That's my father's car." Then she spotted the police cars and her heart skipped a beat. She began to panic. The people standing by the cars noticed them as they continued down the hill.

One of the two police officers pulled his revolver from its holster. He was young, Joe noticed, and looked scared. Suzanna's father stared in disbelief at his daughter and Joe. His fists clenched and unclenched, his jaw was tense with anger. Suzanna's ex-boyfriend, the one who had warned her to stay away from Joe, started yelling at him.

"You dirty rotten killer! What did you do to her?"

"Would you shut your mouth," Suzanna said to the young man. "He hasn't done anything."

"Put your hands up and lay face down on the ground," ordered the policeman with the drawn gun.

Joe looked at them in surprise, then asked, "Why?"

The second policeman drew his weapon as well. Both Joe and Suzanna heard the click as he cocked the gun.

"On the ground, Sir. Now!"

"I asked you why?"

"Mr. Walks-Bear, I said on the ground—and get those hands up."

Joe started to bend down. As he did so, his foot slipped. His body lunged forward and he instinctively reached out his hands. The younger officer, the one who had first drawn his gun, panicked and let off a volley. The first bullet smashed into Joe's shoulder. The next three missed him completely and the fifth hit Suzanna's left thumb as she threw herself between the policeman and Joe. Her father screamed her name then rushed at the policeman, knocking him to the ground. His partner just stood petrified. Suzanna's old boyfriend had dived behind her car when the first shot was fired. When he stood up he was sobbing. He stared in disbelief at the scene in front of him. Joe lay on the ground writhing in pain. Blood gushed from his shoulder. Suzanna knelt on the bloodstained grass beside him trying desperately to stop the blood that spurted from the bullet hole. Her father told the second policeman to call an ambulance. The young police officer did as he was commanded. The other cop was dumbstruck. He sat on the ground shaking his head. "I thought he had a gun. I thought he had a gun," he kept saying over and over.

Both police officers were given five-week suspensions without pay. Suzanna's old boyfriend bought a used Honda motorcycle and left town. Her father got involved in the investigation of Joe's trial along with her uncle. Between the two of them they were able to locate witnesses who gave testimony implicating a former county sheriff. Vincent Mascetto testified that he had seen the three people run from the store after he had heard shots fired. For his silence, Vincent had been put on the short list for county plumbing contracts. He identified the robbers as three local teenagers—two females and one male. One of the young women was currently in prison serving time for prostitution and armed robbery. The other had been killed in a shoot-out with police in Los Angeles. The killer was identified as a nephew of the former county sheriff. Another county employee came forth to testify that he'd been ordered by the sheriff to send all mail from Brenda McFarley to Joe Walks-Bear back to the sender. Brenda McFarley testified that the sheriff's officers had told her that her Native American boyfriend was dead. The man who had killed the storeowner was arrested outside his home in a nearby suburb. He admitted having taken part in the robbery although he tried to blame the shooting on the woman who had been killed in California.

Joe Walks-Bear received a pardon from the governor of Illinois, but only after a year-long battle in the courts. He suffered emotionally from the experience and for several years had to undergo counseling. In an interview with a Chicago-based free-lance writer, Joe lashed out at society. The writer portrayed him as a bitter man, angry at the world for an innocent mistake. Following the interview's publication, Joe was arrested for drunk driving and resisting arrest.

Although Joe did win a large sum of money in a wrongful jailing suit, the decision was appealed and took years to settle. In the meantime, he fought a daily battle with depression as obstacle after obstacle had to be overcome in his struggle to become a truly free man.

Suzanna stuck by his side through it all. Often the one Joe lashed out at during his fits of depression, she nonetheless remained steadfast in her belief in him. Eventually they were married and moved to Portland, Oregon, where nobody knew about their past and where they hoped to build a better life.

Joe took up wood carving and began showing his work around the country. He met and befriended a medicine man. Things began to turn around for Joe.

Suzanna chronicled in writing the painful series of events in Joe's past, but she was unable to interest a publisher in publishing the account as a book. Eventually she had to set the manuscript aside. She took a job as a reporter in a small town outside of Portland.

After five years of marriage, Suzanna became pregnant. The couple felt blessed. Joe was finally granted the monetary award from the State of Illinois. Under the guidance of the medicine man, Joe was adjusting to society. Suzanna finally found a small press that was interested in publishing her book. The layers of frustration were peeling away. Although it happened slowly and painfully, Joe was able to forgive, and when he did, he began to find the true definition of freedom—his freedom.

SAME OLE, SAME OLE
THE INDUSTRIAL EDUCATION OF A
REDSKINNED MACHINIST

It's a great place—your country, my land.
—*Alvin Harper*

Alvin Harper thought the bastard was choking to death. His face was turning red and his eyes were bulging and beginning to water. His safety glasses slipped down over his nose and fell to the floor between the brake and gas pedal. He reached over, turned the volume knob on the radio down, then picked up his glasses. "What the hell did you say?" he asked.

"I said she called it her box," he repeated for his friend Wally, then added, "Can you imagine that?"

"No shit!" He thought about it for a moment then continued, "Well, I guess it beats calling it a cunt, a snatch, or a pussy. Women don't dig that at all."

"Just straight out asked me if I ever wondered about her box."

"What did you say?" Wally asked.

"I told her no—and I meant it."

"What did she say then?"

"Nothing for a couple of minutes. She looked at me real funny-like and told me that I would now. And you know what? She's right. I can't keep my mind off of it. She walks past the machine shop department, looks over at me, and asks, 'What you thinking about, boy?' in that sweet-sounding southern accent of hers. I want to sit her down and tell her that I'm thinking about lots of things—like what happened to

Raymond Yellow-Thunder in Nebraska. I want to tell her that as an Indian man I'm sick of the injustice that my people go through. I want to tell her that I feel like telling this whole place to screw themselves and hook up with the American Indian Movement and kick some racist ass. But you know, Wally, to these people this is the world. Getting up every morning, showing up at this factory and standing at a machine—hell they become part of the stinking machine. I want to tell her I'm sick of punching a clock and responding to bells like some kind of Pavlovian dog."

"What's that?"

"See Wally! See what the hell I'm talking about?"

"Well hell, you gotta have a job. Everybody does. That's just the way it is, Chief."

"Maybe for you, but not necessarily for me."

"So what are you going to do?"

Wally reached over and turned up the radio like he really didn't want to hear the answer. Just to spite him, Alvin turned the volume back down. He knew Wally hated it when anyone messed with his radio.

"I already got a woman."

"You mean that hippie girl that was here waiting for you to get off last Friday night?" Wally traced the outline of a woman's figure in the air to indicate he liked the way she was built, whistled softly, and grinned at Alvin. "Are you in love with her?"

"I don't know about love, but I do care about her."

He laughed quietly to himself. Alvin braced himself, waiting for a smart comment. Then Wally asked, "Does she got a job?"

"No."

"So who pays the rent?"

"I do."

"I figured as much." He puckered his lips and nodded his head. "Let me ask you something, Chief. Do you sleep with her?"

"Most of the time. We have kind of an open relationship."

"What the hell is an open relationship? Is that what those hippies call free love?" He made a screwing motion with his hips and laughed when Alvin frowned.

"Does that mean I could come over there and get me some, aw, you know, some of her box?" He burst out laughing like he'd just told a great joke or something.

"Could I come over to your mother's house and get some of your sister's?" Alvin asked, waiting to see if he'd react. He didn't, at least not the way Alvin expected.

"If she was into it I wouldn't care. She's nineteen. I doubt if she'd go for it though. She doesn't like you hippie types."

"What the hell are you talking about, you hippie types?"

"Well, you're a hippie aren't you?" He looked at Alvin with a lopsided grin. "You wear a headband and those bell-bottom blue jeans."

"Does that make me bad?"

"Not in my book."

"So tell me Wally, what do you think I should do about Dana?"

"I heard her talking about you in the cafeteria yesterday. She got her eyes on you, brother. I heard her call you her cute little hippie Indian. Then she started whispering and that table full of women started giggling. Those women started talking dirty after that so I got out of there as quick as I could. I didn't want to be listening to that kind of stuff."

Wally was planning a fishing trip and wanted to know if Alvin, whom he called Chief, could give him any advice on how to catch a lot of fish. The Indian told him that the best way is to set a gill net just before it gets dark, go home and make love to your old lady, then pull the net out in the morning. The young Native American didn't like fishing with a rod and reel and when he told Wally that, Wally said he couldn't believe he'd heard what Alvin had just said. Wally was disappointed because he thought every Indian was a sportsman, that they had these fishing secrets that got an Indian all the fish he wanted. Alvin laughed and told him he was right: skins set a net, go home and make love, and in the meantime catch so many fish they throw most of them back. Wally started losing interest in the young Indian as his fishing consultant once he realized that he wasn't about to share the "Indian secret." Neither man said anything for a few minutes as they finished eating. Alvin was lost in thought. He wondered about rumors circulating of an "Indian uprising" in the Dakotas. If and when it kicks off, maybe I'll head out there and get involved, he thought.

"Hey! Isn't that the work bell? What time is it anyway?" Wally asked.

"We better get back inside."

"Yeah, you're right. What they got you working on today?" Wally asked.

"Turning shafts for Bohman Electric," the Indian answered.

"What you going to do about the hillbilly chick? She likes you, you know. I bet she'd give you some of that sweet hillbilly loving. You should know that Bob likes her also. Just letting you know."

"What should I do?"

"Ask her out for a drink. Screw that redneck Bob. A lot of people go to the bowling alley lounge after work. It's pretty cool. You want me to tell her to meet us there?"

"No! I can talk for myself."

"I know girls like that. They like to party."

"Have you ever partied with her? Have you had her? Be honest."

"No," Wally answered, "but I sure would like to."

"Has anybody that you know of?"

"Not really, man. I don't know anything about her as a person except that she's a hillbilly."

"Don't say hillbilly. She might just be from the South."

"Besides Bob the redneck been trying to get her for the longest time. He may not like you copping his stuff."

Alvin heard the bell ring. "Oh shit, there it goes. See you later, Wally. By the way, I don't give a shit about that redneck asshole. What's he gonna do? Whip me?"

"Okay, Chief. I'll see you at break time. Hey, should I talk to her?"

"I told you I would."

The two machinists each went back to their departments to work the rest of the shift. Alvin worked in the machine shop. Wally was a set-up man in the grinding department. They worked on the second shift for a large company that produced small electrical motors. The second shift consisted of about one hundred and twenty people, mostly younger women who worked on the assembly line or operated punch presses. Everyone in the plant was surprised that Alvin and Wally had become buddies, for they were as different as day and night. Until you got to know them it was virtually impossible to imagine them sitting together in a bar.

Alvin had long hair and dressed in blue jeans, motorcycle boots, and a leather jacket. It was his long hair and deep-set eyes Dana found attractive. Wally sported a crew cut and wore work uniforms with safety shoes. He carried a six-inch scale and a small calculator in his shirt pocket. He also had a keychain attached to his belt that had about twenty keys on it. He could be heard rattling down the aisle in the factory even when the roar of the machinery made it hard to talk. Alvin lived in a sort of commune in the New Town area just off Addison and Broadway. He shared a small apartment with a young woman he'd met at a concert. She had come home with him after the concert and had ended up staying.

Wally lived with his mother near Central and Grand Avenue. He was a third-generation Polish guy who still had a bit of an accent. His mother barely spoke a word of English. Wally had been with the company for eight years. He never missed a day and his encyclopedic knowledge of the grinding machines surprised nearly everyone. He had started as an assistant on the line but through sheer dedication had moved up until he was the lead set-up man. Whenever there was a problem with a machine, they consulted Wally and when they needed a part to fix it, Alvin was brought in. As a result, the two worked closely together and began eating lunch together. They talked about everything under the sun—work, women, and family. Wally would bring his lunch in an old metal lunchbox he said his father used to use. Alvin teased him about the old box until Wally told him that his father had been killed by some black muggers near Western and 42nd Street.

The Indian had worked at the company for less than a year. He understood machines and liked to work without supervision. For him the job was just that—a job. Shortly after Alvin started working there he and Wally discovered that what they had in common was that the redneck foreman didn't like either of them. For that reason alone they usually ate lunch together. They were two outcasts in the lunchroom which belonged to the foreman and his ass-kissing buddies. Their boss and his friends sat like a group of vultures at the front table and made rude comments to women and other workers they didn't like. After hearing a racist remark made by one of these men, which the foreman insisted was only a joke, Alvin rarely entered the lunchroom except to use the Coke machine. When he did go in, the men would sit there staring silently at him. Everyone knew they didn't like him and he couldn't have cared less about them. The result was tension. The foreman didn't like Wally because he felt threat-ened by his mechanical ability. Like his newfound buddy, Wally had no love for those men, and did not hesitate to let them know how he felt.

ANOTHER CHAPTER OF SAME OLE, SAME OLE—
FORTY-FOUR DAYS LATER

They were lying in her bed. He was reading and she was busy clipping her toenails. They weren't living together but he spent so much of his time there with her that she washed his jeans and he folded her pants in the basement laundry room. They both joked about it. He even kept his own toothbrush in her bathroom.

Although they tried to keep their relationship a secret, everyone on the second shift suspected they were carrying on. When questioned, they would each reply that they had gone to a movie then dancing once. Of course, everyone interpreted that their own way. One rumor was that they had interracial orgies on weekends. Dope and sex always creeped into the conversation about them. The orgy rumor had started when Dana, Alvin, and Ruth were picked up by Ruth's husband one Friday night to go out partying. Wally and his date had joined them at the restaurant. They'd only gone out to eat and have a few drinks but the rumor mill started to grind. They ignored the whispering as best they could but problems were beginning to develop with their coworkers.

When the situation at Wounded Knee happened in South Dakota things intensified—especially for Alvin. Suddenly he sensed hostility from guys who had always been civil with him before. At first he couldn't understand what was happening but then it began to dawn on him that those workers were brainwashed when it came to Indians and their rights. The first incident was when he heard war whoops as he walked down the aisle, then he found a note hanging from his toolbox that said, The only good Indian is a dead Indian. He reported it to the union but there was nothing anybody could do.

"Look here, Chief," the Union steward had said. "People call me Dago all the time. Ain't no harm meant. I think you're being sensitive."

"Do I have to get outside sources?" Alvin asked.

"Do what you want, but there ain't no witnesses. So what can I do? Chief, just forget it."

"Don't call me 'chief' anymore," Alvin countered.

That was the prelude to the blowup that was to follow.

As she clipped her nails, Dana talked to her lover about his writing.

"So you read good writing and try to imitate it? That's what you do? Then you ain't really a writer at all—just a machinist who imitates good writing," she commented.

The young Indian man closed his book and put it down. "Well actually, Dana, I think of myself as a writer who works as a machinist. It's my day job. I imitate the style of other writers so I can become a better writer."

"By imitating. Isn't that copying?"

He smiled, reached over, and began to rub her bare leg. He noticed her skin rising into goose bumps. "I don't copy the stories or the words—just how the stuff is presented."

"That's wild. Why do you do it?"

"I guess I'm trying to get away from the excrement of all the judgmental assholes that surround me. To me it's like a medicine. I get to purge myself of these antisocial thoughts in a socially acceptable way. Everybody got something they do to make themselves feel better. Writing is my medicine."

"That's a weird thing to say," she replied, swinging her legs to the other side of the bed. "Sometimes you're so strange."

"I thought that you liked that about me," he answered.

"I do but other people don't and they're really starting to talk about us. It's getting to me."

"And?" he asked.

"And what?"

"What do you want to do about it?"

"I don't know. It's just getting to me. What is it that you want from me?"

"What do you mean, Dana?"

"You know—from a lover"

"You want to be my lover?"

"I am your lover," she said as she reached over and kissed him playfully.

"Well, I want to be accepted, not worried over. I want a sense of kinship where I can feel normal." He paused, lit a cigarette, then continued. "I want a situation where I'm not misunderstood or resented when I find comfort in silence. Can you understand that?" He looked at her and she nodded. "What do you want from a lover?"

"I want a lover who thinks about my box," she replied as she moved closer to him.

"That's what started all this trouble in the first place."

They both laughed as she lay down on top of him for the fourth time in two hours. She liked it on top.

AND YET ANOTHER CHAPTER—LATER THAT SAME WEEK

He hadn't seen the paper that morning so he didn't have a clue as to what Snider was talking about when he asked, "What the hell you Indians doing in South Dakota?" The Wounded Knee thing had made the front page.

When Snider handed him the paper, Alvin felt a burst of pride. "It's about time they did something out there."

Snider gave Alvin a strange look then continued. "You know, I was in the Army. I'm proud to be an American and don't like anybody putting this country down."

As Alvin walked back to his work area like he'd done a hundred times before, no one wished him good morning or said a single word. He began to feel uncomfortable, ill at ease. That got the muse flowing so after he got the large LeBlonde lathe set up and running, he grabbed a pencil and began writing a poem. He wrote as the machine worked.

> The bad-assed foreman is glowering at me
> in an old testament sort of way.
> he be makin' me feel like
> a major sinner, his friends 'n' him.
> this place is going to be
> kinda like clearing my throat . . .

so new air can get in, I guess.
trouble wrapped itself around
him 'n' me because a woman
he desired, desired me instead.
then those militant Lakotas
made front page news
by kicking America's head.
told 'em things hurted ears 'n' egos.
I cheered and chanted with
my LeBlonde engine lathe . . .
chips was flying up 'n' 'round.
little blue C's flying
America got caught in a lie
upside down flag flapping
in western winds stinkin'
of reactionary . . .

"What the hell are you doing?" It was Bob.

"I'm working. That's what I'm doing."

"No you ain't. You're writing one of them damned riddles again. I'm sick of this shit. You grab a broom and while this lathe is cutting you be cleaning up the area or pulling chips. You're not paid to write." Bob's face was beginning to turn red.

"Get out of my face. I'm doing my job. I'm not paid to pull chips or sweep the floor. I'm paid to run this machine. Look at the contract."

"I'm writing you up." Bob grabbed the paper with the poem on it as evidence.

"You can't just take my stuff like that. This ain't Nazi Germany."

"It's a good thing for you it ain't," Bob countered. "This shit you write is anti-American. If you don't like this country so much, why don't you go somewhere else?" the redneck asked.

"This ain't about no poem. This is about Dana. Go ahead and write me up, jack-off. I'll have Dana say you're sexually harassing her."

"I'm writing you up all right. Everytime I see you, I'm writing you up. You're history in this place."

"Hey, man, I'm screwing the woman you wish you had. She told me about you coming on to her. I should call your wife and tell her."

"You're asking for a major problem and you're going to find it right here, you dirty Indian."

"What if I just kick your ass right now? Me and you, man to man—right now."

"You threatening me?"

"No, Bob, I'm promising you."

"That's it. Let's go to the office. Right now."

On the way to the office two of Bob's friends joined them. They fell in step with Bob as though they were bodyguards. As they got to the door of the personnel office one of the men grabbed Alvin and tried to push him against the wall. He knew immediately that he was being set up. He put his hands up to show that he wasn't resisting. The secretary sitting by the front door saw it all and came to his rescue. Both Alvin and the foreman's thugs were given a verbal reprimand by the personnel manager. The following day, Alvin got written up again for making a defective part. The process of getting rid of him had been put into place. That did not surprise him much but when Wally started eating his lunch in the lunch-room with some of the other guys, Alvin was somewhat disturbed. To make matters worse, he and Dana had their first real argument.

"Why'd you have to say that to him?"

"It's true. You told me he's been hitting on you."

"Now everybody's pissed at me. Don't you understand? I need that job," she said.

"Why? You can find another one."

"But I want that one. It's close to my house and I know everyone there."

"It doesn't bother you that he's always hitting on you?"

"He just talks. He doesn't do any harm," she countered.

"Maybe you like it."

"Maybe I do," she shot back, then began to fold the laundry. "Listen, maybe it would be a good idea if we didn't see each other every day. Maybe we need a break."

"Is that what you want?" he asked as he pulled the wet clothes from the washer and stuffed them into the dryer. "Is that really what you want?"

"I don't know what I want anymore. Anyway, I have to go down South to get my kids next week."

"Your kids? I thought you said they lived with your mother."

"For the summer. They been spending the summer with their grandmother in Kentucky. I told you about that. I have to pick them up. I'm taking the week off. When I get back, I don't think we should see so much of each other."

"If that's how you feel," he answered.

"That's all you have to say?"

"What more can I say?"

"Don't you even care?" she asked.

"You know damned well I do."

"About the sex, right?"

"That too," he said, nodding.

"About me?"

"Yes, about you."

"Do you love me?" She wanted to know.

"You know damned well I do. I told you that."

"We can still see each other but not like it is now. I think we should date other people."

"Just like that, huh?"

"Well."

"I tell you I love you and you hit me with this. What is this—a game or something?"

"Of course not. I never thought the situation would get this heavy. The people at work—"

He cut her off. "Screw them. I don't give a shit about any of them."

"I know you don't, but I do. Was it necessary to broadcast that we were sleeping together?"

"The way I understood it is that getting me in your bed was a challenge to you. You and your girlfriends started this shit, not me."

"Don't flatter yourself," she answered.

"Just because I'm an Indian you had to do this? Bed the chief—right?"

Dana was silent for a minute. "Well, I'm the one that comes out looking bad. Like a whore or something."

She started crying. He took her in his arms and tried to comfort her. They made love all that afternoon but he knew in his heart that it was the beginning of the end. He slept very little that night. What little sleep he did get was interrupted by bad dreams. He could hear the garbage picker's cart through her open window. It was a small crackling noise. Then he heard the rattle of cans and the metal clang of garbage cans being opened. That's a lonesome sound, he thought, and one that has become so familiar. A comment on the state of things. He noted that he had seen more and more garbage pickers wandering into the nightmares that were their lives. Their sweat-stained shirts reminded him of rats. Why he made that association, he didn't know. They surely held a stench that attracted rats and flies and lice. He thought it was the stink of sweat and rot. The demeaning odor of dreams that had decayed and left only the shell of a human being wandering the alleys in the night. They were like stories floating through the big city alleys or seeds in the wind tossed this way and that.

He rolled over on his side and looked at Dana.

She was pretty. Her chopped black hair and green eyes were startling to look at. Her smile signaled a woman who took life to be an adventure, an exciting woman to be around. She was breathing in small gasps, as if even asleep she was excited to be alive. And when awake, she was a real southern lady with some down-home southern opinions and attitudes. He found her a refreshing change from the hippie girl he had been living with until he caught her with another woman and a skinny hippie guy in his bed. He touched Dana's face softly, then ran his hand gently to her breasts and began circling them slowly. Her nipples hardened, she opened her eyes and smiled.

"What are you doing?"

"Thinking about your box again," he reminded her.

"It's getting to be a habit."

"You told me it would," he smiled

"I did, didn't I? Well, you started it."

"And Momma, I can finish it too."

"Oh don't I know it," she replied as she climbed on top of him.

Three days later he was pushing the last of Dana's suitcases into the back seat of her sister's car. Dana came out of the apartment with a bag of munchies for the trip. She put her hand on his arm. He stopped and looked down into her face. A tear rolled down her cheek. He kissed it away.

"I'll only be gone for ten days," she said. "I'll be back. We'll get together then. Just think how we'll tear up that bed."

He didn't say anything.

"Damned hippie. It was sure nice between us, wasn't it?"

He nodded his head and chewed on the inside of his mouth.

"Aren't you going to say anything?" she asked.

"What's to say?"

"I don't know."

"Neither do I, Dana."

She got in the car and put it in gear. He felt a sudden surge of emotion. Panic grabbed his heart and squeezed. "Dana!"

She stopped the car.

"Dana, I love you."

She started crying again. "I know you do, you damned hippie."

They stared at each other for a long time. Tears flowed down her face. He chewed the inside of his mouth but said nothing. He was afraid he would cry too. He reached out and touched her face. "I'll see you in ten days, baby doll."

She put the car in gear a second time and pulled away. He smiled and blew her a kiss.

That was Sunday afternoon. Monday afternoon, when he reported to work, he couldn't find his time card in the rack. He walked into the personnel office to get a card and was told to see the manager.

"I'm looking for my time card."

"You've been dismissed. We're letting you go because we've had two reports of sexual harassment against you," the personnel manager said.

"You've got to be kidding."

"Unfortunately I'm not. They're right here on my desk."

"Who's charging me?" Alvin asked.

"One is from a Fran Wochowski. The other was made by a Miss Dana Lawrence."

"I want the union in here. You can't do this. It ain't legal. I wouldn't screw Fran Wochowski with your dick. Get the goddamned union in here!"

"Well, that's your right of course, but it might interest you to know that one of the witnesses against you is Wally, your union steward. Wally said that he talked to you about it. Advised you to stay away from Dana Lawrence."

"This is all bullshit. Dana was forced into this and so was Wally. I know it."

"Can you prove that Mr. Harper?" the personnel manager asked. He looked at Alvin and waited. Alvin shook his head and the man continued, "Miss Lawrence signed it, pal. That's all I know. I'll have security escort you to get your tools. We don't want no trouble. I hope you'll cooperate."

"What about my check?"

"Here it is," he said as he handed an envelope to Alvin. "We even gave you your vacation pay. Of course it had to be prorated because you weren't here a year. Good day and have a good summer."

Alvin took his tool box and left. Twenty years later he ran into Dana at the Century Mall. As he walked by her he nodded but he said nothing. He looked back and saw she was crying.

TREACHERY IN THE GHETTO

"If I've been to one demonstration, I been to a hundred but I have never been to a demonstration quite like the one where we Indians joined with the Greens to demonstrate against Hydro-Quebec in Chicago. Son-of-a-bitch it was hot as hell out too and there we were—at the wrong address."

"That's what made it special?" Robert asked.

Gerald and Robert were sitting in McDonalds on Sheridan and Foster. The two Native Americans hadn't seen each other in several days and were catching up on things.

"Well, first off, like I said, we were at the wrong address. That whole day started out kinda messed up. My old lady woke up grouchy as hell. When she saw me getting ready to leave she said she had plans and needed me to stay around the house to watch the kids." Gerald paused to sip his cup of coffee. "Hell, the last time she did that she was gone for two days. My little girl was running a fever and I was out of Tylenol for her. Wanda ran out to get some and didn't come back for two days. She even took the goddamned checkbook! There I was, stuck in the house with no money for medicine, groceries, or cigarettes. Man was I pissed."

"Well, where did she go?" Robert asked.

"To tell you the truth, I never found that out. I threatened to kick her ass, but she knows better. I think she's seeing another guy. Probably a white guy too." Gerald laughed bitterly then looked into his coffee. He swirled it around for a second then took another sip.

"Oh come on, man. You're just being paranoid," Robert said as he stirred his own coffee.

"No I ain't. I know she's fooling around on me. It's only a matter of time before I catch her."

"Well, how do you know?" Robert asked.

"She's always bitching at me. No matter what I do she's got to bitch. Nothing I do is good enough for her. I'm telling you, man, that's a sure nuff sign. I do all kinds of things for her but nothing makes her happy. She's seeing somebody."

"Like what kinda things do you do?"

"Well, like just the other day. I painted this Hindu's back porch for him and when he paid me I went out and bought a couple of toys for the kids. They'd been good and I thought they deserved something special. Man, she freaked out on me and took those toys right back. She said we needed other things that were more important."

"What did she get?" Robert avoided Gerald's eyes as they talked. He didn't want to see the pain he knew he would find reflected there.

"I really don't know. I didn't want to start a war by asking."

"Yeah, I think I know what you mean. So anyway, what about that demonstration you mentioned?"

"Oh yeah! That. Well, it was organized by these activists from Greenpeace or something like that. They were demonstrating against that hydro dam they're building on Indian land up there in Quebec. They wanted some Indian involvement and so they called Rudy and he let the rest of us know about it. He said at least some of us should show up. So I decided to go down there. I had my demonstration clothes all laid out and then Wanda comes downstairs and sees me getting ready. 'Where the hell do you think you're going?' she asked me."

"Your demonstration clothes," Robert asked. "What do you mean?"

"You know, ribbon shirt and choker. Then I got this little backpack that I carry other things in. When she saw that she knew what I was up to and she just wanted to mess with me. I told her where I was going and I even asked her to come with me."

"What did she say?"

"She started bitchin' of course. Cussed me out for wanting to take her and the kids to a violent demonstration. Even though she knew it was gonna be nonviolent. I told her a million times I don't believe in violence. She knows I'm a pacifist." Gerald leaned back and looked out the window. He shook his head and cursed silently. Robert leaned forward.

"So what do you carry in the backpack? Why did she get mad at you when she saw it?" he asked.

Robert knew Gerald was a sensitive kind of guy. Those are the suckers that always end up getting screwed by women like her, he thought. She sure as hell wouldn't get away with that with me. I'd put her in line real quick or I'd be out of there. But this guy, he thought, has to go the whole route before he'll wake up.

"There's a gas mask and some magic markers in it. I keep some sage and sweet grass, just in case," Gerald answered.

"And what happened?" Robert asked as he drained the last drop of coffee from his cup.

"I called my aunt to see if she would take the kids. It cost me ten bucks but she agreed to baby-sit for me. Then I went by your house to get you but your roommate said some woman had come over and you were gone for the day. Who were you romancing anyway? You never told me nothing about a new girlfriend."

"I don't remember who it was," Robert replied as he got up to get a refill. He waited a second as Gerald drained his cup and handed it to him. As he walked to the counter, Robert took out a hankie and wiped the sweat from his face.

What a lucky sucker, Gerald thought to himself. Robert don't have to answer to anybody. I should have stayed single.

Son-of-a-bitch can't even remember what woman he's fooling around with. That's playing the field, boy. Gerald smiled to himself as he thought about his friend's luck. If it wasn't for the kids, he thought, I'd be so far gone that bitch wouldn't know what to think.

Gerald loved Wanda, but she had been really hard on him these last couple of months. They hardly ever had sex anymore and when they did it felt empty and mechanical. Not like it used to be. Whenever he asked Wanda about it she reminded him that she had two of his babies and what did he expect anyway. She had a way of making him feel like the guilty one.

He had suggested they go visit some of his relatives on the reservation in Ontario but she had nixed that idea by saying he was probably going to end up on a drunk with some of his cousins. Besides, she was in no mood to be left alone with his relatives while he ran around visiting.

"So why don't you just leave her?" Robert suggested as he returned to the table with the coffee. He had startled Gerald. "You know, you could just cut out. That's what I'd do."

"The kids," Gerald answered. Robert nodded his head.

"Kids sure can be a problem, can't they?"

"It's not their fault they were born."

"Yeah, I know that, but they sure do clip people's wings," Robert said.

"I couldn't leave my kids. I'd go crazy without them."

"So why don't you just tell her to go and keep the kids? That might be a solution."

"There's too many Indian kids being raised without both parents. It ain't good. Besides, I wouldn't do that to Wanda. She don't deserve that. She's a good mother, you know. Those kids love her and . . ." Gerald paused a moment. "And so do I. I keep hoping we'll work things out. They got to get better."

"What if they don't? You're miserable enough now, man. I bet she's miserable too. That has to affect those kids. They might be better off if you broke up with her." Robert took a long swallow of coffee and watched his friend's face to gauge his reaction to the idea. Then he continued, "I bet she'd let you visit them anytime you wanted."

"No, that's no answer. That's a cop-out. I want those kids to have a family life."

"Well, I'm just thinking about you. You're my pal. I don't like to see you feeling so bad. Maybe you could take a little trip up to Canada for a month or so. Get your head together. Maybe a short separation would do you both good."

"Maybe so but I don't want to be away from the kids that long."

"So take them with you. They'd love it up there. You could let them run wild and not have to be worrying about them all the time. Wanda could get her head together and maybe things would work themselves out."

"You know what? Maybe you're right. I'm gonna think about that," Gerald said, leaning back to light a cigarette.

He shut his eyes. He could hear her voice nagging at him. It was always the same: her voice, edgy with irritation, drove itself against his eardrums and smashed headlong into his nerves. At times like that he wanted to just holler at her to shut her up and make her leave him alone. Instead he usually picked up a book and read or took the kids out for a long walk in the park.

"So you started telling me about this demonstration. What happened?" Robert asked.

"Well, when I couldn't find you I went down there myself and they were already marching around in front of this building on Michigan Avenue."

"How many people were there?" Robert asked.

"Maybe a hundred or so. Quite a few Indians too. Those ones from Aniwin were there. The Indian Center had a few skins representing them. The Institute for Native American Development sent some of their students. Those militant women from W.A.R.N showed up and they were looking good."

Robert laughed and made a sexist comment about the Women of All Red Nations. Gerald replied that they do some very good work for the People. They'd been through this before. While Gerald was the type of Indian who had always been involved in the Indian struggle, Robert didn't believe in social demonstrations. He was against demonstrating and felt any meaningful change had to come from inside the system. He advocated taking over by joining yet he never got to taking over.

"Then there was the usual groups of Communists selling their little newspapers," Gerald continued, "and some Chicanos from the South Side. A couple of old Black Panthers joined in and some radical-looking gay group called Act Up brought some real life to the action. Some pro-lifers were asking people to sign petitions and so was some guy trying to get on the ballot for an election. You know—the usual thing. It was pretty good as far as demonstrations go."

"So what made it so special besides getting all these different kind of skins together? I can't stand the way they always fight each other. Indians just can't get along together. That's how they took our land in the first place. Someone ought to—"

"Well anyway, as I was about to say," Gerald said cutting him off, "we were there about half an hour or so when this little old lady comes up to me and asks if we were demonstrating against the Canadian Consulate. I told her we was and she smiled and said that they had moved about two weeks ago. I couldn't believe my ears. Here was all these Indians marching in a circle and these cops watching us as we hollered at the Canadian government and they had moved up the street. I told the white guy running the thing but he just looked at me with this stupid grin on his face and didn't do anything for about ten minutes. Finally he sent this other guy to verify what I had told him. I guess he couldn't believe an Indian. Well after some discussion he informs us all that we were gonna move the demonstration to another address. Of course all the skins knew what was happening and we were having us a big laugh."

"What did you do?" Robert asked with a big grin on his face. He was enjoying this: imagining all those people demonstrating in front of the wrong place. "You ready for another cup of coffee?"

"So why don't you come on over to the house this afternoon?" Gerald asked. "Wanda's got a doctor's appointment. She said she'd be gone all afternoon. She got another yeast infection and that was her excuse for not getting it on with me last night. I don't know why the doctors can't give her something to take care of that. I'll be at home with the kids. I'm gonna make some chili and fry-bread. I got the whole afternoon free, though, so I'm gonna watch that Mike Tyson tape. You're welcome to join me."

"No can do pal. I got plans for the afternoon. I gotta run over to the Indian Center to get them to do my resume over for me." He shook Gerald's hand, then left to hop the Sheridan bus. Gerald watched his friend leave. The guy sure stays busy, he thought to himself.

Gerald got the kids down for their afternoon nap then turned on the TV.

He put in the Mike Tyson video and kicked back to watch it. It proved to be more violent than he had anticipated so he turned it off. He turned on the Cubs game instead. His mind drifted to Wanda and their problems.

What's the woman's problem, he wondered to himself. She's always complaining and once she said she wanted some excitement—freedom from patterns. "I want experiences that make me react. You bore me, Gerald, you really do. All you want to do is act like an old married couple or something. That's getting to be a problem and I don't want problems to solve, I want excitement." To his way of thinking, she was being unrealistic. People change and their lives change with them. They had the kids to think about. To him it was cut-and-dried but not to her. She seemed fragmented to him. One day it would be this, the next day it would be that. He never knew what was coming. She had these surreal ideas about life that she juxtaposed with actual facts. Trying to deal with her and her problems was quickly turning into a nightmare for him. It's true what Robert says, he thought. Maybe I should just book. But the kids need me. I could take them with me though. They would be better off on the reservation . . . We all would.

Gerald's thoughts were interrupted by the urgent ringing of the doorbell.

It was Robert and he was obviously shook up.

"Man, it's your old lady."

"Is she okay?" Gerald was afraid she'd gotten run over by a car or something.

"Yeah, she's okay. But if I was you, I'd go over to the Wooden Nickel and get her."

"Why? What is she doing?" Gerald asked as he mechanically began picking up the toys scattered around the room.

"Why don't you just go over and check it out?"

"I can't. The kids are sleeping," Gerald answered.

"Go ahead. I'll watch them for you. You gotta get over there as fast as you can. She's acting the fool, man."

"The Wooden Nickel? Is that what you said?" Gerald asked. He began stuffing the toys he'd picked up into a wooden toy box.

Robert nodded to Gerald, who was becoming distraught.

"Why the hell would she go there?"

"I don't know but man, she's there all right and making a fool of herself." He paused a moment to let the words sink in then added, "And of you. She's really high on something. You go ahead, I'll watch your kids." Robert sat on the couch. He picked up a pillow and put it next to him. "You need to get her out of there before she does something you'll both regret."

"What the hell is she doing?" Gerald asked.

"Gerald, why don't you go see for yourself?"

"Why don't you tell me?" Gerald picked up a plate and glass of water that were sitting on the coffee table. He walked into the kitchen. Robert followed and stood in the doorway.

"She's coming on to everyone in the joint. I mean, both men and women. She's really drunk and dancing around showing what she's got. I tell you, you better get over there."

Gerald stood in the kitchen and looked out the window. He was quiet. In the front room the television previewed a special report that would be shown on the evening news. Outside, in the alley, the sound of a garbage truck being loaded filtered through the walls of the building. Robert watched as Gerald wrestled with what to do. Robert noticed the ticking of the clock. It was one of those wind-up clocks. It was two fifteen. He read the Big Ben label printed on its face. This is rougher than I thought it would be, he thought.

"Okay, Robert. This won't take me very long. If the kids wake up I got a bottle made for the baby. It's on the counter." He pointed to the bottle in the glass container. "Give the two bigger ones a granola bar and put them in front of the TV. They'll be all right." Gerald walked over to where Robert stood, looked him straight in the eye, and then hugged him. "Bro, I want you to know that I really do appreciate this."

"Don't think nothing of it. What are friends for? You'd do the same for me."

Gerald took his jacket off the nail by the back door. As he put the jacket on he glanced at Robert and quietly said, "I owe you, bro." Robert smiled as his friend left.

Robert waited a minute or so, then glanced out the kitchen window and saw Gerald hurrying down the alley. Then he walked through the quiet apartment to the front door. He looked around the living room and shook his head. He stood by the doorway for another minute then finally opened it. Sunlight pierced the cool quiet darkness of the room. Robert noticed the specks of dust dancing in the shafts of light. He felt the rush of warm air and heard the hard noise of the ghetto life outside. He felt tempted to shut the door again, but instead looked outside. She stood there smiling.

"Is the miserable bastard gone?" Wanda asked. Robert nodded. "Good," she whispered. "By the time he figures this one out we should already be on the expressway heading south." She moved closer to Robert. He felt her warmth. She pressed against him and he marvelled at the softness of her body. She put her arms around him, then kissed him. Robert hesitated for a moment, then responded to her deep kiss. She ran her tongue around the inside of his mouth. Robert moaned softly, yielding to her demand.

"What did you tell him?" Wanda asked.

"To go see a demonstration," Robert answered.

"At the wrong address again. Dumb shithead will never learn," she laughed as she began emptying the front closet.

SLOW WALKER: HERO OF THE MUD FLAT BATTLES

It would have been the perfect ambush except for this slow-walking, fast-talking little white boy named Muffin. He was the slowest kid on earth and for us, on the day of the big battle, his lack of speed was a blessing. He saved our asses and became the hero of the hour. Muffin was the most unlikely kid in town to become anybody's hero, but that's exactly what happened—and oh, how that kid enjoyed it!

It all started when Rowina LeSage, a hot-tempered Métis girl, got into an argument with Roger Harper, a friend of Dougie, the most racist kid in Sapawe. It's not that racism was in short supply in Sapawe—there were white racists and Indian racists and everything in between—but with some people the racism just was so undisguised. With people like Rowina, Dougie, and Roger everything was about racism. Their perspective made life a bit difficult for their friends at times. Rowina didn't like white kids and didn't hesitate to say so. To top it off, Rowina had a tongue on her that reminded me of Lash LaRue's whip. She could be one mean girl when she wanted to. Another thing about Rowina was that she had five brothers and so she could box as good or better than most of us boys. She knew it and she used it.

"You and your pal Dougie are both stupid slobs," Rowina snapped at Roger, with whom she'd been arguing all day.

Roger gave her his meanest look but it didn't phase Rowina in the least. There is no way in hell that Roger could hope to intimidate Rowina. She was just too tough. But he was trying.

"If you were a boy, you know what I'd do to you?"

"Anytime you're ready, punk."

"Yeah, well you don't know how lucky you are," he responded.

"Roger, you're scaring me," Rowina teased as she stood there, feigning fear.

"Don't push your luck, girl."

"Any time you feel brave enough to try it, just hop your ass on over here. I bet I could knock you out."

"I wish you were a boy," Roger snarled, "I'd kick your ass all over this town."

"Yeah, sure you would!" Rowina laughed. "You and whose army?"

"Now that you mention it, I do have an army." He paused for a moment, grinned an evil grin, then added, "If I need one."

"You call that ragtag bunch of sissies you hang around with an army? Don't make me laugh," she sneered.

"We'll take you and your Indian war party on anytime and kick your asses real good."

"I really doubt that you little punk," she shot back.

What Roger was referring to by "Indian war party" was a group of us that hung around together. We weren't all Indians but most were, to varying degrees. At least once a month we'd get into a fight with Dougie and his group of friends. Usually it happened spontaneously but this time it would be different: this time it would be planned and anticipated. This time it would be serious business. Most of his group was white but there were some Indian kids that hung with them too. The division in Sapawe was not so much racial as it was by class— the management's children against the workers' kids.

"Okay, why don't we find out?"

"We're ready, anytime you guys are," Rowina answered back.

"Okay, big mouth." Roger stopped talking for a moment as though debating what to say next. " Saturday! Noon at the mud flats."

The mud flats were the stretches of fields between the railroad tracks in the Canadian National Railroad yard. The yard had been built on top of clay fields where nothing seemed to grow. It was rumored that the land was barren because it was saturated with mysterious chemicals someone had dumped there. As a result, people avoided the mud flats. Isolated and desolate, the mud flats were the perfect place to fight battles to the bitter end. The mud flats were where we went to settle our most serious issues. We didn't take any old argument there, it had to be something major. And in most of our eyes, the challenge Roger and Rowina had taken up was a serious matter. We were going to the mud flats.

"We're gonna kick your Indian asses," Roger warned.

"We'll see about that."

"Yeah, we sure will. You know the rules say anybody who is on the flats is in it. Even girls. You're gonna get it just like you was a boy. I'm gonna personally get you, Rowina."

"Like I'm supposed to be afraid," Rowina taunted.

"Talk your shit now because I'm kicking your ass on Saturday. When I finish kicking your ass, I might decide to do something else to you. You know what I mean?"

"You ain't man enough now and you never will be."

"Yeah?" Roger looked at Dougie and smiled a devilish grin. "We'll see what comes down on Saturday."

Every kid in Sapawe would get involved in this conflict before it was over although only a handful would actually fight. The kids had been pretty much cooped up over the winter months and this was going to be a great opportunity to let off some steam. The argument had taken place on a Thursday morning so there was some time for all of us to get ready for the big day. Preparations included recruiting kids to take part in the battle.

The politics involved in a battle of this magnitude were surprising. Favors were called in and some people were actually threatened—especially by Rowina who wanted to make sure she had a good-sized army. Preparations also included selecting our arsenal, a serious matter.

Rowina had worked out the details regarding weaponry with Dougie and Roger. A formal agreement had been reached—or so she thought. We chose slingshots for our long-range battles but when the battles raged closer, slingshots were ruled out because someone could get hurt. The next line of defense was what we called "flingers." These were long flexible poles we used to hurl clay balls. There was always much discussion about what kind of wood made the most effective flinger. Some kids liked ash, but others preferred birch, poplar, or cedar. The Indian kids chose poles with a fork in them. They would weave pouches onto them out of buckskin much like you would make a lacrosse stick. The flingers worked better that way. And the most close-quartered battles were fought by hand. No weapons could be used. It was here that wrestling and boxing skills plus personal bravery were of utmost importance.

Thursday and Friday were days of frenzied recruitment. Lines were being drawn among the kids and some of the decisions about which side this or that kid took didn't always have much to do with the original argument between Rowina and Roger. This year's battle would be a doozy as even girls on bad terms with each other got involved, deciding to settle their arguments on the flats. Anticipation was running very high. Chains of command were being defined and rules of war established. Rowina turned into something like a bitch goddess and played the part to the max.

Her first recruitment efforts were directed at a group of boys that included myself; my younger brother Ivan; Grant, an Italian boy we called Sammy; and her own brother, Vernon. We were each assigned duties and thus became her officers. Grant was second-in-command because he was good at planning. Ivan and I were given the responsibility of getting the weapons together and making sure every kid in our army was properly outfitted. The Italian boy was responsible for organizing support units. These were groups of smaller kids who made the mud balls we flung at the opposing army. Another group of noncombatants included three girls who would prepare lunch. No battle could be fought without a lunch break as part of the plan. As her army grew in number, Rowina delegated recruitment responsibilities to others. My brother and I, along with Vernon and Grant, were responsible for recruiting and getting volunteers. And that's where Muffin comes into the story.

Muffin was a volunteer. He wanted to be with us—he always wanted to be with us—but there were some in our ranks who felt he should be with the other side since his father managed the company store. In another place and time Muffin might have been known as "white trash" because of whom he associated with, but in Sapawe he was often referred to as an "Indian-lover," especially by Dougie and his group. There was much discussion among our band as to whether or not he should be allowed on our side in this fracas. Of course it would be decided upon by a vote. Much to her credit, Rowina believed in the democratic process—at least when it served her purpose and went her way.

"Muffin wants to join us," my brother Ivan informed the group.

"Why?" asked Grant.

"Because he's mad at Dougie for not having invited him to his birthday party."

"That's a good reason, but he's so slow," Rowina said.

"He's a crybaby too," Grant interjected.

"He's not a crybaby either," Ivan replied.

"What about the time he got hit with the ball?" Grant countered. "He cried for an hour and wouldn't stop until I bought him a cone."

"Well, what about the time you fell out of the rafters in the horse barn? You cried all the way home."

"Falling out of the rafters and getting hit with a baseball is two different things. Don't you think?"

"But you still cried. You didn't even get hurt," Ivan said to Grant.

"At least I don't pee in my pants like someone I know." Grant was getting down and dirty. That had been an accident and he knew it. I was about ready to come to my brother's defense when the Italian boy spoke up.

"Let's stop arguing. I say we let him in. We need as many people as we can get," Sammy said.

"Don't forget what his dad does. He's part of the bosses," Grant reminded us.

"But his old man doesn't hang around with the bosses. You all know that and Muffin don't hang with their kids very much," Ivan said.

"Only because they don't let him. He's too slow for them. That's why he comes to us," Rowina pointed out.

"He could work with the little guys," another boy offered.

"He won't go for that. He wants to be up front," Ivan continued. Turning to Rowina he asked, "What do you say? You're the leader. It's up to you."

"Well, like Sam the Man said, we need all the help we can get. Let's put it up to a vote."

"Should I call him in?" Grant asked.

"Yeah, he's got a right to know," she replied.

Muffin was brought into the clubhouse to witness the casting of votes that would decide his future as a warrior with our group. He had been waiting patiently outside. As he entered he looked around at each of the members of the inner circle. Everyone was stone-faced. No one but my brother smiled at him. They were pretty good friends. There were eight of us present and each of us was dead serious about what we were doing. Rowina explained to Muffin that some of her people were not in favor of him being with us because they felt he should be with the management group since his father was a manager. Of course he was ready for that.

Muffin was known as a fast talker and he now lived up to his reputation. He explained that his dad hated the book-keeping job and would rather be out cutting timber with our fathers if he had a choice. Grant reminded him about the baseball incident and Muffin countered by reminding us that he was a half a year older now and far more mature. That seemed to satisfy everybody except Grant who muttered obscenities under his breath.

Rowina called for the vote. It was a four-to-four tie, so Rowina offered him a chance to prove himself by working with the little guys making mud-ball ammo. But Muffin insisted that he be allowed to be on the front line because it was a known fact that he could use a slingshot real good. He reminded us of the time he killed a partridge with his sling-shot, which none of us had managed to do. "Not yet any-way," he added, being the diplomat. We needed a tiebreaker, and it came about in a somewhat odd way.

"I guess we'll have to wait until tomorrow to make a decision," Rowina stated. "We have to have more people present."

"But I want to know what side I'm gonna be on before I get home."

"So, we can do it tomorrow at school before the bell rings," she replied. "That's the best I can do."

"That's bullshit. I want to know now!" Muffin insisted.

"How we gonna do that? It was a tie."

Things were not going too well for Muffin at that moment. I could see the kid was breaking into a sweat and getting angry. I liked him and wanted him on our side. I was half afraid that he might start crying to convince us. I realized that if he didn't get in with our group he might just join the other side even though he wouldn't be any too happy about it. I also realized that this kid wasn't about to let this battle get by him. He was going to participate one way or another. I decided to help him out by making a suggestion. "I know what we can do." I offered. "We can let Chum decide."

"Chum? Are you crazy? How's a dog gonna decide something like this?" Grant said.

"Well, you guys all know that dogs have this instinct about who can be trusted. They know more than we do about what people will do. How many times have we trusted Chum out in the bush?" Turning to Grant, I added, "You said yourself that he was the smartest dog in town."

"Yeah, but not smart enough to vote," Grant countered. "This is serious business."

"How could we do it?" Rowina wondered. She sensed that this Muffin incident could lead to dissension in her ranks and she wanted a solution.

"Well, we can put Chum and Muffin in the middle of a circle and if Chum wags his tail or makes some kind of friendly signal, we'll know Muffin can be trusted. We'll trust the dog's instincts."

"I don't know about this," Grant said. "Trusting a dog to vote? I think it's crazy."

"Hey, we trust him to guard us when we're on camping trips. You don't think that's crazy," I said.

"But Chum likes everyone. You know he's gonna wag his tail or something," he argued.

"What about it Rowina? Does Chum get to vote?" I decided to apply some pressure of my own, and you know, play some politics, so I added, "If you can't trust my dog, I'm not so sure I can trust you guys. I just may decide to sit this fight out myself."

"That's a dirty trick!" Grant complained.

"This is politics, my friend. You've known this dog since he was a pup." Turning to Rowina, I pushed the issue. "Well? Does he get to vote?"

She winced and shot me a dirty look. I smiled at her. We both knew I had her.

"Okay. We'll see what happens." Rowina turned to Muffin then added, "You can't do anything to get his attention. Do you understand, Muffin?"

"I understand." At this point he was ready to do anything to be a part of the action. "I'll accept Chum's decision."

"I'll be goddamned," Grant muttered with disgust.

A few words about my dog Chum are appropriate here. I mean, after all it isn't every dog that gets to be a part of the democratic process in the way that Chum did. You know he had to be something special and, in most of our opinions, Chum was. Basically he was a mutt—part Labrador and part English Setter. No one but me ever called him a mutt and I only did so with love in my heart. He was special all right, and he looked special. He had the long flowing hair of his Setter ancestors, but his face and coloring were those of a Lab. His shoulders were broad and solid. His ears hung down in just that certain way that made him look intelligent. He used his expressive eyes to communicate all kinds of things to me.

From day one Chum was my constant companion. He'd wait outside the schoolhouse for me everyday, no matter what the weather was like. He came with me everywhere I went. He protected me and other members of my family too. If my older sisters had to go out at night, they always wanted Chum with them even though they often liked to tease me and say he walked lopsided. You know how intense sibling rivalry can get. No one could get anywhere near any of us if he suspected something wasn't right. He was friendly most of the time though, which was true to his Labrador breeding.

I've heard it said that when a dog has been raised around children from birth he seems to understand what those kids are thinking. The day Chum stepped into the circle of eight kids in Sapawe, Ontario, to decide the fate of a little slow-walking, fast-talking white boy, I truly believe he somehow understood the nature of his undertaking. I think he understood his decision might just possibly have a life-long impact on the kid.

Now a few words about Muffin. He was a good kid, smart and by no means a nerd. He had nerve and would go along with most of our schemes, but he couldn't walk through the bush. Try as he might, he could never keep up with the rest of us in the bush. I mean, this kid had proved himself on several occasions. He could spit as far as anyone, he could smoke without coughing much, he could fart pretty loud, and would even light one on occasion. And as far as long-distance pissing went, Muffin had placed second only to Grant in that winter's piss-off. He had pissed nearly five-and-a-half feet. Not too shabby considering he wasn't much more than four feet tall. The only trouble with him was that he was slow in the bush. As for the cry-baby bit, I secretly didn't blame him for crying. He got hit right in the eye with a hard-ball that Grant had thrown. I was pretty sure we all would have cried if we'd gotten hit. Grant was just pissed about the ten cents for the ice cream cone. I considered Muffin a stand-up guy. I was just hoping my dog liked him as much as I did as I explained what he was going to do.

Chum was up to the task. That dog had a natural flair for the dramatic. Like a politician out for votes, he walked from kid to kid, sniffing hands. He greeted each and every one of them, then walked to the center of the circle and looked at Muffin for a moment. He cocked his head to the left then to the right as though measuring up Muffin. We all held our breaths. The mutt looked at me and I pleaded with him silently to wag his tail. A few moments later he jumped up and placed his paws squarely on Muffin's chest. Muffin, true to his word, stood as still as a statue. Then Chum began wagging his tail. A cheer went up from the group.

Every kid in that circle was totally convinced we had done the right thing by Muffin. Muffin was overjoyed. He practically bubbled over with excitement as he promised, under oath, that he would fight to the end, that he would be faithful and obey Rowina's commands. He also promised he would not drag ass through the bush but somehow we all knew better on that count. So now the battle lines were drawn. All that was left was for the weather to cooperate. We all prayed for rain so that by the next day the clay in the mud flats would be soft and gooey and great for making mud balls.

Our prayers were answered on Friday afternoon just before school ended. Most of us had spent the day peering out the window to see what the sky was doing. Roger had made a remark to Grant about doing a rain dance and that had quickly escalated into a pushing match. Both sides were ready to go at it and we had a hard time not doing it right there in the classroom. I think the teacher suspected what was coming because we were given a big lecture about peace and community. While she was lecturing a few drops of rain hit the school window, then a few more. Pretty soon a sheet of rain streamed down the glass. A cheer went up from several of the students. We were gonna have a war, by golly, and spirits were running high. Rowina called a last-minute meeting on the way home to urge each of us to be ready for tomorrow. It was totally unnecessary because every one of our guys was raring to go—or at least we thought that was the case. My brother and I got up early the next morning, finished our chores, then headed out to meet Rowina and the rest.

The sky was overcast. The air was damp and just a bit chilly. I noticed goose bumps on Ivan's arms. I could smell the dampness of the leaves and moss as we walked to meet our friends. It smelled like a spring day. Clouds were rolling in from the west which meant that it would probably rain a little. It was a perfect day for a battle. When we got to the baseball diamond where we had all agreed to meet there were several boys and two girls already there. The girls had packed us all a lunch.

There were only ten in our group. We had expected at least twenty people but for various reasons our numbers had been cut in half. Of the ten, six were Indians. As I looked around the small but determined group, I noticed that every Indian was wearing something that would signal their heritage. Even I had decided to wear a beaded vest and a string of red beads. Muffin had put on a headband and a seagull feather sticking up in the back. He looked comical, of course, but none of us said anything. Rowina paced back and forth, cussing at the ones who hadn't shown up. She looked at Muffin for a moment and I figured she was going to insult him for the way he looked, but she didn't.

"Well, what do you think, Muffin?" She smiled as she spoke. "Are you ready?"

"I'm ready," he answered as he looked around proudly.

"I bet those other guys will have something to say about that there feather you got on your head," Grant commented.

"Does it look stupid? Should I take it off?" Muffin asked.

"Hell no. Don't take it off," Rowina spoke up.

"I just feel like it will give me good luck. I found it when we went on that camping trip to Big John Island. Remember that?"

"You'll be lucky if you don't get killed today," Gary Spoon joined in. "We all will."

"Well, I'll tell you this much. If you go down, Muffin, we'll go down together. I really do appreciate you being here," said Grant. We all felt the same. Grant didn't give praise very often, so Muffin must have known he was really welcome. It also meant Grant had decided to accept Chum's opinion of Muffin and that made everyone feel good.

"I think him and that feather are gonna bring us some luck," Rowina said as she smiled at Muffin. "Well, I guess we should get going. If anybody else shows up they can join us on the flats. I wonder how many of their people showed up?"

"You know what, I bet they got the same problem we do," Grant said to Rowina. "Well, let's hit it everybody."

"Wait! Before we go, I want you all to know that I consider you people to be my best friends. Can we do some kind of cheer together?" Muffin asked.

"I think that's a great idea. Okay everybody repeat after me," said Rowina as she pulled Grant and several others into a circle. "All for one and one for all! By the sacred power given to us as keepers of Mother Earth, we promise to fight all evil and not abuse the earth or the weaker beings. This is our pledge."

"And we promise to kick some ass," Muffin added. Everyone laughed.

From the ball field, which in reality was just an old corn field or something, to the mud flats was about a mile and a quarter. There were two ways to get there. One was to follow the road. The other was a more scenic route—a path that meandered through a valley and skirted several rather steep hills. Rowina had us fall in single file. She chose the scenic route and somehow it felt like that was the way we should get there. As we marched along, I kept noticing that Muffin was falling farther and farther back. Chum was also lagging behind. Perhaps he was watching over Muffin but I think he was just exploring the area. He was, after all, a hunting dog.

As we went down a very steep incline, walking became difficult. From this point on the path practically plunged down at about a sixty-degree angle. The granite rocks that served as our stepping stones were slippery and so we had to be very cautious or risk falling. The granite rocks had been dropped there by a glacier about a thousand years before— or at least that's what I'd been told. When we reached the halfway point, I looked back and noticed that Muffin wasn't even in sight. Grant and Ivan both saw me looking back.

"Don't worry. He knows the way to the flats. He'll get there at his own pace," Ivan assured me.

"What if he turns back?" Grant asked.

"No way!" my brother said.

"Why not?"

"I just know. He got more balls than you think."

"We'll wait at the bottom," said Rowina. "We need to take a rest anyway. Don't want to be worn out before we get to the flats." She looked up at the sky then continued, "I'd say we're a little ahead of schedule. I want to get there first so we can get the higher ground." We all started walking again.

"Watch your step," my brother warned everyone. "This is where Old Man Beaver-Heart fell and broke his hip. It was right here on this hill."

"Yeah, he's right," Rowina said. "We don't need no accidents so be real careful."

We heeded their advice. We were each carrying several weapons plus supplies so walking required total concentration. No one spoke as we labored slowly down the hill. One of the girls fell and started sliding down the mud. Two of the boys grabbed her and helped her to her feet.

"I said to be careful," Rowina said.

The small band of warriors nodded agreement. The girl smiled sheepishly and muttered a thank-you as the others helped her pick up what she had dropped. The group continued down the hill.

Everyone was so focused on what they were doing no one noticed how quiet things had gotten. There wasn't a single bird singing or squirrel scolding us for invading his territory. Things didn't feel natural: it was too quiet. Under other circumstances one of us would have noticed the signs immediately. I mean, after all, this group was made up of Indian kids who had been raised in this area. But because we were concentrating so hard on walking none of us noticed anything out of the ordinary. Eventually one of us would have sensed something was wrong but it never got to that point because all of a sudden the silence was shattered by Muffin screaming from the top of the hill behind us.

"Watch out!" he hollered. "On your left! On your left!"

Suddenly the girl who had slipped on the hill grabbed her elbow and let out a yowl. Grant got hit on the thigh at the same moment.

"Shit!" he screamed. "They're on both sides. They got sling shots. What are we gonna do?"

"Find cover!" Rowina ordered. We all obeyed, some of us before she had spoken.

"They ain't supposed to use slingshots. Not this close."

"Did you believe they'd go by your 'Rules of War'?" Grant asked. "Shit, Rowina, you can't be that stupid."

"Don't call me stupid," she replied.

"Never mind arguing. What are we gonna do?" Sammy asked.

"They got us pinned down here pretty good."

"There ain't nothing we can use to shoot back. Maybe we could rush them," he suggested.

"We can't. We'll never get up this hill," Rowina replied.

"Well, you're the leader. You wanna surrender?"

"No way!" she said. "We'll figure something out."

"Can you see how many of them are up there?" Grant asked.

We were spread out on both sides of the trail. I huddled next to an old stump. Grant, Rowina, the girl who'd gotten hit, and Sammy were all laying flat on their stomachs behind a rotten log. The others and my brother had taken cover behind a big boulder. Sammy let out a yell. He'd been hit on the leg. Immediately after that Ivan cursed as a rock hit his shoulder. I heard one whiz past my head. I tried to hide my head behind the stump.

"Those dirty bastards," Rowina cussed.

"Hey, Rowina, can you hear me?" It was Roger.

"What do you want?" she hollered back.

"What do you think I want?" he asked, followed by a loud laugh.

"Me too! I want the same thing," Dougie chimed in. We could hear them laughing and bragging about what they were gonna do to Rowina and us.

"What about our agreement? We said no slingshots this close," Rowina said, stalling for time.

"There's at least five of them up there," Grant whispered. "I'm gonna try something."

"Be careful," Rowina urged.

Grant got up to try and dash to better cover, but before he could, he heard someone let out a holler of pain and surprise. It came from the other group. It was Dougie. Then someone else screamed out.

"It's that goddamned Indian lover! He's at the top of the hill. Ouch! He got me. That little bastard," someone hollered. "Look out—he's getting ready to shoot again! That little bastard's good with that thing."

I took a peek. It was true. Muffin was running from one spot to another, shooting as he ran. I heard someone else get hit.

"You better get the hell out of here, Muffin. I'm gonna kick your ass for this," Roger warned.

"Go to hell. Here take this, asshole," Muffin answered the boy with a well-aimed shot.

Roger yelped as a stone bounced off his right arm. "You're gonna get it boy."

Muffin responded with another volley of rocks. Dougie and his friends scrambled for cover, hollering threats as they did so. Muffin ignored them and continued to assault their positions. Grant, who always carried a pocketful of rocks, began picking the guys off from our side. The others found things that they could use as well. Ivan shot a pine cone that found its mark on the back of Roger's neck. The tables were turning. Muffin had them pinned down from above and we were getting off some real good shots from below.

"Hey Muffin!" It was Dougie. "You know you're supposed to be with us. These guys don't care about you. Let's talk this out."

"Nothing to talk about."

"I'm telling you, if you don't stop you're gonna be in for some big trouble. What's wrong with you anyway?" Dougie said, trying a new tack. "They're are a bunch of Indians."

"They're my friends," Muffin answered as he let loose a shot that made Roger cry out in pain as it caught his right leg. He jumped back to hide from the wrath of Muffin's slingshot and as he did so, he came right into my sights. We had him in a crossfire. My small rock found his back. He cursed as he searched for shelter but there was none. Rowina got him next. Then Grant and Sammy both got him. That got us going real good. The juices were flowing and we could smell victory. We took our time and aimed well. Their trap had been turned around on them and they now were caught in it. We kept up the attack.

If there is one good thing that could be said about both Roger and Dougie it is that they both had a lot of spunk. When their friends took off, neither of them flinched as they continued to shoot back. They were both getting hit but wouldn't quit and didn't cry. It became obvious that they didn't have a chance. Rowina tried to give them a chance to surrender and admit defeat but they were both too stubborn and tough to accept.

"Had enough yet?" Grant asked as he hit Dougie with a nice shot. "You ain't got a chance. We got you. What are you gonna do?"

"We ain't giving."

"Okay, but it's your funeral," Grant hollered back, then turned to Rowina. "We could rush them now. What do you think?"

"Just give me a minute to think. Everybody hold your fire," she ordered.

"Don't wait too long," Grant advised. "We need to move on them right now."

"Don't tell me what to do," Rowina barked.

"They're gonna get away. You don't know these two like I do. They're really sneaky."

As if to verify Grant's advice, both Dougie and Roger dashed from behind their cover and made a headlong rush for the hilltop. They figured they could rattle Muffin's cage and get past him. Muffin, however, had other plans. He threw down his slingshot and waited with his slinger, ready to use it as a war club. Dougie and Roger didn't have a prayer to get past him. They realized it, stopped, looked back, and threw their hands up in surrender. Muffin stood his ground, poised to swing the club if necessary. It wasn't. With a certain amount of pomp and circumstance, he announced that they were now prisoners of our group.

"Lay on the ground," he ordered the two prisoners.

"Go to hell," Roger snapped back.

"Okay! You asked for it," Muffin said as he swung the pole at Roger. Roger—well, he ducked and hit the ground.

"Okay, okay. I'm on the ground."

So it was over and Rowina had made her point. But it was never really over because in less than a month we found ourselves back at the mud flats locked in combat.

As we grew older and began to learn to live together, the mud flat battles became less important, but the younger generation continued to "take it to the mud flats." Our group, however, had changed. Roger Harper's family moved away after his father was caught embezzling company funds. My family eventually moved to the metropolis of Atikokan where my life changed considerably. I don't know whatever happened to Muffin. Someone said he eventually joined the Canadian Navy and went overseas. My brother Ivan was killed in Viet Nam. Grant was convicted of rape. Dougie stayed in Sapawe until the company folded. Rowina got married several times and had lots of kids—at least that's what I was told. I always planned to go back to the old homestead in Sapawe, but I never did. Maybe the saying, "You can't go home again" really does have some truth to it. Nevertheless I'll always remember with affection that collection of kids that made life so eventful growing up in Sapawe.

CONE TREES AND BIG DEALS

"I'm a red-headed Italian." No one said anything. We just stood there looking at the kid, so he shrugged and continued, "You know, an Italian guy—like Columbus." Still no response so the kid kept on talking. "Okay, okay, a dago then, depending on who you're talking to."

"C-C-Columbus, a dago?" Vernon asked, with a puzzled look on his face.

"What's that got to do with us?" Grant asked.

"The guy who discovered this here land? You know, Columbus." The kid stopped talking, thought a moment, then snapped his fingers and started reciting a verse we all knew: "In 1492, Columbus sailed the ocean blue, he hit a rock and broke his cock, in 1492."

The kid bowed at the waist with a grand flourish, like a Mexican bullfighter.

Everyone started laughing, except Grant. He sized up the guy with a hostile eye. "I ain't never seen a red-headed dago before."

"Most people haven't but they've been in my family forever."

"Columbus didn't come here to Sapawe. Indians discovered this place. Our people were always here. From the start." We could all see that Grant had every intention of maintaining his hostile attitude. Whenever he got into one of his moods there wasn't much you could say to him. Sometimes I could pull him aside and try to reason with him. I didn't want Grant to blow our deal so I knew I had no alternative.

The boy looked at each of us three Indians, one after the other, then shrugged. "Who knows? I don't know anything. I only know what they tell me in school. My dad says half of that is bullshit. You know what I mean?"

You may be wondering how it is this red-headed boy calling himself a dago and a little on the rebellious side happened to meet three Indian boys of a similar nature just outside of Sapawe, deep in the backwoods of northwestern Ontario. As unlikely as it was, it was no accident, you can bet your bottom dollar on that. There were actually four of us boys but one was sitting high on a ridge watching—just in case. It was like that in Sapawe between us Indian guys and them white boys that summer. It was the year the army worms or caterpillars came through the area. They got on everything. There were so many of them crawling on the railroad tracks that even the trains had trouble moving. Those caterpillars made a mess of everything. I think it was 1954.

One thing about living in a small community—and Sapawe certainly was a small community—is that everyone knows what you're up to. Maybe sixty people called Sapawe home, and one-third of them were kids. So, as you can imagine, there weren't a lot of secrets. We knew everything—except where Jimmy the Rat, the local bootlegger, hid his booze. We were determined to figure that one out and that's how this whole situation with Jimmy got started. We wanted to find out where he hid his stash.

We found it out quick enough. From our vantage point on a high hill behind his shack we spotted Jimmy the Rat digging under an old barrel in a field. We had him. It was all so easy. We wondered why the Ontario provincial police could never catch the guy. They were always supposedly trying to bust him. As my dad would say, "The bugger is greasing their palms, that's why they can't catch him." No one ever knew if that was true or not, but go figure. Well, we'd got him easy enough but now we had the problem of what to do with the stuff.

"We could have a party and drink it all," Gary suggested. "Invite every kid in town. It would be a big blast. Just think of it.

"Are you cr-crazy or something? We'll kill ourselves, aye. There's too much there. We got to ge-get rid of it," Vernon argued. Vernon was Métis. He talked with an accent and a slight stutter. He always wore a beret that someone had told him came from France with his ancestors. Nobody believed that story.

"You want that son-of-a-bitch on your ass?" Grant piped in, shuddering. "If we had a party someone would sure as hell tell on us. You can be sure of that. And I don't want him on my ass. No way! He's one mean-looking bastard." Then he added, "He don't never take a bath. I bet he's killed people before. That guy's got some mean-assed eyes in his head. I mean to tell you!" "I mean to tell you" was his favorite expression.

"You ever smell the guy?" Gary asked. "They say when he lifts his arms you can whiff his BO from five feet away. Now that's nasty, ennit?"

So what are we going to do with the wine? I think we should drink some of it and try to sell the rest," Grant suggested. The problem at hand was how to get rid of the stuff quickly and with no questions asked. That counted out anybody we knew. Aside from it's being illegal for kids to have booze, we all sensed there was physical danger as well.

No one said anything for a few minutes. Grant sat on a stump, chewing a piece of grass like he always did when he was thinking. He was a big kid, on the verge of being fat. He wore a shirt that was two or three sizes too big for him but he liked it because it had pockets and lots of them. When a boy is ten years old, pockets are important. All kinds of important things could be carried in them, like rocks for your slingshot, candy, even comic books.

Gary was the youngest of all of us. He was tall for his age. Because of his pouting lips and brooding eyes everyone called him Pretty Boy—a name he hated. He took a jackknife out of his cowboy boot and started whittling on a stick. His family had moved from North Dakota a few years before but he still wore western clothing. Although he wasn't Anish- anaabe he was accepted as a shinob even though he was a Sioux Indian. He always said that the Sioux and Ojibwa must have been distant cousins and that's why they always used to fight. We had a hard time figuring out why our ancestors fought so bitterly because we all got along so well. Vernon looked at the two of them with an impatient glint in his eyes.

"Well?" he asked, "W-w-what are we going to do?"

"I say drink it," Gary spoke first.

"We'll sh-sh-sure as hell get caught."

"I think you're sc-sc-scared," Gary said, imitating Vernon's speech impediment.

"No I ain't," Vernon retorted.

"Bullshit too. You're sc-sc-scared." Gary kept it up.

"You better watch out, Gary." Grant warned him. "He isn't going to take that teasing too long. I mean to tell you."

"Hey! Hey! I got an i-i-idea!" Vernon exclaimed. "What about the explorers?

"Hey, that's a good idea. We can sell some of it to them. We might as well make some jing." Gary slapped Vernon on the back. "The only thing is," Grant said, "I don't trust explorers."

"What do you mean? You've never met one—none of us has," Gary countered. Grant had no argument for that.

The plan was simple. We had to find a black sheep: a kid who could keep his mouth shut. With that in mind we set out to find that one explorer who was cool enough to make the grade. To our surprise we found him pretty easily. He stuck out like a sore thumb. He turned out to be the red- headed Italian kid, our black sheep explorer.

In case you're wondering what explorers were, I'll explain. Explorers were these people—almost always white— canoe enthusiasts who went on excursions through Quetico Park. One of their base camps was at the end of the lake where we lived. Sometimes there'd be fifty or sixty of them camped at the end of Sapawe Lake. We viewed them as intruders. Of course you understand what that meant in terms of mischief-making. Opportunities abounded! Cutting tent ropes, setting canoes loose on the lake, pretending to be bears in the night, and conducting Indian raids were only a few of our pranks. We used to climb a high cliff that looked across the cove and watch them. They never knew we were there until it was too late That's the way we liked it. We set out to meet our new objective with optimism. We positioned ourselves atop the ridge and watched the explorers, looking for our candidate. We'd been there less than an hour when the action started.

"Look at that guy! What's he doing anyway?" Gary wondered. We riveted our eyes on one boy who was obviously sneaking away from the crowd as they sat in a circle reading.

"Look at that b-b-bugger. He's ditching the r-r-rest of them," Vernon said, pointing out the obvious.

"I wonder what they're doing," Grant said.

"B-b-bible study," Vernon replied.

"You don't know nothing about Bible study. I bet you haven't even got one in your house," Gary teased him.

"And you'd lose. I know when I see a B-b-bible. That's what they're reading. They m-m-must be Holy Rollers," Vernon answered.

"Well never mind them. What's the kid up to?" Grant whispered. "He could be our guy. Just look at him. He could be the one. I mean to tell you."

"Look at how they're dressed." Gary pointed at the group.

They all wore short pants and tennis shoes. They seemed extremely well organized. We watched as the boy stealthily slipped away. He was dressed just like the rest of them but he wore his little uniform with a big attitude. From our lookout we could see everything that was going on in the Holy Roller camp.

"Okay guys. Let's do it," Grant whispered. We set out to make contact and strike a deal.

My heart was beating fast, my palms were sweating, but I felt good about our mission. I held the big stick I always carried on these missions loosely in my hand. You see, it was my job to carry that stick, dubbed "the shit-stick," because I had a proven record of not being afraid to use it. It was our weapon—just in case any shit started. Making contact with the red-headed boy wasn't much of a mission. We walked right up behind him. The ground was moist so we made very little noise. On top of that he was totally into smoking a cigarette. We stood there a full half minute before he noticed us.

"What the hell? Who are you? What do you want?" he stammered.

"Don't worry, we're friendly," I assured him.

"Who are you?" he asked again.

"He said we're friendly, didn't he?" Grant said to the boy in a voice thick with hostility. "What are you doing over here all by yourself?"

"Smoking."

"W-w-what's your name?" Vernon asked.

"Vincent—Vince for short. What do you want?" He eyed the stick I was holding in my hand.

"To talk to you," I replied.

"Who are you? You got names? " he asked.

"Don't matter none. Don't be such a chicken," Grant answered him, then looked at the rest of us and grinned a knowing grin.

"You shouldn't sneak up on people like that," he said to Grant.

"Did we sneak up on him?" Grant asked. We all shook our heads no. "You just didn't hear us because we're Indians."

"I can see that. That's what I'm worried about. What are you going to do to me?"

Of all of us, Grant was the most distrustful of whites. His mother once had a white boyfriend who turned out to be a freak of some kind. Our parents used to whisper that the guy was a child molester. He would go after Grant's little sisters when he got drunk. Eventually his mother beat the guy half to death with a frying pan. She spent five days in jail for that. Since then he was always distrustful of whites—any whites.

"You think we're going to scalp you or something?" he asked.

"I don't think that. Anyway, my dad said that it was the white guys who started with the scalping shit. You guys just got better at it. But why does he have that big stick? Indians make me a little nervous and Indians with big sticks make me real nervous. It could be a war club. In fact, it looks like a war club."

"It is a war club. We call it 'the shit stick.' He has it just in case. He's got orders to use it if he has to—and he will," Grant told the boy.

"Well he don't need it now. Tell him that."

"Put the shit stick away," Grant told me.

I leaned the stick against a pine tree. I wanted the kid to relax so I asked him for a puff on his smoke.

"We just came to talk to you," I assured him.

"About what?"

"A deal."

"What kind of deal?" You could tell his interest was piqued.

"We gotta see if you're cool first," I answered.

"They call me the Ice Man. Ain't no stool pigeon. I'm cool. I'm as straight as that there cone tree," he bragged smiling. He had an interesting accent. I liked him. I liked the way he started strutting around. He seemed to be much more relaxed now.

"C-c-cone trees?" Vernon asked, "What do you m-m-mean, c-c-cone trees?"

"Those are cone trees aren't they? I figured they'd be called cone trees. They call apple trees apple trees because they got apples on them. Could a person eat those cones? You know—if they was lost and desperate?"

"Those are called j-j-jack pines," Vernon informed him as he straightened out his beret.

"Why are they called that?" he asked.

Vernon just shrugged. "I don't k-k-know."

"Nice lid," the kid commented.

"Lid?" Vernon asked.

"Hat. Nice hat you got. Where I come from we call hats lids."

Vernon beamed. "My ancestors w-w-wore it when they c-c-came here. They c-c-came from France."

I could see that Grant was growing impatient and I knew when he got like that he could blow the deal. He was looking at the red-headed boy with disgust.

I decided to jump in.

"Look, we didn't come here to talk about no jack pines or hats. We came to make a deal. Are you interested?"

"So what is it?" the boy asked.

"We got wine. We'd be willing to sell you some." Grant studied the boy intently, gauging his reaction. "If we decide you're cool enough," he added with a challenge.

"You mean vino? Where'd you get it? I am most definitely interested. Why hell, Italians and vino go together like—"

"So let's talk," Grant cut him off.

"Like I was going to say, like love and marriage."

"We got f-f-four bottles. We want three d-d-dollars each," Vernon said. "You got m-m-money?"

"Not on me, but I can get it. It won't take me long. I'll be right back. Don't leave."

Vince started to leave. Grant blocked his way.

"Man, what's your problem? You want to do business or what?" Vince asked Grant.

"Don't bring anybody back with you. Understand? Our deal is with you. We're not interested in meeting anybody else. You got that, kid?"

Vince laughed as he stepped around a scowling Grant.

"No problem. These guys are all from the Chicago area. Not me though." He stood back and patted his chest. "New York City, born and bred! Most of them don't like me and I don't like them."

Ten minutes later he was back. He knew how to haggle. In a matter of minutes he convinced us to let him have two bottles for five bucks. Other than that, the deal went down without a hitch. We were happy and so was he. We thought that was the end of it and we were really quite proud of ourselves. That should have been the end of it, but it wasn't.

Later that night the explorers managed to get themselves busted with just over half a bottle of the wine still on their hands. Vince had thrown a big blast. Things got noisy during the night and the instructors found out what had happened through a snitch. Vince had been bragging about his Indian connections and the snitch told them everything, as snitches do. Vince, however, wouldn't say a word. So he and the snitch were brought into Sapawe to try and identify who had sold the wine to the boys. Bootlegging was a serious offense. We were all rounded up and put in a line-up. We felt like criminals. This was organized by some of the local men, but Jimmy the Rat was trying to supervise the whole deal. He wanted to find out who had stolen his wine.

Both Vince and the snitch looked like they'd been dragged through a pile of shit. They were a mess. I can't remember much about the snitch except that he wouldn't look anybody in the eye. I learned a lesson that morning: snitches never look you in the eye—least not for long. And talking about eyes, Vince's were a mess. They looked like two piss holes in a snow bank but damned near as red as his messed-up hair. We all figured we were busted. I mean, think about it: if the kid did tell, how could we defend ourselves? We weren't ever going to see him again so he didn't have anything to lose.

They had all us kids line up and Vince walked up and down, looking at all of us. Jimmy the Rat stood nearby and as Vince walked by us he overheard Jimmy threaten to kick our asses to kingdom come.

Vince heard him and raised his eyebrows in a question. I shrugged. Vince's hair, carrot-red, stood on end. We couldn't help but laugh. Even the kids who had nothing whatsoever to do with the wine caper laughed. Vince had a hangover, we could all tell that much. We'd seen plenty of hangovers in our lifetimes: most of us came from alcoholic families to one degree or another. Vince looked us over and kind of cocked his head. Then the kid did the damnedest thing any of us could have ever imagined. He turned to one of his instructors and asked if he could talk to him alone. We all figured this was it. So anyway him and this staff guy walked a few yards away and Vince started crying. I mean the kid was wailing. The instructor turned around and looked at Jimmy the Rat with the most stern look on his face.

"You should be ashamed of yourself," he said to Jimmy.

Well Jimmy gets this surprised look on his face. "What the hell are you talking about mister?"

"This child just told me that you were the one who sold him the wine and that you told him to blame these kids. You should be ashamed of yourself exploiting these kids like that. I have a good mind to call the provincial police."

"Hey! That little bastard is lying. It was these kids right here." Turning to us with a look of rage, Jimmy added, "Why, I ought to kick your arses into next week!"

He started to come after us. He might have gotten away with putting his boot to our butts because most of the local guys were into him for money but there was a second force there to stop his stinking ass. The instructor, an image of good health and righteousness, stepped between him and us.

"Don't even try it. Pick on somebody your own size—like me."

I glanced over at Vince. He winked and started wailing again.

"Don't let him get his hands on me. He said he would kill me. He said to blame the Indian kids. That's what he told me. Please keep him away from me."

"Don't worry, son. I won't let him hurt you. Are you sure he's the one?"

"Yes, yes. That's him." Vince wailed. "Don't let him get hold of me."

Some of the local men began to look at Jimmy like he was scum. Most of them, however, just laughed. Jimmy the Rat? Well, he was glaring at us but the creepy-looking scumbag didn't say another word—at least for the time being. He wasn't about to tangle with the muscle-bound Mr. Righteous, and none of us could blame him. But that was not the end of Jimmy the Rat. The son-of-a-bitch held a grudge for a long, long time.

The crowd broke up and Jimmy stormed off. Vince whispered, "I'm gonna get my ass kicked for this when I get home."

"Not me," I lied. "It's not the Indian way. Columbus should have discovered that when he came here. We don't hardly get whipped. But we sure as hell get lectured a lot."

"No shit!" he grinned.

We all agreed that Vince was a real cool guy. The best of tourists. He'd have been one of us if he lived in Sapawe. Even Grant had to agree he had style. "Unusual in white boys," he declared. We all had lots of laughs about the cone tree bit, especially the way Vernon told it. We speculated on why Vince chose to do what he did to Jimmy the Rat. As for Jimmy, we gave him a wide berth for a long time.

We were talking about Vince and his mannerisms for weeks.

"You know w-w-what we should have d-d-done?" Vernon said. "We s-s-should have g-g-got his a-a-address."

We should have. We could have written him a letter, a thank-you note.

Such is life! Such is life, indeed. You hustle, you take chances, sometimes it pays off and sometimes it don't. With Vince it had paid. We all learned something from that rebellious red-headed dago. People are people, and most of them can be pretty cool when offered the right opportunity. Vince sure was! Columbus should have been half as cool.

NUMB-NUTS AND THE
CHEESE-HEAD HAT

There were four of them that day—not counting Numb-Nuts Greenside, who had just returned to Sapawe from a trip to Chicago. The boys all climbed onto this old tractor where they liked to hang out. It was the middle of one of those hot, humid July afternoons in 1953. People still talked about the war in those days but it wasn't war these boys were talking about. It was Numb-Nut's trip.

"So Numb-Nuts, tell us about your trip to the big city," Grant said to the nine-year-old Indian boy who sat perched on the driver's seat of the old rusty tractor.

"Yeah, tell us about that," Muffin piped up. "Did you have fun?"

"Did I have fun? Heck, yeah, I had fun," Numb-Nuts replied, then after thinking about it for a moment, added, "some of the time anyway."

"So tell us," another boy urged.

Numb-Nuts Greenside sat on the old, saddle-like tractor seat as though he were in control of the world. His hands clutched the steering wheel like a racecar driver might. For that moment, the kid was in the power seat and he was truly enjoying it.

"I will but first give me some of those chips," he answered as he reached a chubby hand into the bag.

"Hey! Take it easy would ya? Buy your own chips," the boy protested.

"If you don't give no chips, I won't tell nothing," Numb-Nuts warned.

"Give him some chips, asshole," Grant ordered the boy. He wanted to hear Numb-Nut's story. We all did. The kid knew it and used that fact to his advantage. He reached over to my brother and helped himself to a piece of the black licorice he was eating. Under normal circumstances Numb-Nuts would have started a major fistfight by being so bold. My brother Ivan would have punched him right between the eyes. But today Numb-Nuts held an ace, which gave him all kinds of advantages.

"Well, it all started when my aunty got that big check in the mail. It was treaty money or something like that."

"She's only a quarter-breed. Why does she get paid?"

"Okay. So anyway, my aunty got this money," he said, wisely ignored the question. We'd all heard our parents making the same arguments whenever Indian money was about to be released. Indians seemed to come out of the woodwork at treaty payment time. Numb-Nuts was diplomatic enough to stay away from the topic. He continued with a shrug, "And she goes out and buys this car. You all know how she is."

The boys nodded in unison. Grant let out a snicker. "Not as well as I'd like to. You know what I mean?"

"Hey! Don't be insulting my aunty or I ain't saying shit."

"Okay, okay. I won't say nothing about your aunt's nice ass."

Everyone broke into a roar of laughter. This was a running battle between the two of them.

"I could say something about your sister's big tits, you know," Numb-Nuts said. He was pushing his luck: Grant wouldn't think twice about slapping him upside his head. I figured he probably would do just that after we heard the story. Within three days, someone was going to beat this kid's ass. I knew it and so did he.

"Well anyway, back to my story. You all know how she can be. Once she comes up with an idea, nothing can change her mind. That's how we got to the city of Chicago."

"Yeah, but that's nearly a thousand miles away. How long did she drive?" someone wondered.

If there was one thing about his aunt Sugar, it was that she liked to party. Another important thing to know was that she and Numb-Nuts were tight. She was his aunt, but not much older than he, and she was his favorite.

Numb-Nuts's real name was Walter. People all said his dad was a Jewish guy who'd passed through the area. Numb-Nuts was accepted as an Indian even though he was less than a half-breed. This acceptance was based on his mother's history in the community. Now that's something odd about some Indian communities. If people knew your Indian relatives, they accepted you without question. I never knew Sugar's real name but we all knew the real color of her hair. Sugar lived with Numb-Nuts and his mom, whose nickname was High-Pockets because she was a short woman. Now High-Pockets had a man Numb-Nuts told us was not his real dad. They didn't get along real great. They called him Shine-and-Glitter, but I can't begin to tell you why because no one ever told me. There was one thing about living in that town and that is that everyone had a nickname. It's like that in a lot of Indian communities. They called Sugar Sugar because she was a good-looking woman and a real charmer. One sweet example of Indian womanhood, according to the men that lived in the bunk house. That's where the single men who worked in the saw-mill were housed. In the interest of literary integrity, I'll let you speculate as to why Numb-Nuts was given a moniker like Numb-Nuts.

"She picked me up at the house with this new car. I mean it wasn't brand-spanking new, but it was newer than most Indian cars around here. Heck, the radio even worked."

"What color was it?" a boy we called Bum-Bum asked.

"What do you mean?"

"What color was the car?" Bum-Bum repeated.

"What does that matter?" Numb-Nuts asked as he picked up the Coke I'd been drinking. The kid was making us pay for this story but I figured that was just the way things were—the way life is for that matter. To me it was worth it to have him slobber in my Coke. I wanted details. Details that would fuel my own dreams. I wanted to visit a city real bad and this kid had been to one. I wanted to hear everything about it.

Two girls walked up. They were both cute little white girls we sometimes let hang out with us. Notice I said "sometimes." They always had to do the dirty work or play the bad guys when we let them play with us. Numb-Nuts wasn't about to let them hear the story without paying. One of the girls had some peppermint candies and agreed to hand them over to him if they could stay. Of course he wouldn't share any of them with us, a detail we all noted.

"We drove all night long. Sugar said we stopped for a while somewhere in Wisconsin so she could catch a little sleep, but I didn't really know about that because I was out like a light. When I woke up she told me we were just about to cross the state line into Illinois. She had a map and showed me where we were. It was a town called Madison or something like that. It was named after some famous president."

"What's a president?" one of the little girls asked.

"That's why I hate girls," Numb-Nuts said, his voice filled with disgust. "They don't know anything. You don't know what a president is?"

"I bet you don't either," her friend said in her defense.

"Of course he does," I interjected.

"None of you do," she stated. "Tell me what it is then."

"Cities are named after presidents," I explained. "So there. Now would you be quiet so he can tell us about his trip."

"What was it like?" Grant asked Numb-Nuts.

"It was nice. I can tell you that much," Numb-Nuts said.

"What's that supposed to mean?" Grant demanded.

"Not as many trees as around here but still, it was nice."

"Was it like a desert or a prairie?" Bum-Bum asked.

"There were farms all over the place. Before we left Wisconsin my aunt bought me a hat that says 'I'm a Cheese-Head' on it. It's really cool. Maybe I'll show it to you later. It's kind of goofy but I like it because ain't nobody else around here got one."

Everyone nodded their agreement to that. Ain't no one got a hat like that. Not in this town. That definitely places a value on it. Everyone valued uniqueness in Sapawe.

"Where is it at?" someone asked.

"It's at my house."

"I bet he ain't got no cheese-head hat. I bet there ain't even such a thing," the smaller girl said.

"Do so!" Numb-Nuts responded. "Anyone want to bet? Come on, chicken asses. Let's bet. Who wants to bet?"

Well nobody was in a betting mood that day, so he told us, "I'm gonna let you see it—at least the ones who pay."

"You want to charge us? We're your best friends."

"I ain't payin' to see no cheese-head hat," my younger brother stated, but we all knew he would pay.

"What's a cheese-head hat for anyway?" one of the girls asked.

"You wear it. That's what it's for," Numb-Nuts responded as he made a face like she was the stupidest person in the world.

"Is it made out of cheese or something?" Grant asked. "The cheese would melt and it'd stink worse than shit."

"Oh phew! Who stinks? What's that smell?" It was the same girl again.

Bum-Bum laughed and added, "It would make one of my dad's beer farts smell like French perfume."

Everyone laughed. One kid made a comment that Numb-Nuts was the only one dumb enough to wear a hat made out of cheese.

"That's why he's called Numb-Nuts. He's a dummy," said the girl.

Numb-Nuts held his ground. He knew what they were doing but it didn't matter because he also knew the value of what he had and he was going to exploit it to the max.

"It's not made out of cheese," Numb-Nuts informed us.

"Well, what then?"

"Regular hat cloth, stupid," he answered.

"Why's it called a cheese-head hat then?" the girl asked. She could get away with asking stupid questions because she was a girl.

"Geez, you're stupid. Quit asking dumb questions. Because that's where all the cheese is made at."

"No way!" Bum-Bum piped up.

"They're known for that. Don't you guys know anything at all? Geez, what a bunch of local yokels."

He had hit it. Without knowing it, this cross-eyed, buck-toothed bastard had tickled us and stirred up a hunger in each and every one. He had lowered this mixer into the very center of our curiosity and whipped it up like we was a mess of pancake mix. We all knew that travelers know more than regular people who never go no place. Home folks—or as Numb-Nuts had put it, local yokels—just didn't know the things travelers did.

The teacher in our one-room schoolhouse, Mrs. Lawrence, was a world traveler. Every year she went somewhere different and we'd sit transfixed as she told us about her trip. She was our passport to the world and oh was she good at telling us the very details she knew would pique our interest. She sure knew how to tell a story. "Hell she'd even been to Carl's Bad Cavern and seen millions of bats," Grant once declared in her defense. In our young minds there wasn't no one who knew more than her.

Now Numb-Nuts had traveled to Chicago and in one stroke was able to lord it over us. He had joined the ranks of world travelers and knew something the rest of us could only daydream about. So he was gonna tell us about his trip but in his own way and in his own time. Now about that cheese-head hat. We had to see it.

Somehow, seeing that hat would make his experience more personal for each of us, would magically make us each more worldly as well. I can tell you this much: I was delirious to see it, feel it, try it on my head. I knew in my heart that the hat would let me sail to a place I'd never been. Things like that stimulated our imagination like crazy. One of the things we did when we got bored was to sit by the highway and watch the cars go by. We'd read all the license plates and the ones from far away places like Illinois and Florida would really set our imaginations afire.

"So after we left Wisconsin we got into Chicago and they had these highways. Boy, I tell you, they were big enough for six cars side by side."

"No way!" the girls shouted.

"I'm telling you, they were that big."

"You're lying now. There ain't no road that big," the littler girl said.

"How would you know? You ain't never been there. You ain't never been nowhere."

There it was again! That attitude only travelers can assume. They've seen more than you have and by virtue of that fact, they deserve a special place in the world. It was highly unlikely Numb-Nuts would ever be the last one picked for a team now. Each of us decided then and there that we would become travelers. No one said it but the feeling floated in the air. You could tell by the way we looked at each other and by the way we looked at Numb-Nuts. You could sense it in the way we all leaned forward waiting for another detail about his trip, another fact that would somehow move us onto a higher plane of knowledge. The atmosphere was vibrating with our curiosity.

"There were so many cars I got dizzy trying to figure out where they were going or where they'd just come from. They had these turn-offs that were just crazy. There were cars on top of cars. They was underneath us and beside us but on another road. Some was going in the same direction and others were heading straight at us. At least that's how it felt. Sugar said they were called cloverleafs and I can see why. I never knew there were so many cars made. They looked kind of like ants. Remember when we was messing with that ant hill over by the horse barn? Well that's what it looked like. That's the best way to describe it. Just shut your eyes and remember them ants but instead of ants it was cars. And you know what? Every car had only one person in it. What a waste, huh? If there was two people in each car it would have been only half as crowded."

"So what else did you see?" Bum-Bum asked. "Is it true about the houses being real big?"

"Skyscrapers!" Numb-Nuts answered in a knowing voice.

"Did you see any of them?" someone asked.

"There's more people live in one of them skyscrapers than there is in the whole Rainy River district."

"Come on, that can't be true," Grant interrupted. "Do you have any idea how many people that makes?"

"You'd have to be there to see them," Numb-Nuts said, discounting Grant's doubt with a wave of his hand. "We pulled in about seven-thirty in the morning. People were going in every direction and they hardly even said a word to each other. Sugar said it was called rush hour."

"Rush hour! Why did they call it that?" the girls asked in unison.

"If you saw it then you'd know why," he said to the girls. "There were so many people—rushing and pushing and shoving. Car horns and hollering everywhere. I was a little afraid but not for very long. You had to see it."

Now we had another word, another gem to add to our arsenal of city words. "Rush hour!" The word sounded business-like and cosmopolitan. Everyone tried the word on for size.

"We drove down this street called State Street. It's so famous they even got a song about it."

"I ain't never heard it," Bum-Bum countered.

"I don't doubt that," Numb-Nuts replied, "Before I traveled to The Windy City I didn't know about it either. The song is called 'State Street that Great Street.'"

"And? . . ." Grant urged the boy on.

"Well, there's so many things to tell about." He hesitated and thought for a moment. "Did you ever hear of an El-train?"

"Big deal! We have trains around here," Bum-Bum laughed.

"But no El-trains." Numb-Nuts emphasized.

"So what's so special about them?" the small girl asked.

"They drove right through the busiest part of town. You should've heard the noise. They're on these tracks that go above your head and they even go through tunnels. When they stop all these people get off them. They push and shove each other like they're gonna fight, but they don't. They hardly look at each other. I went to a zoo. Lincoln Park Zoo. That was fun."

"You went to a zoo?" we all asked.

None of us had ever seen a zoo before. Oh we'd read about them, but here was a kid—one of our own—who had actually visited one. He told us about it in detail.

"I'm telling you, I stood that close to a real lion. I saw a tiger and all kinds of big-assed cats."

"What was they doing?" someone asked.

"Did they roar?'

"Well, mostly they paced back and forth like they'd like to eat someone. Some of them just looked like they wanted to sleep but that's how they fool you. A boy thinks they're asleep and gets near, and bingo, he's one dead boy!"

"Yeah, right!" My little brother was getting tired of hearing his stories. He had started to play with some marbles. Grant joined him. Our attention was beginning to wane. Numb-Nuts saw it coming so he made a move.

"Who wants to see my cheese-head hat?" he questioned.

"I ain't payin to see no cheese-head hat."

"Me neither," Bum-Bum chimed in. "Besides, you ate most of my chips."

"I ain't got no money," I lied. My brother looked at me funny because I'd just gotten whipped the night before for lying to my mom, but I guess he figured this was different. He knew I had a quarter in my shirt pocket. The cheese-head hat didn't excite me enough to pay to see it. Grant, however, wanted to see it.

"Look," he said, "I ain't got no money either, but I want to see that hat. Can I owe you?"

"If I give you credit, you gotta promise you'll pay me. Will you shake on it?" Numb-Nuts asked. "If you don't, your sister wears falsies."

We all agreed to the same terms but I can assure you that there were little fingers crossed and other actions that would negate our words should something go wrong. Then we all walked over to his house. His mother must have sensed we were coming because she had Kool Aid ready when we got there. Numb-Nuts went into the house and when he emerged we all burst into laughter. So this was it, huh? This was the cheese-head hat? A symbol of superiority? Hardly, pal!

Of course we all tried the hat on, and yes, just like Frosty the Snowman's hat, it was magical because it worked. We sailed away, each in our separate worlds of make-believe. Numb-Nuts enjoyed a few more days of fueling our dreams but eventually his edge wore off and he got his ass kicked a couple of times for being rude, but still he got picked far from last when we played ball. Of course he always insisted that the team he was on be called the Chicago Cubs. And even that helped fuel our dreams and added a bit more substance to our days of what ifs. The name Chicago became synonymous with adventure in my mind.

And eventually I would live the dream that Numb-Nuts and his cheese-head hat helped fire up in my young Indian mind that year in Sapawe. I left for Chicago in the summer when older girls swam naked in the lake and the year the Lyons house burned down. Overall, that was a good year. I drove on the big highways. I rode the El-trains, visited the zoo, and even played my guitar on State Street during rush hour. And always I remembered Numb-Nuts and that cheese-head hat.

BILL AND GLENDA

Bill and Glenda thought of themselves as second-generation urban Indians. Their parents had moved to Chicago's South Side during the 1950s in accordance with the Relocation Act. They met at Red's, a blues bar on Thirty-fifth and Archer Avenue. It was love at first sight. They dated a couple of weeks then decided to live together. Their families disapproved so they moved to the more liberal North Side. Both had been raised in working-class homes. Both regarded their families as being provincial, not with the times.

It was a Tuesday night, just before Christmas, and Bill and Glenda were having serious doubts about their relationship. Some people refer to this doubting as "the seven year itch," but they'd been together a lot less than seven years when it hit them. Maybe because of the way the North Side is, you know. A place where people just seem to stay strangers by choice. In their old neighborhood they knew everyone and everyone knew them.

"So just what the hell do you think love is?" Glenda demanded as she stood in front of the kitchen stove warming her behind.

Bill hated these conversations. They made him uncomfortable. Guilty!

"Well? Are you going to answer me?" she asked. "Do you even know?"

"Of course I do," he replied. He moved his head around in a circle several times. His shirt collar felt tight. He undid the top botton and removed his tie. He hung it over the back of the chair.

"Well?" She leaned closer, bending at the waist. He shifted, reached for his coffee, and looked out of the window. It was just starting to snow again. She moved back an inch closer to the hot stove and rubbed the cheeks of her butt in anticipation.

"Boy, I really want to hear this. Should be a doozy."

What is it she wants to hear? he wondered. If I really told her what I'm thinking, she'd just get upset. Better say nothing.

"You really want me to tell you?"

"For the last quarter hour I've been trying to get an answer out of you. Yes, Bill, I want you to tell me. How do you feel about us?"

Shit! She knows. How could she possibly have found out? It wasn't like they could run into each other at Jewel's Supermarket or something. It was a one-time thing.

She waited a minute then cupped her right hand to her ear.

"What? What did you say? Why don't you speak up, sir?"

"Aw, why don't you just stop with that shit, okay?"

"What shit are you talking about, sir?" she asked.

"I'm telling you no matter what I say you won't like it. It's always the same," he replied.

"Like what Bill?" she asked.

"What I was going to say," he explained.

She leaned back and rubbed her chin.

"You mean to tell me that you only say what you think I'd like to hear? Is that what you're saying, Bill?"

He nodded. "Essentially."

"Bill, that's not very honest of you."

"I guess you're right."

"You guess I'm right? For Christ's sake, Bill! What I'm trying to do here is to get us to have a decent conversation. We hardly talk anymore."

"Hey, we talk a lot. More than lots of people," Bill said.

Bill could see Glenda was irritated. She leaned forward from the waist again.

"You bastard! I want an answer and I want it now!"

"You want an answer? I'll give you one then." He shifted again and took a swallow of hot black coffee. He thought for a moment about how he could frame his reply.

"Well?"

"Don't start okay? I'm going to give you an answer. You want to hear how I feel? Then just be quiet. Okay? You talk and you make me pissed, so just be cool. Okay?"

What am I going to say? What can I tell her? I love this woman. It's best I don't say shit, he decided.

"I'm waiting." She tapped her foot on the bare floor. Bill noticed she didn't have shoes on. She followed his gaze. Her toes curled defensively. Bill smiled and she noticed. "Well?" she demanded loudly.

"Are you sure you want to hear this?" he asked. "Oh by the way," he added, "I love the way your toes curl. Always have."

"Bill! Just answer the question, would you?"

He picked up his empty coffee cup, waved it in her direction, and said, "Refill, please. I will not answer questions without my coffee. It's just a thing with me."

She turned toward the stove and picked up the coffee pot. As she filled his coffee mug she thought about how they'd met. She wondered what it was about him that had attracted her. They had been so honest with each other right from the start. What happened to that honesty, she wondered. Where did it go? Time had changed so many things—for both of them. The move north had been nice: new restaurants, new clubs, and new people. Maybe that was what went wrong, she thought.

"What was the question again?" Bill asked with a flourish of his mug. He was clowning, trying to lighten the mood. She knew exactly what he was doing.

"About us. How do you feel about us? And you can quit with the clowning. I'm serious!"

"I can see that," Bill mumbled.

She leaned forward again. She reached across the small wooden kitchen table and knocked softly on his skull. "Hello Bill! Is anybody home in that head of yours?" As she bent down her butt stuck out. Bill saw it coming but didn't have time to say anything to warn Glenda. Her butt touched up against the stove and her eyes opened wide with surprise. She cursed, jumped forward, and spilled some of his coffee. He couldn't help but laugh. For a moment she was livid with anger. Then she started laughing too as she rubbed her ass. Bill hoped that would be the end of the conversation but soon she stopped laughing and got serious again.

"Stop evading the question, Bill. Answer me now!" She had suddenly raised her voice a full octave.

"Don't start hollering. That's one of the reasons we never talk," he said.

"Don't go into your Stoic Indian act, Bill. Just answer my question."

"I just want to go to bed. I'm tired."

"Is that all you can come up with?" she asked.

"That's where I can show you how I feel about you," he replied, hoping she'd soften up. He could see she wasn't going for it. Again he wondered, What now? I don't dare tell her. She'll freak out. Suddenly Bill felt really tired. He remembered his father telling him when he was a boy that the truth is always the best option. Bill didn't think so in this case. Delay tactics, he thought. I'll use more delay tactics. Eventually she'll get tired and quit asking.

"Can you tell me what the point of this conversation is anyway?" he asked.

"The point is, Bill, that I'm feeling kind of insecure about our relationship. That's the point."

"Did you visit with your sister today?"

"Bill! Just answer my question, would you please? God you make me crazy."

"Well you drive me nuts with your questions. Are you on your period?" he asked.

"Okay, Bill, if that's how you want to play it. You never tell me how you feel about anything. I'm really beginning to feel insecure about us. All I am to you is a piece of ass—and not even that very often anymore."

He began to feel really bad about not coming clean with her about this deal. He wanted to but the consequences were too high a price to pay. It had only been one time! He felt trapped. It's best not to say anything. Maybe it will go away like the flu or something. He didn't want to hurt her. Evasive action, he recommended to himself.

"It's your fault, Glenda. You always have some excuse when I want to make love to you. Sometimes you leave me feeling like a rapist."

"And sometimes I feel like a piece of meat," she shot back.

"Baby, what do you want?"

"I want you to tell me what you think about our love. It's simple Bill, really simple."

"That's not the way I am, Glenda. I don't just throw words around. I'm Indian," he answered, hoping to side-track her. She'd always been taught that being Indian didn't make her any different than anybody else. Bill believed differently. He claimed that being born Indian in this country automatically set him aside, especially as an Indian male.

"What the hell is that supposed to mean anyway? Just tell me what the hell you feel love is, okay, Bill?"

"Okay then! It's one person feeling more than the other."

"What kind of answer is that? That's one weird philosophy. I wish I'd known about that a year ago."

"Well, I wasn't exactly finished. It's like one person protecting the other one."

He watched her face change. Her bottom lip trembled. Her eyes narrowed. Now she's pissed off, he thought.

"You mean you feel like you're protecting me? I don't need to be protected Bill. I'm a woman. I need to be loved."

"Well, come on to bed then. I'll show you some love."

"Is that all you can think of? You insult me and that's all you come up with." She was nearly crying with rage. Bill knew she was right, but it was started now, and there was no way he could turn back, however badly he wanted to.

"See? You always have to personalize these things. I'm speaking in general, Glenda."

"Go on then."

"Sometimes love seems like it's someone requiring a safe harbor or maybe permission to be that for someone else."

"Say what? Hello, Bill! Wake up and smell the coffee."

"I didn't start this conversation. I'd be happy to drop it right now," he responded, but he knew there was no way that was going to happen.

"Is there more? You want to insult me some more?"

"Insult you? What the hell are you talking about?" he asked. He was beginning to get angry at himself for not having the nerve to tell her. She must sense it, he thought.

"You must not be very happy with me Bill , especially if you feel like you have to protect me."

"There's nothing wrong with that, Glenda. Listen, baby, society puts us in that role. It's what being an Indian man is all about. No, I don't mean that. What I'm trying to say is that a man in general, regardless of race, feels like he's the hunter and protector."

Glenda walked across the small kitchen. She didn't say anything. She put a piece of bread in the toaster, then walked to the refrigerator to get the jelly. Bill watched her as she spread jelly on her toast.

"You want some?" she asked. He nodded and she cut the bread in half, handing him a piece.

"Thanks, baby. You ready for bed yet? I'm really bushed."

"Bill? Did you ever think about having an affair on me?"

She knows! Shit, how could she know? His mind raced in circles. He clawed at his memory to locate any hint that he may have unknowingly dropped. There was nothing. He looked at her face, searching for a clue. He saw tears well up in her eyes. Shit, he thought, I'm going to have to tell her. She brushed at her eyes with the back of her hand. He racked his brain to think of words that would make things all right. There was nothing. He wondered how she could know. He opened his mouth to speak. But she put her hand over his mouth.

"Bill, do you still love me?"

He nodded.

"Oh Bill, I'm so sorry what I did to you."

"What's that?" he asked as he silently counted his blessings. Oh did he ever love her. More than she could know. He wanted to hold her close and smother her with kisses.

"Bill, I slept with another man."

"You what?" He jumped to his feet. She fell to the floor. He was tempted to reach down and help her up but the shock of her announcement numbed him. He couldn't think straight. "What did you say?"

"It was only once. I don't know why I did it. I am so sorry. Will you ever be able to forgive me?" she asked.

"I never would have guessed," he replied.

"Being with him made me realize how much I love you. I really do love you, Bill. If you leave me because of this I'll be heartbroken, but I'll understand. I wronged you."

"Come here, baby." He reached down to help her to her feet. He sat on the chair and pulled her onto his lap. He kissed her gently on the cheek. She turned her head and met his eyes. He saw her need, the love that was there.

"Can you ever forgive me?" she asked.

"Hell yes. Yes, yes I can. I understand how you feel," he assured her.

"Oh Bill. I don't deserve you."

"Oh yeah you do. We deserve each other. I love you, Glenda. So much." He kissed her full on the lips. "Maybe we should get married. You know, make an honest woman out of you. It sure would make our families happy. What you think? Huh? Will you be my blushing bride?"

"Oh Bill. I would be so proud to be your wife."

"Okay then, we'll get hooked. First we'll do it the white way. You know, to make it legal and all. Then we'll go up north and get married with an Indian ritual. Okay?"

"Bill, I'll marry you any way you want."

"Okay then," he said with a happy laugh. She thought he sounded as if he were relieved about something but she wasn't about to ask questions.

She dropped her toast on the kitchen floor as he picked her up and carried her to the bedroom. He laid her gently on the bed and began to kiss her passionately. She returned his kisses. They made love that night like two brand-new lovers. Bill never did admit his affair to her although he was tempted to once or twice. It's best not to say anything, he reasoned.

They got married shortly after that, then went up to Wisconsin and married again in the Indian tradition. "For ourselves," Bill always said.

Bill and Glenda got past the premature "seven-year-itch" and settled down to raise a family. When Bill was offered a much better job that required they relocate to a different part of the state, they did so without question. Five kids later, Bill won the Illinois lottery. Always a hard-working couple, their lifes were altered drastically by the money. They decided to get away from all the temptations of a big city and start over. Bill wanted to move his family to a small town in Canada. He purchased some land and contracted to have a house built to their specifications. That small town, so far away from the south side of Chicago, was where his family had come from originally. For Bill it was a return to his roots. The small town was called Sapawe.

BENNY RED-BEAVER

"Cigarettes and whiskey and wild, wild women. They'll make you crazy, they'll drive you insane." Benny Red-Beaver clung to the street sign and began to sing. He was drunk and didn't care. Two white women passed him and frowned. They edged to the curb of the sidewalk. Benny struggled to focus his vision. When he did he noticed the two women. They both wore disgusted expressions on their made-up faces.

"Up yours!" he muttered as they hurried away. "Couple o' well-fed heifers if you ask me." He watched the cellulite jiggle like jelly as they hurried up Broadway. Both had more than ample butts. Fat-assed bitches, he thought, as he held a bottle up to the sun and eyed its contents.

Benny squinted at the sun. Another hot day, he thought. He had been heading north on Broadway in the Uptown District on Chicago's North Side, staggering and sweating profusely. He held onto the street sign with a tighter grip to keep from falling. His vision had blurred again.

Benny noticed his blurry reflection in a vacant store window and grinned at himself. He hung onto the post, staring at his image. He shook his head, squinted his eyes real hard, then started thinking. When he drank, which wasn't too often by some people's standards, Benny would get philosophical. He knew he got that from his grandfather, who had raised him. He could remember the old man's words but not what he looked like. Someone that important to me and I can't even remember what he looked like when I shut my eyes. He shook his head and wiped the perspiration from his forehead. That always made him feel sad. The things time does to people, he thought.

"There ain't no limits but your imagination," the old man had said to Benny on his twelfth birthday. "You have to understand that. You got to see the world as a place of possibilities, and the only way you're going to do that is if you understand that everything is connected and nothing is dormant—everything is in constant motion." He handed Benny his birthday gift. It was a hunting knife, a beauty he would treasure for many years to come.

"Twenty years ago," Benny whispered. "Twenty years ago to the day."

He leaned weakly against the street sign. He held the bottle up to the sun again. An impulse of self-preservation gripped him. Alcohol is a demon, he thought, grimacing. It's a terrible thing with a million little demons swimming around inside. The bottle was half empty and it was ten-thirty in the morning.

"Yeah right, old man. This goddamned whiskey has a limit—and me too. I think maybe I'm reaching mine." He took a swallow. It tasted nasty so he spit most of it back out and dropped the half-empty bottle to the ground in disgust. It bounced three times, spun once, and was still.

Benny was an artist. His work was valued highly by those who knew it. He did paintings about the streets and the people he met, and he was good. This ritual of drinking he would go through about once every six months seemed a part of his creative process. It would be followed by an intense period of research. He might spend a week or so reading up on a subject before he would ever put brush to canvas. He would take an idea, absorb as much information about the topic as he could, let it gel for a week or so, then begin to develop it. Generally he could go for months without a drink but when he dried up creatively he would go out onto the streets and get to "drinking with the boys" as he called it.

"Just like that, pal. I had enough of your shit. You're out of here," he said to the bottle. Rays of sunlight bounced off the greenish glass. The traffic roared past him as Benny clung to the sign. The morning sun felt good on his face and he was beginning to feel sleepy.

Chicago police officer Rubin Wallace sat in his cruiser on the east side of Broadway at Wilson and watched the Indian leaning against the street sign post. He recognized the Indian as a guy he'd once arrested for disorderly conduct in a barroom brawl. He got out of the squad car and approached the Indian carefully. Never can be too careful, he thought. No telling what a guy will do, especially when he's drinking. He picked up the bottle, which he noticed was half full. Benny's eyes focused on the police officer, then opened wide in recognition. Rubin smiled at Benny.

"Had enough, huh Chief?"

Benny didn't answer. He looked down at the ground and noticed an ant carrying a crumb. He smiled at the irony of such a small insect carrying a crumb so much bigger than itself, then he turned ever so slowly to face the officer.

"Well, well! If it ain't—" Benny leaned closer to read the officer's name tag, "—Ossifer Wallace." He slurred the name on purpose and held tighter to the post. "Here to serve and protect, I assume."

"We try," Rubin grinned.

"It's all a man can do," Benny replied gesturing grandly with his left arm. He nearly fell on his face. Rubin reached out to help him but Benny waved him away.

"What were we talking about? Oh yeah! The evils of whiskey, cigarettes, and wild women. You ever get drunk, officer?"

"More often than I should have," Rubin answered. Now he remembered what it was about this guy that had stuck in his mind. He was a philosopher and a bit of a comedian. A likable guy.

"Whiskey is evil stuff. Drags your ass down. Breaks a man in half. Eats his soul." Benny paused for a moment, then got serious as he continued, "Today's my birthday."

"Happy birthday! You're right about whiskey, Chief," Rubin said as he removed his sunglasses. "Where do you live?"

"What?" Benny asked.

"What's your address?" Rubin asked.

"I can't go there. My old lady is pissed at me. It's my goddamned birthday and she's pissed off."

"You look like you're going to fall asleep. You can't stay out here on the streets. Might get yourself hurt. What's your address?" Rubin asked again, then added, "I don't want to lock you up. You'd have to stay there until tomorrow morning. That could get pretty miserable because it's hot in the lockup."

After several more minutes of coaxing, Benny gave the officer his address. When Shirley sees me with a cop, he thought, she's going to freak. She's afraid of the police. Probably wanted by the law someplace for busting the Major Crimes Act—all twelve of them! The bitch. He smiled to himself. He got into the police car without any further arguments.

"Well, ossifer. Tell me, how you been?" he asked from the front passenger's seat of the police cruiser.

"Actually I've been doing okay," Wallace replied. He looked over at Benny, who had his head down.

"You okay?" he asked Benny.

"Yeah."

"What the heck are you doing? Don't puke in this car."

"I ain't going to puke in your car," Benny assured the officer as he sat up straight. "Trying to get my ass sobered up before we get to the house. A little bit anyway," he added, pushing his long hair back from face. "Sometimes it works."

"I doubt it. That would make all the blood rush to your head," Wallace said.

"Yeah. So?"

"Well, think about it, Benny. If all the blood rushes to your head and the alcohol in your blood goes up there, what's going to happen? You're going to get drunk all over again, right?"

"I'm sorry, ossifer, but the world's spinning around and I can't think," Benny laughed. The officer laughed with him. He pulled the squad car onto Benny's street.

"What'd you say the house number was?" he asked Benny.

"That's it right there. The one with the bike chained to the fence." He pointed at a three-story brownstone. "It's my bike. I lost the key."

Wallace steered the squad car to the curb. He got out and walked around to help Benny out of the car.

"Come on, guy. I'll bring you to the door."

"No, that's okay," Benny answered.

"It's my job, pal. I'm just protecting you."

Benny laughed. "I'll probably need it too. You got earmuffs? This woman can swear. I tell you."

"I'm used to it. My ex-wife was the same way."

"From what I hear, that's the best kind of wife," Benny said. "I once heard that the reason a woman marries is so she can change the man. The reason a man marries is that he hopes she don't change."

"You ain't got that quite right, Chief. Think about it."

"I can't. I swear, ossifer."

"Yeah, right."

The two men went in and climbed the stairs. Three children were playing on the second floor landing. They grew quiet as the two men walked by.

"Tell me why Indians can never find an apartment on the first floor?" Benny complained. "There must be some kind of plot going on in this city. You know, I helped three people move this month and every one of them got third floor places. Well this is it," he said as he struggled with the keys. The door opened and the two men entered the apartment.

"Mi casa, su casa!" Benny joked as they walked through the door. Rubin grinned at Benny's lame Spanish accent.

They could hear noise coming from the bedroom.

"She must be watching the talk shows. I'll surprise her," he whispered as he crossed the living room quietly but quickly. He turned and smiled at the policeman who stood somewhat uncomfortably at the front door. Officer Wallace wanted to tell Benny not to open the door, but he let it slide. Benny grabbed the door handle and opened it quickly. "Got ya!" he yelled. The woman screamed and a man cursed.

"What the hell is this?" Benny stammered. He looked totally shocked.

"You bastard! Get out of here! I said get out!" the woman screamed.

"Oh man, I'm sorry," the man said.

Benny turned to look at Rubin. The officer saw that the color had drained from his face. Benny's voice and hands were shaking. He stumbled toward the couch. Rubin crossed the room to help him to the sofa.

"You sneaky bastard!" his woman exclaimed. "What are you doing coming back here? Are you drunk?" They could hear her in the bedroom moving about the room, putting on some clothes. They could also hear the man's voice. He sounded scared. He was complaining about something. She told him to shut up. The woman came out of the room. She froze when she noticed the cop standing next to the couch where Benny sat, his head in his hands. The man came out of the room behind her. He looked scared. He bumped into the woman who had stopped in her tracks. When he saw Rubin his face fell and he looked as if he wished he were dead. Benny looked up at the guy.

"You? You and her? I thought you were a friend."

"Benny, I'm sorry. I didn't mean it."

"The hell he didn't," the woman added, a cruel grin on her face. "We've been going at it hot and heavy for six months. You ain't been taking care of business, so I found someone who could."

"Six months?" Benny's voice was little more than a whisper. He and Shirley had been together about nine months. Officer Wallace shifted uncomfortably. The woman turned to look at him.

"What are you doing here?" she asked.

Rubin stiffened. He looked at her with a steady gaze. Oh man, he thought, what a bitch.

"I brought this man home. He didn't want to come home and I guess I can't blame him."

"Yeah? Well if you're finished with your business, you can go. And take this useless piece of shit with you," she said pointing at Benny. "Throw him in an alley somewhere. I don't care what you do with him. I don't want him here."

"Shirley, you don't have to be rude to the man," Benny said quietly. "He's just being nice. But you wouldn't know much about that, would ya?"

"That's all right," Rubin said. "I deal with weirdos all day long." Turning to Shirley, he added, "Every day."

"Well whoop-dee-do for you!" she answered, pulling the robe around her more tightly. "I want him out of here and you too."

"You got money for a room someplace?" Rubin asked Benny. "I can drive you to a hotel."

Benny nodded.

"And don't bother coming back here. Take your clothes." She was practically spitting at him.

"What about the T.V and stuff? It's all mine," Benny said. "And," he continued, "my art supplies."

Normally Officer Wallace wouldn't have said anything, but he liked Benny and he definitely didn't like Shirley. She bugged the hell out of him. He decided to intervene on Benny's behalf.

"I'm just wondering, whose name is the lease in?" he asked on a hunch. Oh he knew these kind of women. User, he thought. She's a goddamned user.

"Mine," Benny replied.

Officer Wallace looked at the woman. He saw the look of hate burning in her eyes. She turned her head and stared angrily at Benny.

"Yeah, it's in his name, but I paid last month's rent."

"And this stuff is his?"

"Can I go, officer?" the other guy asked timidly.

Jerking his thumb toward the guy, Officer Wallace turned to Benny and asked, "You know this guy?"

"Yeah, he's the janitor," Benny said.

Rubin looked at Shirley, opened his eyes wide, and grinned. "The janitor?"

"That's what he said, isn't it?" Shirley wasn't liking the way this was going at all.

"By law," he said, emphasizing the words, "if the lease is in his name, you can't kick him out."

"Is it okay if I go?" the janitor asked again.

"Just hold your horses a minute okay?" Wallace spoke sharply. The janitor was shaken. "You better put on those pants or I'll arrest you for indecent exposure. You got any ID?"

The janitor nodded and began to dig in the pockets of his pants.

"Didn't I tell you to put them on?"

The janitor struggled to get into his pants. The police officer watched him for a moment then turned to the woman. She looked away.

"It is the law, lady. You cannot kick this gentleman out of his own apartment."

"But I paid the rent," she replied.

"One time out of nine months," Benny said, then added, "I had to bail her out of jail with the rent money."

"Jail?" Rubin looked at Shirley and asked, "For what?"

Shirley didn't answer.

"What were you in jail for?" He repeated the question.

"Resisting arrest. She was drunk and they kicked her out of the Saxony," Benny answered for her. "She started raising hell."

"It was all your fault," she said to Benny.

The janitor finally got his pants on. Rubin glanced over at him and asked for his identification again. The janitor reached into his pants pocket and pulled out his wallet. He handed it to Rubin. Rubin handed the wallet back to him and told him to take out his identification. The man handed the police officer a driver's license and a Social Security card. Wallace glanced at the documents, handed them back, and pointed to the door. The janitor bolted out of the apartment. Rubin looked over at Benny who was sitting with his head down, looking dejected.

"Look, she doesn't have the right to tell you to go. In fact, you can tell her to get out if you want. She doesn't seem like she would want to stay around here anyway. Why don't you tell her to go?"

"Shirley," said Benny, "I don't think it's ever going to work out between you and me. Maybe we should go our separate ways."

"You can't just tell me to go. I have rights, you know," she answered.

"Look what you just did. I mean, the guy's supposed to be a friend and that's what you do with him."

"Grow up would you? He don't mean anything to me. He was nothing but a dick. That's it. I don't have no feelings for him."

Probably doesn't have any feelings for you either, Benny, Rubin thought. He was amazed at her brashness. It was hard for him to picture the two of them as a couple. Benny was quiet, a nice guy. In fact, he was the exact opposite of her. If she had balls, they'd be made of brass, he thought.

He looked around the room. It was small with a clean sort of clutter about it. Oil paintings in various stages of completion leaned against the wall. Nice work, the officer thought, as he waited for Benny to respond to Shirley. That's how Benny made a living, he figured.

"No, Shirley, this can't work. Why don't you just get your stuff and go?"

"You heard what the man said," Wallace said, turning to Shirley. She was starting to look almost desperate.

"I don't think this is police business. Benny, why don't you tell him to leave? We can work this out between us. I know we can."

"I don't want to. I just want you out of my life. This ain't the first time and it won't be the last. You're a whore, Shirley."

"Who the hell you think you are calling me a whore?"

"Why hell, woman, I just caught you in my bed screwing a guy who's supposed to be my friend. Get your ass out of here! Hit the road, Jack, and don't ya come back no mo'," Benny started to sing, faking drunkeness. Officer Wallace grinned.

She looked at Benny with a "poor me, the victim" expression on her face. Benny sat completely still for a half a minute and studied her face. He thought about what had just happened. He felt the center of his heart go hard. She read it in his eyes.

"Fuck you then!" she said. He waved goodbye. I'll get the bastard, she thought. She stood up, let the robe fall from her body, and walked into the bedroom to get dressed. She left the door open so she could continue to talk.

"You'll regret this. I'll get you for this," she hissed.

"Are you threatening this gentleman? Don't give him a reason to arrest you," Rubin warned. He turned to Benny, "You want her locked up?"

Benny smiled at her and asked, "Aren't you even gonna take a shower? Wash that stinking thing?"

Her face turned a shade of red as a look of pure hate washed slowly over it.

In the end, Shirley packed her few belongings. She tried to argue her way out of it, but Benny had had enough. He wouldn't budge an inch. She stormed out of Benny's place. Rubin hung around long enough to drink a Coke Benny offered him. After Rubin left, Benny made himself an egg sandwich, switched on the television, then went to sleep. He spent his thirty-second birthday sprawled on his bed with the TV blaring.

Officer Rubin Wallace got off duty at four. By four-thirty he was on his way to the lake for a relaxing swim.

Arthur Coleman, a black, chronically unemployed bi-sexual, and four other hard-drinking men listened as Shirley spoke. "I'm telling you guys. He's got to have at least a thousand in that apartment. All's we got to do is make sure he's not there, then we go in the place and get it. Simple as riding a bike. He got other shit up there too."

"Like what?" one of the drunks asked.

"Stereo, VCR, videos, and tapes. Man, he's got over a hundred tapes. Blues, jazz, and rock. We could sell those anywhere," Shirley assured them. "He also got a lot of artist's supplies up there."

"I don't want to be involved in no burglary," the same drunk protested. "I'm outta here."

"Well go on then. We don't need you," Shirley answered. "Too lazy to work, and too afraid to steal. Useless fucker."

Two others agreed with their friend and left. Arthur and his friend Dude decided they would join Shirley in her plan to go to Benny's apartment and rob it. They were an odd couple, dangerously faithful to each other. Some say that the most dangerous combination of criminals is blacks and whites working together. Each one tries to outdo the other. That's how those two were. Dude was from West Virginia. His family had come north looking for work when he was a ten-year-old boy. They had come with a dream of a better life but it turned out to be an illusion. Living from day to day, never finding steady work, his parents had turned to booze and split up years ago. His mother had run off with an alcoholic country-and-western musician and drunk herself to death. His father lived in a halfway house. Life and alcohol took its dues on him and he lost his mind. Dude had spent most of his life roaming back and forth between Chicago and West Virginia when he wasn't in jail for some petty crime.

Dude had met Arthur in the county jail and despite the racism in each of them, they managed to forge a steady love-hate relationship. Many people suspected they were lovers because they were always together on the streets. Of course they both denied it. In reality, Dude was afraid of Arthur. Arthur knew that and used Dude in every way possible.

The plan was simple. As soon as it got dark, Arthur would go to the front door and if Benny answered, he was to ask for Shirley. If Benny didn't answer, then they would go around to the backdoor where Shirley knew a key was hidden. They'd go in and take what they could carry.

Arthur was interested in the cash. He certainly didn't relish carrying a stereo down the street. He had plans of his own about the cash; he was going to grab the money and then he and Dude would ditch Shirley. Dude, on the other hand, pictured himself in possession of all those tapes. He doubted Shirley's claim that there was a thousand dollars in the apartment. He couldn't picture a thousand dollars. In his entire life he'd never had more than three hundred dollars at any one time. And Shirley had an agenda of her own. She just wanted to get some kind of revenge on Benny for kicking her out like the way he had done. She knew there wasn't a thousand dollars in the place. Of course, he did have a lot of tapes but nowhere near a hundred.

The three approached the building on Kenmore Avenue and walked upstairs. Arthur rang the door bell several times. No one answered. Inside the apartment, Benny was still sound asleep with the TV going. The combination of alcohol and heat had gotten the best of him. He didn't stir as Shirley and the two intruders entered through the back door—not even when Dude stumbled over a kitchen chair.

Arthur immediately began to ransack the kitchen cupboards looking for cash. Dude walked into the living room and spotted the stereo set and tapes. He quickly went back into the kitchen to get a brown shopping bag for the tapes. Shirley needed to use the bathroom.

Benny began waking up when Dude unplugged the television set. He moaned softly and covered his head with his pillow. He had a monster of a hangover. In the meantime, Arthur found 125 dollars hidden in the breadbox. He began searching with renewed vigor, sure now that Shirley had told the truth about the thousand dollars. He finished searching the kitchen and went into the living room. He opened the closet next to the bathroom and began rifling the shelves. He found a small, 22-caliber pistol Benny had bought and hidden there several months ago. He had always intended to buy some bullets for it but never had, which, as you'll see, turned out to be a major blessing. Shirley, in the meantime, had finished in the bathroom. Benny heard the flushing, but it took him several seconds to react. He knew it was Shirley. In his befuddled state, he didn't remember having told her to leave. He got up slowly, shook his head, and walked drowsily toward the bedroom door, stretching and yawning. He thought he heard a man's voice. Then it all came back to him in a flash—the argument earlier in the day, the whiskey, the cop, and then him telling her to leave. That bitch! What the hell is she doing back here, he wondered. I guess she didn't believe me when I told her to leave. Probably here with her janitor again. Well she's outta here and that's it.

"What the hell are you doing here?" he demanded as he walked through the door. Dude was the first to react. Scared, he ran toward the kitchen. Instinctively Benny started after him. He hadn't gone three feet when he saw Arthur, who had just grabbed a lamp with a heavy base. Everything seemed to be going in slow motion and without sound. He tried to stop and get his bearings, but he was too late. Arthur swung the lamp and caught Benny on the left side of his head. He started to go down, wincing from the sharp pain in the back of his neck. He tried to catch his balance. He heard himself groan. He saw flashes of extremely bright light as he hit the living room floor. He sensed another blow to his upper back, then another to his head. Shirley, who had just walked out of the bathroom, saw Benny struggling to regain his balance. He had managed to get onto his knees. If I can just get up, Benny thought, maybe I can get out the door. First Shirley froze, but then she stepped forward and kicked him in the stomach. Arthur swung the lamp again hitting Benny on the back of the head. By now Benny had managed to get into a crouching position. The last blow did it. He fell back onto his knees. Shirley kept kicking him in the groin and stomach. Her fifth kick broke several of his ribs. He tried to get to his feet once more but couldn't. He groaned again as another blow cracked his skull. Dude, seeing that Benny was down and unable to do anything, got brave. He emitted an almost hysterical laugh, picked up a kitchen chair, and hit Benny across the back. It wasn't necessary because Benny was already unconscious by that point. Arthur, cussing and swearing, began beating Benny on the head with the lamp.

"You bastard!" he screamed. "You fucking bastard!" Finally he collapsed into a chair and sat there breathing hard. Dude looked around. He bent over and studied Benny up close.

"Man, I think you killed the guy," he whispered.

"What do you mean, I killed him? If he's dead, we all did it. You hit him real hard with that there chair. That's what probably killed him," Arthur said.

Shirley stood in the middle of the room saying nothing. She just stared. Her breath came in short gasps as if she had just finished having sex. The bastard deserved it, she was thinking, but deep inside her a fear was welling up that blocked her ability to reason. She had never seen so much violence and had never been involved in it either.

"I only hit him once," Dude protested.

"Yeah, that's because your sissy ass was breaking for the door," Arthur countered.

"You didn't have to go off on the guy," Dude whined.

"Would you shut the fuck up?"

Shirley still hadn't said a word. She stood there looking at Benny. He wasn't moving at all. He's dead, she thought. So easy, it was so easy. Dead! Dead! Dead! She wanted to laugh. Is this what I wanted—him dead? We used to make love. Oh Benny, when did it all change? We were in love and now you're dead. So easy. Then her mind went blank.

Dude started putting the tapes into the bag. Arthur looked at him with disgust. Petty motherfucker honkey, he thought, but didn't say anything. Dude noticed the look on his face.

"What? What the hell are you looking at me for? This is what we came to do, isn't it?" he said to Arthur.

"Where does he keep his money? Where's the thousand dollars you was telling us about?" Arthur asked Shirley. Panic was beginning to seep into the room.

She didn't reply.

"Hey, snap out of it! Where he keeps the thousand dollars you was telling me about?"

Shirley still made no reply. Arthur was getting angry, and when Arthur got angry, things got ugly.

"I want my money, bitch." He jumped to his feet and grabbed her by the back of the neck. "Come on, get with it. What the hell's wrong with you anyway?"

Shirley stood frozen in the middle of the room. Arthur began to increase the pressure into his grip. "You said there was a thousand dollars up here. Where is it?"

He was beginning to get irrational. All he could think of was the thousand dollars she had mentioned. He wanted it. I want my money. This bitch owes me. I want my money. Dude was scrambling on hands and knees trying to get all the tapes. He glanced at Dude and felt very angry. Damned punk, he thought. He turned and looked at Benny on the floor. The he saw the corners of Shirley's mouth twitch and he knew: the bitch had lied. She stared at Benny.

Blood was oozing from his head and ears. He'd received more than a dozen extremely hard blows with the base of the lamp. A puddle of blood surrounded his head. In his mind, Arthur blamed Benny and Shirley for what had happened. Goddamned Indian and his half-breed bitch. She's the one. She's the one made this happen, he thought. And now look at her. An image of her testifying against him and Dude flashed through his mind. In that instant he made up his mind. Arthur had managed to stay alive by relying on his instincts.

Shirley stood staring at Benny's crumpled body. She recalled how they had met. How nice he'd been to her. She'd been living on the streets, turning ten-dollar tricks in order to eat and have a roof over her head. She shuddered involuntarily, remembering how the men had pressed money into her young hands. It came back to her in a flood of memories—the fear, the desperation, the shame. Then she met Benny and things changed. He was well known in the neighborhood as an artist of promise. She had been very flattered that he wanted to paint a picture of her. She insisted it be in the nude. At first he'd been embarrassed by her nakedness, but eventually he got over it. His embarrassment had pleased Shirley.

Arthur slapped her across the face. "Bitch, I want my money! You said there was a grand in this place. Where does he hide it?"

Shirley still did not say or do anything. In the back of her mind she realized this thing had gotten out of hand. She realized that both she and Benny were in danger—more danger than she had imagined possible. She wanted to do something to help Benny, but she was frozen with fear.

Dude finished packing the tapes. He watched Arthur trying to get Shirley to react. He kneeled down next to Benny and began going through his pockets, searching for cash. He found fifty dollars, took thirty, and handed the rest to his friend. Arthur reached over and grabbed the money, then quickly pushed Shirley onto the couch.

"This bitch is going to tell me where the rest of that money is," he said to Dude. "You know what I mean?"

"She's kinda freaked out," Dude said.

Turning to Shirley, Arthur slapped her again. "Where's that money?"

"I bet he keeps it in the bedroom," Dude suggested.

"Maybe you're right," said Arthur. He grabbed Shirley roughly and pushed her into the small bedroom. Dude began to unplug the television and stereo speakers. He heard Shirley scream, then begin to plead with Arthur. Dude could picture what Arthur was about to do. He started to go into the bedroom. When he opened the bedroom door Arthur told him to get out. He heard the sound of cloth ripping and Shirley's cry. He saw a flash of white skin and experienced a moment of intense excitement. He went into the kitchen and made himself a sandwich. He sat quietly at the kitchen table and ate. He couldn't get the image of her bare skin out of his mind. He started singing a jingle in an eerie voice. Dude started fantasizing about Shirley and himself.

"Well, she jumped in bed and covered her head and said I couldn't find her. I knew damned well she lied like hell so I jumped in bed behind her. She opened up her pretty white legs . . ." He started laughing as he ate.

About ten minutes later Arthur walked out of the bedroom, buckling his jeans.

"What the hell you singing?" he asked Dude.

"Just thinking about Shirley," Dude answered, then asked, "Where is she?"

"She's in there. You want some of her? She's butt-assed naked."

"What about the money? Did you get it?"

"There ain't none. The bitch admitted she lied to us. She had to be punished for that." Arthur answered. "I'm hungry too. What they got in this funky-assed kitchen?"

"There's some bread and shit."

"You wanna get some of her?"

"Maybe I will," Dude replied with a big grin on his face.

"Well, go ahead. Get you some and then we got to split."

Dude turned and walked into the bedroom. Shirley lay on the bed crying. Her torn clothes were scattered on the floor. She was bleeding from the nose and her eyes were beginning to puff up. She looked up as Dude walked in.

"Don't you touch me," she hissed.

"Why not? You let the nigger get some."

"He raped me."

Dude saw she had been tied up the bed posts. How convenient, he thought. He laughed as he unbuttoned his jeans. He started singing the jingle again.

Shirley started crying, then she started screaming. Dude wasn't sure what to do.

Arthur came running in. He grabbed Shirley by the hair and slapped her three times. She kept screaming. Arthur jumped up and landed on her stomach with both knees. Dude heard the breath rush out of her body. She stopped screaming as her eyes rolled back in her head. She passed out momentarily.

"Bitch, I'll kill you if you make another sound," he snarled.

She opened her eyes again and Dude saw the fear. He smiled and punched her in the face twice. He looked over at Arthur for approval and got what he'd hoped for.

"That's all you got to do," Arthur said to Dude with a big smile on his face. "Don't you know how to handle a bitch like this? What's wrong with you? I gotta show you everything, man. Now you take some of her and if she even whispers, you beat her half to death. They like it like that,"

Arthur told Dude. "If she resists, just beat her senseless. Like this." He hit Shirley on the back of the head. She moaned but didn't cry out.

Arthur walked through the living room and stomped on Benny's head. "Fucking Indian bastard. I just screwed your lying-ass white woman. She wasn't shit." He laughed loudly as he entered the kitchen to open a can of Spam and make sandwiches.

Dude was scared, but excited. He forced Shirley's legs open and laughed. She reacted by kicking him. He got angry and started punching her in the face. He laughed as blood poured from her mouth and nose. Suddenly he turned into a madman. He grabbed her hair and yanked her from the bed. The cloth that Arthur had tied her with snapped. She landed on the floor with a thump. She kicked at him again and started screaming. Dude grabbed her by the neck and started choking her.

"I'll kill you, bitch!" he hollered. She continued screaming loudly. Dude tightened his grip. She stopped screaming but continued to struggle. She brought her knee up hard into Dude's crotch. He hollered and she broke free of his grip. She jumped to her feet and bolted for the door.

In the kitchen, Arthur had heard the struggle. He cursed and ran toward the bedroom. Oh she's gonna get it now, he thought to himself. As Shirley rushed out of the bedroom, Arthur kicked her in the stomach. She fell flat on her face. He stomped her head against the carpet. Dude came rushing out and joined him. Shirley was out like a light. The two intruders continued beating both Benny and Shirley for several minutes. Blood was spattered on all four walls. The two men methodically took turns beating the bodies as if they were possessed by some kind of devil.

"We better get our asses out of here," Arthur said to Dude between gasps. "I'm sick of this shit, man."

"I didn't get none of that bitch," Dude complained.

"Yeah, but it looks like you got something out of it." Arthur laughed and pointed at Dude's crotch.

Dude looked down and saw that he had an erection. "Wow. That's freaky isn't it? Man, I got a goddamned hard-on from this shit."

"You sure did. You was getting off on this shit." Arthur's eyes were ablaze with excitement. "Look, you're my best friend. You sit back on the couch and let Arthur do you a big old favor."

"What you got on your mind?"

"I'm gonna give you some satisfaction," Arthur said. He looked at Dude, waiting to see how he would respond. When Dude offered no negative response, he continued, "You like head?"

"Oh! Are you sure?" Dude grinned stupidly at Arthur. He'd always wondered about Arthur's sexual preference and now he knew.

"So you like pole as much as you like hole." Dude grinned as Arthur nodded. He sat back on the couch, his pants down to his knees. He sat rubbing himself expectantly. Arthur had another idea.

"Grab that bitch and put some hurt on her while I do you. This will be so freaky."

"I like freaky!" Dude said, laughing. He grabbed Shirley's limp body, pulled her onto the couch and started massaging her breasts. Her body was limp and she was barely breathing. Both men were making small noises as Arthur began bobbing up and down. Dude laughed hysterically as he climaxed. He twisted Shirley's head until he heard her neck snap. He moaned loudly as he ejaculated. Arthur began laughing also. At that very moment the Chicago police kicked in both front and back doors. They were shocked by what they saw. The two men made no effort to resist arrest.

Officer Rubin Wallace heard about the incident at roll call the next morning. Even before the victims were named, he knew one of them was Benny. He felt shocked, then angry, and then he began to feel a sense of guilt. He wondered if he had made a mistake in the way he dealt with the couple the day before. He requested and was given the day off. He went to the hospital to visit Benny but the Indian artist was in a coma. It was three days before he regained consciousness. When he did, the first person he saw was Rubin. At first he couldn't remember anything at all. After several hours he could remember his name and Rubin. He asked about Shirley. Rubin told him what had happened.

Investigators were shocked at the cruelty and violence the two men had committed. Shirley had died instantly from a broken neck. Dude and Arthur had signed confessions in which each blamed the other. They were charged with several major crimes, including breaking and entering, rape, attempted murder, and murder.

Twenty-nine days later Benny was released from the hospital. Relatives picked him up and took him home to a small Indian reservation in northern Michigan. He spent several months traveling back and forth to Chicago to see the doctor and go to court. During his stay in the hospital, he and Rubin Wallace had become good friends. They made plans to visit each other. Throughout Dude and Arthur's trial, Benny stayed at Rubin's apartment when he would come to the city for court dates. During his vacation, the police officer went to Michigan to visit with Benny's family and get in some fishing. On the final day of the trial, Rubin and Benny paid a visit to Shirley 's grave.

Arthur was sentenced to ninety-nine years in prison. He testified that Dude had been the one to commit the murder. Dude was given a one-hundred-year sentence. One year into his sentence, Arthur was murdered in a jail-house love triangle. Dude committed suicide about five years later by hanging himself in his cell.

"So what are you gonna do now?" Rubin asked Benny at the end of the trial.

"I think I'm gonna hit the road for a while. You know, get my head together. Bastard scrambled the hell out of my brain. Sometimes it's hard for me to keep things straight. I get confused. I want to do some serious traveling," Benny said. "I haven't painted anything for a long time. I need to get out there and get me some inspiration. Maybe I'll try writing some poetry.

"How you gonna get around?"

"Hitchhike, I guess."

"I wouldn't advise it," Rubin said.

"Well you know how that goes."

"You know what? I got a Triumph 650 I never use. I could let you have it for pretty cheap. You interested?" Rubin asked.

"I am if the price is right. How much?"

"How about a c-note?"

"You can't be serious."

"I'm telling you, I am. I never ride that motorcycle. You'd have to get it tuned up but it's almost like new. I rode the thing for one summer. It was just this phase I was going through. I want you to have it Benny. It'd be just what you need. Do you know how to ride one?"

Benny laughed.

"Well, do you?"

"Honestly?" Benny asked.

"Now why would I want anything but the truth?"

"No, I don't," Benny smiled. "But I can learn real fast."

"Do you even have a driver's license?"

"Nope. Never did," Benny laughed.

"It's going to take you at least a week to get everything together. You know I can't let you take off unless you're completely legit," Rubin said.

"Once a cop, always a cop?"

"You got that right, pal," Rubin grinned.

"Okay, we'll do it your way."

A week and a half later Benny had learned to ride the bike. He passed the permit test with flying colors. On Saturday morning he and Rubin went out to have breakfast at a local Steak 'n Egger. After eating they returned to Rubin's apartment to say a final goodbye. It wasn't yet 8:00 A.M. when they quietly loaded Benny's gear onto the back of the bike.

"Remember to call every now and then, okay?"

"I will. You know what? Out of all this the only thing that I can really grasp is that it's going to take a long time before I can ever let anybody get next to me again like Shirley did."

"Yeah, but you got to remember that not all people are like that. I mean there are good people too. You know?"

"And those are the ones I'm going to try to meet. I want to believe they're out there. Really I do."

They shook hands, hugged, and Benny took Lake Shore Drive to Highway 55 heading south. He came back to Chicago three years later, met an Indian woman named Chili Corn, and married her a year after that.

NOMAD

"I go wherever I feel like going. If people leave me alone, I don't bother them," he said, summing up his philosophy. "I know how to survive, so I don't have to ask anybody for anything. I ain't no burden."

Eddie Hoyte was a person of the road, an interstate nomad wandering through a domain of strangers. Twenty-two years old and he still looked at the world with innocence. Of course he wasn't thinking about himself in those terms the day he got out of a car at Peterson's corner, somewhere in rural Ohio, but the fat woman who watched him sure as hell was thinking about what she saw. And what she saw she didn't like at all.

She sat behind the counter in the small country store, eying Eddie suspiciously.

"Another one of those hippies comin', Kitty. We best be careful. This one looks like an Indian. Hell, I think he really is, Kitty. Now we got trouble," she said softly to the fat striped cat curled up next to her. She heard the roar of a motor as the car that Eddie had gotten out of sped away.

"He's one of those hitchhikers, Kitty."

She watched as the young man consulted a road map. She watched as he shook an army canteen, opened it, and took a swallow. She eyed him suspiciously as he shouldered his back-pack and headed toward her store. She watched the whole thing from beginning to end. Nothing happened on that corner she didn't know about. She was proud of that. It was, in fact, her claim to fame.

As Eddie Hoyte turned to walk toward the store, Esther Peterson, the fat woman, spat into an empty Hills Brothers coffee can that sat on the floor. PING! She smiled and reached under the counter to move the twenty-two caliber pistol to where she could grab it quickly if she needed to. Can't never trust those goddamned hippies, she thought. Especially an Indian hippie. She squinted her eyes at him. He was an Indian, she could see that, and if the red-skinned devil tried to do anything—anything at all—he was going to get the surprise of his life.

"Make my day, redskin!" she said softly and smiled. She just loved Clint Eastwood in that movie. PING! She spat into the can again.

Esther chewed Copenhagen snuff. A rivulet of brown juice trickled from the left corner of her mouth. Her graying, greasy hair was pulled back into a tight ponytail. She wore a faded, dirty smock with polyester slacks that looked as if she'd slept in them for several nights. Eddie Hoyte walked into the store and looked around. The odor of the place assaulted his nose.

Dimly lit, small, and not well organized, it was a pathetic excuse for a store. The space was nearly filled to capacity by a row of display shelves in the center. The store looked crowded. He turned to the woman at the counter and smiled.

"Good afternoon. Sure is hot out, ain't it?"

"What's so good about it? If you was from around here— which I can see you ain't, bein' that Indians bin run out a here a long time ago—you'd know this ain't no 'ceptional weather for this time of year." She turned her head slightly and let loose another shot of spit. Eddie heard the ping as it landed in the can. Her hostility took him aback. He looked at her closely. She returned his stare.

Small, beady-blue eyes glared hatefully from among the countless freckles that dotted her oval face. Her sagging jowls and chin were defined only by layers of massive flesh. Eddie wondered if she had ever been pretty. He thought about telling her to shove her store up her fat ass and leaving, but he needed supplies for the night. He walked up the first aisle, the one nearest to him. There was dust everywhere and it made him feel caged in. He just wanted to buy what he needed and get back outside into the fresh air.

A small selection of dusty articles was displayed on the dusty shelves. Dusty canned goods, dusty boxes of crackers, and dusty packages of baking items. Dead flies, mouse shit, and pieces of dried leaves littered the spaces between the items. A shiver crept up the young man's spine. "Holy shit!" he said softly to himself.

"What'd you say?" Esther asked him.

"Nothing," he replied. Agitation colored his voice. He wanted to tell her to go to hell but decided against it again.

"Ya said somethin'. I done heard ya."

"Talking to myself."

"You ain't no escapee from a loony bin are you?" She emitted a high, squeaky laugh.

Eddie thought he heard her pass gas. I oughta say something to her. Really get her going, he thought with a smile. But he continued down the next aisle without responding. She spat into the can again. Eddie shook his head in disbelief.

A refrigerated butcher's showcase stood at the back of the store. It reeked of half-rotted meat. Blood and water formed a puddle at the bottom. The motor made a grinding sound. Bad bearings, Eddie thought. When he wasn't traveling, he usually worked as a mechanic. He looked into the case at the meat inside. He caught his breath and turned quickly away. He moved quickly away into the last aisle. He wondered how the hell she managed to get past the health department inspections, if they had such a thing around here.

Esther craned her neck to watch Eddie as he checked the prices of items on display. Her body shook like jelly with every movement. She reached under the counter and touched the gun for reassurance. He'd best not try anything, she thought, because I got him covered. Thieving redskins, always tryin' to take what decent white folks worked so hard to get. She had a hard time breathing, always had.

"This goddamned heat ain't helping it any," she cursed softly to herself. "Maybe I should go see a doctor. Get me a checkup." She squinted suspiciously at Eddie as he turned the corner, his hands empty.

"Are you gonna buy or you just gawkin'? I ain't in business to have no-count folks in here gawkin'. I gots overhead ya know." She reached under the counter again to touch the gun. "Just in case," she whispered to the cat, then turned back to Eddie and continued, "and don't be fixin' to steal nothin' either. The last hippie come through here who tried that is down in the county jail. My cousin be the law in this here county. Got the thievin' bastard ninety days, he did. Cried like a baby in front of all the county folks. Nobody give a shit cause we don't hold to thievin' around here. So don't you be thinkin' of stealin' nothin', cause I can fix you up too."

She giggled. Eddie went back to pick up the items he'd decided he might be able to stomach. He had intended on buying a pound of lunch meat, but after looking at the meat case, he had changed his mind. If it wasn't sealed tight in a can he didn't want it.

"I'd like a can of Spam, a can of these here Rosedale peaches, a can of pork 'n beans, a loaf of bread, and a liter of coke. Oh yeah! And a package of that there black licorice. I was raised on candy like this. You like it?" he asked, smiling and laid the items on the counter.

"Don't eat no candy like that. I can only eat a few cause they don't agree with my system—I get the shits. You know what I mean?" She picked up the stub of a pencil, put on a pair of eyeglasses, licked the lead, and began totaling the items.

She reminded Eddie of a pregnant sow. In fact, he thought, she even smells like one. Her smell seemed to permeate the room. The small ceiling fan was not strong enough to remove the pungent tang of her body odor. Eddie tried to hold his breath, but there was no way to avoid taking in the smell. He wished to hell she'd hurry up.

"Ya know that there hippie boy I was tellin' you about? Well, he walked in here, just like you. He faked me out for a while cause he was pleasant and all, but the little son-of-a-bitch snuck some gum in his pocket. I see'd him do it. You never know what they're gonna do," she said, scratching the back of her neck. Her arms were huge and jiggled as she moved. Eddie was amazed and uncomfortable.

"Like you now. I can't be sure of the likes of you. Bein' a woman out here in the country, I has to be on guard. You may be polite as all get out, but I know you be thinkin' of rapin' me or somethin'."

Eddie was shocked. He was offended and was getting sick of her rudeness.

"Raping you?" he asked, amazed. "You think I'd rape you?"

"Well, I'm a woman way out here by herself. Ya can never tell."

"Don't worry, I'm not a rapist."

"Maybe you be thinkin' of robbin' me."

"No, I'm not thinking that either. How much do I owe you?"

"'Cludin' taxes, it comes to four dollars and ninety-eight cents."

As Eddie counted out the money, he saw her reach under the counter and move something. The cat lifted its head to look at Eddie.

"You sure you ain't got no bad designs in that head of yours?" Esther asked. "I know the devil talks to your kind. Makin' you do evil things to decent white folks. Especially us God-fearin' white women. You likes white girls, Indian boy? You like that there white poon tang?"

"What the hell is poon tang?"

"You know, white pussy."

She looked at him with a challenging smirk on her face. Eddie shook his head.

"Here's the money." Eddie wanted to get out of that store. He didn't like what was happening. This woman is crazy, he thought.

"Well I'm surprised—ya bein' Indian and all. Most folks knows that you heathen redskins don't have no love for us white folks. John Wayne sure enough had the right idea with y'all. He put ya in your place all right. Now there was a man make most any white woman get a damp spot on her bloomers." She roared with laughter that shook every ounce of her as she bagged the items. "Done made your ears red. You're a bashful boy."

Eddie was speechless. As he watched her put the last of his purchases in the bag, he became acutely aware of her heavy breathing and the whirring sound of the fan overhead. He only wanted to get out of her store as quickly as possible.

Esther watched him pick up the bag. She spit into the can again. PING! The hollow sound reminded her that she was in charge. This was her store, her home and this hippie son-of-a-bitch didn't belong here. She resented the way he looked at her. It made her angry because he wouldn't argue back, and she interpreted it as meaning he was being judgmental. She hated judgmental people—especially those dark-skinned devils with their long hair.

"Can't speak huh," she sneered. Eddie stopped in his tracks and half turned to look at her. She reached under the counter. She could hardly breathe. Her eyes squinted and her body tightened. Eddie saw her change. He sensed she had a gun under the counter and wouldn't hesitate to use it. Yeah, screw you, he thought as he turned and headed for the door.

"The truth got hold of your tongue. Makes you silent. That's how you Indians are. Yeah, I know in your head you be thinkin' things though. You thinkin' of rapin' me? Wanna make me pay for what us white folks did to you. We should've kilt the whole bunch of ya," she shrieked as he bounded out the door and down the two steps to the street. He didn't stop until he was a good distance from her store. Then he noticed his hands were shaking and he was sweating.

"Rape her? Holy shit! Where did she get that idea? In her dreams! White poon tang? Do I like white pussy? What a racist bitch, talking to me like that. She should have her throat cut."

He looked up at the sun. It was heading toward late afternoon. He needed a place to settle in for the night and make a campsite.

Esther sat in the store. She watched the young man standing at the intersection. She swore to herself and let loose of a thick glob of the slimy brown snuff. PING! It landed in the coffee can just like she knew it would. Her piglike eyes squinted against the bright sunlight outside her gloomy store. She focused her vision and watched Eddie fish in one pocket then another.

"What's he lookin' for anyways? Don't suppose that hippie Indian gots a gun do ya, Kitty? Maybe he's gonna come back to rape me and kill ya? What's he lookin' for anyways?"

Eddie was looking for a pack of cigarettes. After that crazy woman in the store he needed to smoke, to mellow out. He found it. As he was lighting one, he glanced back at the store window. He saw movement at the window but paid little attention to it. Esther, on the other hand, was paying close attention to him.

"He's smokin' that there marijuana, Kitty. It's that wacky tobacky! Stuff makes Indians go crazy, almost like firewater. Communists give it to them, so's they'll do bad stuff to decent white folks. When they smoke that, they go rapin' and killin' and scalpin'." She turned and spit into the can again. PING! She squinted her eyes in Eddie's direction. "Ya know, that's what they smoked in their peace pipes, but when the Communists got involved, they put a chemical on it makes them crazy. I wish John Wayne was round here. He'd handle that hippie like he weren't nothin'. Oh that John Wayne!" She reached under the counter and grabbed the gun. She rubbed the gun against her cheek and smiled dreamily at her cat.

"Oh boy, that John Wayne was a real American. They don't make them like that no more and that hippie is a prime example." She pointed to the roadside. "Look at him Kitty, he don't give a shit at all. He's just standing there puffin' away and lookin' over here. He's thinkin' of comin' back after us. I know he wants to rape me, a woman out here by herself. I got a good mind to call the law."

She pondered a moment and then made a decision. The woman waddled over to the telephone that hung on the wall. The cat stood up, arched its back—you know, like cats do—and waddled behind her.

ON THE RUN

You never could have convinced the young Indian sitting
in the waiting room in the Chicago Avenue lockup that his
girlfriend was a convicted murderer who had been on the
run, but here she was, sitting in jail. Bobby Steele felt dizzy
and tired. He swallowed the last of the black coffee, crushed
the paper cup, and shook his head to keep himself awake.
They'd told him she'd killed her husband in Ohio. She'd
been a fugitive from justice is what the detective had said. So
now the young Indian understood why she had been that
way—always so secretive, so unwilling to talk about herself.
He sat on the hard wooden bench in the police station. He
noticed how the bench had been worn smooth by other
people sitting right there, waiting. He fidgeted about. After
what seemed like hours his name was called. A sergeant
with an understanding smile approached him.

"Mr. Steele?"

"Yes sir." Bobby straightened up on the bench. He felt
a pain shoot through his left shoulder—an old hockey
injury.

"Miss Petrovelli doesn't want to see you."

"Miss Petrovelli?"

"That's her real name."

"Did she say why?" he asked as his heart sank.

"Look kid, she's probably doing you a big favor."

"And how do you figure that?" Bobby asked, massaging
his shoulder.

"Well, think about it. She's wanted for murder. Hell, she's already been convicted. She's going to prison. She's a fugitive. You don't want to get involved in that."

"I know you're probably right, Sergeant, but it isn't that easy. You know what I mean?"

"She was a hooker. Didn't that bother you at all? She was selling her body to other men, for Christ's sake."

"At first it did, yes, but after a while . . ." Bobby's voice trailed away. "I offered to go to work so we could live like a decent couple, but she didn't want to hear it. I loved her. She knew that. I loved her." The sergeant watched as a tear slipped from the corner of the kid's eye. "I still love her, Sergeant. It can't just stop like that."

"Ain't this about a bitch?" the sergeant thought. "This kid's in a bad spot. Seems nice enough. What the fuck is he doing with a god-damned hooker?"

"Jesus, kid, you gotta get your head on straight. She's been convicted of murder. She had no chance for a good life and she knew it. Did you know she was on the run?"

"No. But I gotta tell you, Sergeant, it wouldn't have made any difference to me, not once I fell in love. She used to cry sometimes, but would never tell me why. Man, she'd be crying from real deep. It used to really get to me."

"Think about how she must have felt. It had to be rough on her, living a life like that, living a lie."

"Couldn't you talk to her, sir? I really need to see her for a minute."

The sergeant knew the regulations, knew them like the back of his hand. But he also knew human nature. Sometimes regulations and human nature, he thought, come into direct conflict. Screw the regulations, he decided. This is real life.

"I probably shouldn't do this, but I will. You seem like a pretty straight guy. Wait here." The sergeant got to his feet, grunting as he did so, and walked into the back room.

Bobby shut his eyes and leaned back against the wall. He felt completely drained. It was as if all his emotions were swirling like rainwater going down a drain on a rainy night—around and around. He wondered if he would ever get over this heavy weight that had just fallen onto his youthful shoulders. His eyes hurt. He squeezed them shut, real tight to ward off the pain. His thoughts drifted off to the day he had met Lynn.

Sergeant Welsh looked into the cell where Miss Petrovelli was being held. She sat huddled in a corner, looking crestfallen and alone. She certainly didn't have the demeanor of a killer, he thought. He wondered why she had killed her husband, but somewhere deep inside, he knew. He'd been a cop long enough to know about those things. It was an old story: abusive husband, desperate wife. Son-of-a-bitch probably deserved what he got, he thought to himself.

"Miss Petrovelli, can I talk to you for a minute?"

"I don't really have a choice, do I?"

"Of course you do."

"I've already made a statement. What do you want?"

"It's that young Indian kid here to see you. He seems to care about you a lot, Miss Petrovelli."

"I said I don't want to see him."

"Why not?"

"What's your point?"

"My point, Miss Petrovelli, is that the kid loves you."

"I don't want him to love me."

"But he does and I think you owe him some kind of explanation."

"What can I tell him?" she asked.

"I don't what the hell you can tell him, but the poor fucker is out there crying around for you." The sergeant paused a moment, then asked, "You do love the little bastard, don't you?"

She broke down crying. Not hard or desperate, but softly and mostly to herself. She looked up at the sergeant. Hell, he thought, this woman isn't a killer. He'd seen killers and looked into their eyes. Her face was soft and gentle. She was actually quite beautiful, he thought. No wonder that kid's out there with a busted heart. Suddenly he felt very tired. I need a beer, he thought as he looked at the woman.

Lynn Petrovelli thought about how she had met Bobby Steele. While on the run, she had supported herself first as a maid, then a waitress, and finally as a prostitute. She and Bobby met in a small bar on Clark Street. They'd spent the afternoon talking and sipping drinks. She'd liked him almost immediately. He had the long hair one would expect from a Native American man. He talked about life on the reservation and what it was like being a Native American in today's society. When he asked her what she did for a living she'd told him she was a hooker. He was shocked by her answer, but then seemed to accept her regardless. That was the start of their relationship. She would meet him for movies and dinner before she went out on Rush Street to walk the streets. He worked nights at a small grocery store on the west side of the city so that never became a problem. Eventually they got more involved. She asked him to move in with her in her small one-room place on Broadway. He did and they got along very nicely there. At first he objected to her being a hooker, but then he accepted it. It had been hard but he'd done it.

"I've hurt him enough already," she finally said. "I just want him to forget about me. He doesn't deserve this. I'm going to prison for a long time."

"That's right, Miss Petrovelli, you are. But he's gonna be out here hurting and wondering about you. Look, just talk to him. He's a young guy. I don't get the impression he's been around much. He's all mixed up."

"Don't matter what I say to him, he's still gonna hurt. It's best he just forgot about whatever we had. He should just go home to his reservation and forget about me. Would you tell him that?"

"You tell him that yourself," he replied, then immediately softened his voice. "He needs to hear it from you. He's a sensitive type of guy."

She nodded and wiped her eyes.

"Why'd you do it?"

"What?"

"Get involved with a guy like him anyway? He's so—well, he's so different from most pimps."

"He wasn't my pimp. Is that what you thought?"

"No," the sergeant said with a short laugh. "I didn't think so, but the world you lived in sure as hell couldn't have suited him. So why that kid?"

"He was a breath of fresh air. You're right, he was different. I wanted to tell him the truth several times and once I even started to but I changed my mind. You think I was wrong?"

"Nobody can say what's right or wrong, Miss Petrovelli, least of all me. Can I ask you something?"

"Sure, go ahead."

"Do you love him?"

"I do."

"Then you know what to do. Do the right thing, Miss Petrovelli. You're like me in a lot of ways, young lady. People like us got to do the right thing, no matter what. Sometimes it's all we have, isn't it?"

She nodded. "Okay, okay. I'll talk to him."

"Thank you, Miss Petrovelli."

"Like you say, 'we got to do the right thing.' It's the least we can do, right?"

Sergeant Welsh watched as the two of them huddled together in the small interview room. They were both crying. The woman held the kid's head in her arms and looked at the sergeant with a sad smile. He knew she was having a rough time. Who the hell wouldn't in her spot? He smiled back. Although he had specified that they only had a few minutes, Sergeant Welsh left them together in the small room for over thirty minutes. He watched through the large plate glass window as the two cried, talked, then cried some more. He felt sorry for them.

She looked deep into his eyes. He had no idea what he'd come to mean to her over the past few months.

"You have to forget about what we've had. Forget you ever knew me, okay? There'll be other ladies out there for you. You're young, handsome, and smart. Go home to your reservation. You said you wanted to help your people. Go home and get involved, okay?"

"I want to know one thing. Did you do it?"

"Yes, Bobby, I did."

"I don't believe it. I know you. You're a very gentle lady."

"It's true, Bobby. I've already been convicted of murder and sentenced to thirty years without parole. You know what that means?"

"How come so long?"

"My husband was the son of a judge in a small town. That means he was privileged. I was a poor girl. I couldn't afford an attorney. You just have to forget all about me. You understand?"

"I can't."

"Oh you can, Bobby. You just don't know it yet. Go live your life. Enjoy it. Live it, Bobby, live it to the fullest."

"I'll get a good job and hire the best lawyer in town."

She moaned softly, so strong was her love for the young man. She brushed back his hair and kissed him gently on the face.

"Oh Bobby, go live your life. Forget about me would you? Just promise me you'll stay like you are."

"I love you, Lynn, I love you so much."

Two burly guards entered the office and spoke briefly to Sergeant Welsh. He nodded and looked sadly into the room at Bobby and Lynn. He walked stiffly toward the door. Lynn saw him coming. She saw the two guards and realized it was time. She hugged the young Indian to her closely.

"Listen to me Bobby. I love you. Very much. You've made my life bearable. I don't know what I would have done without you. Make me a promise, Bobby. Promise me you won't let this get you down. Promise me."

He looked at her and nodded. "I promise you."

The sergeant entered the room with the two guards behind him. "Okay, Miss Petrovelli, it's time. Young man, she has to go. You'll have to come with me." He gently took Bobby by the arm. The guards walked up to Lynn. Bobby looked at the sergeant in desperation. In that second the two men bonded in ways neither of them would ever be able to explain. He started to lead Bobby from the room, but Bobby broke down, crying hysterically when he saw Lynn being taken away in chains. The sergeant put his arm around the young Indian to comfort him and looked out the window. It was raining again.

"You gonna be okay, kid?" he asked.

"Why'd they have to chain her up like an animal?" Bobby asked.

"It's their job son."

"But she's not violent."

"She's a convicted killer and a fugitive. They can't take chances."

"What am I gonna do without her? I love her so much."

"You're young. You'll figure it out."

"I don't know, man. I just don't know," Bobby said.

"Go home and get some sleep. You'll feel better in the morning. Look, here's my card. You need something, someone to talk to, you call me, okay. Look, kid, I know this is rough, but you're an Indian and you come from a long line of people who have made the most out of rough times. Follow your instincts."

Bobby Steele walked out of the Chicago Avenue police station that night a total emotional wreck. For several hours he wandered the streets in a daze. He sat on a bridge near Union Station and was tempted to jump into the Chicago River. The dirty water looked inviting, but he didn't succumb to the temptation. He remembered Lynn's words instead. He would remember them for a long time to come.

Sergeant Welsh sat at the bar talking with two detectives from his precinct. They were discussing the night's events. He told them about Bobby and Lynn.

"You know, I gave the kid my card. Told him to call me if he felt like it. He was a nice kid. Came from a small Indian reservation in northern Minnesota."

"Wasn't a smart thing to do," one of the detectives commented.

"I know that, but this kid was different somehow. There was something about him. You know?"

"Man, Welsh, you know better than that. You can't let these things get to you. Otherwise we go crazy. You gotta keep yourself detached. If you don't you're going down. Keep the shit at a distance. Hell, you been on the job what, about fifteen years?"

"I wonder if the kid will call."

Bobby did call. He called a few days later because he needed a letter of reference for a job. The two stayed in touch, and in time the police officer became like a father to Bobby. He was amazed at the way the young Indian hit the books at school and still maintained a full-time job. He was proud when Bobby invited him to his graduation from college. As a reward for his hard work, Sergeant Welsh gave Bobby a fancy pen and a gold watch that he'd been given when he'd graduated from the police academy.

"So now you got a college degree," Sergeant Welsh said to Bobby, "why don't you think about joining the force? I could sponsor you. You know, pull some strings. I got favors coming. You want me to do it?"

Bobby sat quietly for several moments before answering.

"Thanks, Serge, but I'm going to go to law school. I want to be a lawyer. It's the only way I can help my friends. You know what I mean?"

Sergeant Welsh saw the look of determination in the young Indian's eyes and was glad. It gave him joy to feel that in some small way his influence was at work. The old sergeant smiled knowingly. Idealism, he thought. It keeps the world going.

Lynn Petrovelli was attacked by two inmates shortly after she entered prison. She survived the attack, but it changed her. She became harder. She also began reading books—lots of them—and started writing. A few years later she enrolled in the GED program, then college. When she first entered prison she would receive letters from Bobby every week. Then they dwindled to once a month, then four times a year. She never read any of them because she felt it would be too painful, but she saved every one of them. Sometimes she'd take them out and hold them to her face. She tried hard to catch his scent on them, then she tenderly put them away with her other few belongings.

It was exactly fifteen years later that Lynn received an official-looking letter informing her that an appeal had been filed on her behalf by a Chicago attorney named Robert J. Steele. Lynn could scarcely breathe as she read and reread the letter. Bobby had found a loophole the other attorneys had overlooked. She sat down that night and began reading all his old letters. After college, Bobby had gone on to receive a law degree. In his letters he apologized for taking so long. Every letter ended with his telling her he would find a way for them to be together.

The second time Bobby called the sergeant, with a major request, was three years after Lynn had gotten the notice of her appeal. The phone rang and the now-retired police officer answered.

"Hello," he said.

"I just called to tell you I'm picking her up in the morning," an excited voice said over the receiver.

"Who is this? What the hell are you talking about?" he asked.

"Serge, it's me—Bobby Steele."

The sergeant realized his memory wasn't as sharp as it used to be. "How the hell are you kid?"

"Sergeant, I've never been better."

"You sound real excited. By the way, I've retired from the police force. So tell me son, what's all the fuss about?"

"I'm gonna pick her up."

"Pick up who?"

"Let me start from the beginning, okay? Remember when you told me I'd figure out what I had to do? Remember how upset I was about Lynn going to prison?"

"Yeah, I do remember how torn up you were. I don't remember exactly what I said, but I'm glad you listened to it."

"Well, Sergeant, you told me that I'd figure out what I had to do and I did. I got my ass in school and got myself a law degree. It was rough and it took longer than I thought it would, but I stuck with it and since then I've been working on Lynn's case. I never forgot what you said about being an Indian. How my people made the best out of bad situations. Your words gave me strength when everything looked hopeless."

"You mean the hooker? Nice woman, I recall."

"Right. That's the one. Well, I got her case retried and won a reversal. She's coming home. I got her out."

"That was fifteen, sixteen years ago, kid. You mean to tell me you've been working on it that long?"

"Yeah, and it just paid off. You were right on."

"That sure is loyalty. Did you two ever get married?"

Bobby Steele laughed. "Sergeant, we *were* married. It was just between me and her and the Great Spirit, but we were married."

"You stuck with it that long, with her."

"I had no choice. I love her. She's getting out in the morning. That's why I'm calling. Do you want to come with me to get her out?"

"I don't know, kid. A cop, even if I'm retired, is the last thing she might want to see. You know what I mean?"

"I think she'd be glad to see you. It was because of the kindness you showed us that this came about. You put me on the right path. You'll never know what you did for us. Why don't you come with me to get her?"

"Well, maybe. I don't drive anymore."

"Don't worry about that. I'll pick you up."

"You think it would be okay?"

"I know it would. You're one of the best. I want you there, Sergeant."

"Okay, but under one condition."

"What's that?"

"Call me Walter. That's my name."

Walter looked at the plaque he'd been given upon retirement. It read, "In service to the community. 'Policing is a lifetime job.'" The plaque was among his most prized possessions—a reminder of his years on the Chicago force. He hung up the phone, wiped away a tear sliding down his face, and smiled at himself in the mirror. He thought about Bobby, trying to recall everything about him that he could.

Meanwhile, Bobby sat at his desk in the office he'd rented in a downtown building. He experienced a wave of emotion. Damn, he thought, I have a lot to do before she gets home. Home? He'd never thought much about what home would mean to Lynn. He grabbed the letter from her that lay open on his desk. He reread the words:

When I get home, we'll have to take things slow. Get to know each other. We'll have to repair what the years have damaged, but it will be so good to be home with you again. Bobby, I love you, and I know things will work out. I've learned you're a special kind of man and I want to be with you—to make a home. Do you understand? We'll both be afraid, but you're a strong person—the strongest man I've ever met. We'll find a way. You've already shown me that.

Bobby put the letter down and walked to the window. The city stretched below him. Yes, he thought, we'll find a way.

SMOKING PISTOL SYNDROME

"I'm calling the cops!" she screeched at him. "I god-damned well mean it, you asshole. I want you out of here. I don't want you here when you're drunk."

"I ain't drunk," he answered.

"I don't care. Get out. Now!"

"Why?" he asked.

"You know why," she stated with a firmness that made him angry.

"But I ain't drunk."

"Yes you are. I can smell it," she responded with disgust.

"I'm dog-assed tired and I just want to go to bed."

"You been drinking!" she yelled.

"But I ain't drunk."

Their fifteen-year-old son, Josie, the one everyone said had emotional problems, sat on the floor in front of the television, an empty Coke bottle in his hand. He tossed the bottle on the floor and watched it spin three times, holding his hands over his ears. He silently screamed for them to stop fighting. Of course they didn't. Even if he'd said it outloud they wouldn't have stopped. Josie hated it when they argued like this. It made him afraid.

"So I stopped for one drink. Big deal!" his father hollered from the bathroom.

"I told you I don't want you in this house when you're drinking. You get abusive."

"I wouldn't if you didn't start in on me. Why do you always have to be such a control freak?"

"Control freak? Aren't you the one to be talking about control. I stay in this house all day. I feel like a prisoner. I can't go anywhere, do anything. I'm stuck in here. You have control over me. I stay in this house with your son. He don't communicate to me. The both of you get on my nerves."

"Hey, bitch, I work all day, everyday."

The argument went on and on. Josie sat in the living room listening. He heard his parents' bedroom door slam. His mind was in turmoil. He couldn't straighten things out. He was sure they were arguing about him, because of him. They both hate me, he thought. He wished he were in a regular school instead of the special kids' school. I could run away. Maybe they'd get along better without me. He put his head in his hands and rocked back and forth. He could hear them in their bedroom as they argued on and on.

He got up from the floor and went to the front window. He noticed it had started to rain slightly, a drizzle that made the concrete shine and glitter. He studied the concrete and imagined images dancing across the street. They were Indian images he'd seen in a book. Then he noticed a spider spinning a web in the upper corner of the window frame. After a few minutes he got tired of that and decided to watch the cars going by.

He named them: Chevy, Toyota, Chevy, a pickup truck, and another Chevy. Josie could name every kind of car by sight. His father would brag about that. But Josie couldn't remember the name of the town where he was born and raised and where he spent his entire life. His mother would remind his father about that fact. Then they'd get into a fight.

Sometimes they'd go fishing, the three of them. His mom would pack a lunch and his dad would show him how to cast. His dad always had a can of beer in his hand when they were out there by the lagoons. Josie walked into the kitchen to get some cold pizza from the refrigerator. They had planned to have a pizza party that evening, but his father hadn't shown up for several hours and when he did, he smelled of booze. He wondered why his dad always did that when they planned to have a nice time. It was always the same, he thought. Both of his parents would be all lovey-dovey in the morning before his father left for work. He'd make his wife and son a promise that they'd have a nice evening together when he got home. It looked like he was a happy man in the morning, but by the time he got home he'd be drunk and mean.

Josie poured himself some more Coke and sat at the kitchen table to eat. He accidentally spilled some of the drink on the kitchen floor. Immediately he stopped eating and cleaned it up. His mother would get very angry when he made a mess so Josie kept the kitchen spotless. If there was a crumb on the floor he'd have to sweep the whole floor. If there was a dish in the sink he would wash it. He wanted to make his mother happy. She, however, complained to his father that Josie was a clean freak.

He heard music coming from his parents' bedroom. He heard his mother laughing and the sound of his father's work boots hitting the floor. Josie knew what they were doing. He'd peeked through the crack in the door a month before. Saw them making love. It had scared him that time. Now he heard the bedsprings squeaking and his parents laughing. He knew it was a natural thing they were doing, but he wondered why they always had to fight first. It was always the same, like some kind of ritual. Then he heard that mixture of voices. Sometimes it was his parents' voices but other times it was the others. Those were the ones that scared Josie a lot. They always said bad things to him.

At first they would only whisper, but then they got louder and louder. He held his head in his hands again and rocked back and forth. Then Josie began pacing in the kitchen, back and forth, back and forth. He went to the back door to see if anybody was coming. He hoped someone was, but no one was there. He began slapping at the air, trying to make the voices go away. They stayed and grew even louder.

Josie started to shake. He tried kicking at the voices, but still they wouldn't go away. They only got louder and more insistent. Tears began spilling from his eyes and rolling down his face. He stood in front of the radiator trying to make the voices go away, but still they wouldn't leave. They were telling him to do bad things to himself. He stumbled into the pantry and pulled down the box where his father kept his pistol.

Standing in the middle of the kitchen, fifteen-year-old Josie put the cold, blue pistol barrel to the right side of his head.

The voices began whispering, "Do it! Do it!"

Josie said softly to himself, "Should I?"

"Yes! Do it. Just like that." His mother's voice filtered through the walls. Her voice mixed with the voices he was hearing in his head. He felt dizzy and confused.

CLICK!

"You're not worth living anyway. Everybody hates you," the voices said. "Do it! Do it!" they urged.

"Oh yes. Please don't stop. Do it!" Again his mother cried out with passion.

CLICK! CLICK!

"Mommy and Daddy would be better off without me, he thought as tears rolled uncontrollably down his brown cheeks. He repositioned the gun at his head, shut his eyes tightly, and pulled the trigger again.

CLICK!

"Oh yes! Just like that. Mmmm! Oh baby, like that." Her voice was getting louder. He heard his father grunt, then they laughed and got quiet again.

The other voices, however, were getting more and more insistent, urging him to pull the trigger.

CLICK! CLICK! CLICK!

As quickly as they had started, the voices stopped. Josie stood very still for a moment and listened. He could hear the rain falling softly in the front yard and the swishing sound of tires on the wet pavement, but not the voices. He shook his head and turned slowly to pick up the box from the table. He put the pistol back in the box, returned it to the pantry, then walked over to the window and looked at cars again.

"Ford, Chevy, Chevy, Oldsmobile, Cadillac, ice-cream truck, Chevy, and another Chevy. Chevy wins. What a lucky day."

Josie, the boy people said had emotional problems, could name every car that passed but didn't know you had to put bullets into a pistol. He learned that much later.

RIN TIN TIN OF THE YUKON, OR AT LEAST OF HIGHWAY 80

So I'm walking along this highway late at night, trying to hitch a ride to Chicago, you see, because I got the possibility of a job waiting for me there. In those days you had to grab any chance for work that came along. At least that's one way to rationalize traveling around so much. The last thing I was thinking about was some mangy mutt. It was somewhere near Ottawa, Illinois, on this big-assed bridge that the dog and I first met. It was real dark.

Hell, it was darker than this Choctaw girlfriend of mine used to get in mid-July down in Mississippi. And let me tell you, she was one dark chick. My Chippewa buddies used to hint at me that she was half black. Maybe she was, but that woman gave some good loving, I mean to tell you. The only trouble was she liked to spread it around too much. She was scandalous like that. She was the kind of woman who would totally blow a man's self esteem, then tell you to get out of the kitchen if you can't stand the heat. Well, I hurried my ass out of her kitchen and let the cool winds blow through my soul. It took me nearly a year to find my balance again.

Well anyway, back to the stray dog story. I was feeling miserable and the fog drifting up from the river's surface didn't help my mood any—nor my visibility. You could barely see five feet in front of you. As I walked, my feet were stinging, my legs were beginning to feel numb, and my back was hurting from carrying my backpack and sleeping bag. There was no traffic to speak of and what little there was sure as hell wasn't interested in picking up an Indian from the backwoods of Ontario. Only a fool or a desperado would be out there walking the side of that interstate, especially on a night like that. But you know what? I was actually feeling free. Oh, I admit I was experiencing some pangs of misery but all in all, I knew I had it made. I was free!

Like a lot of other young people during that era, I was on the move. It seemed as if America's youth just couldn't sit still. The war was over and jobs were hard to find. I had hitchhiked to Oklahoma City because I heard a rumor there was a lot of work to be found in the oil fields. They told me the work was hard but that never scared me. As an experienced machinist, I figured that it would be a sure bet I'd get on. Besides, I was a card-carrying union construction laborer out of Chicago. Well, I ended up selling flowers on a street corner to romantic cowboys and disgruntled wives. I stuck around for a month or so, but nothing came along that was more attractive than selling flowers. It was the only gig that interested me. Had I cut my hair I might have gotten work as a waiter, but what the hay—I'm a full-blood Indian. I bet I hadn't had more than ten haircuts in my whole life.

And I missed Chicago. I couldn't get into the cowboy mentality. Even the goddamned Indians talked and dressed like cowboys. Some other people might think it was quaint but it wasn't for me. So I called up a machinist buddy of mine.

"So what's shaking up there?" I asked him.

"Where are you?" he asked.

"In Oklahoma City."

"You're shitting me right?"

"No, for real. But I'd like to come back to the city. I can't handle this anymore. They don't know how to appreciate me here," I told him.

"Ain't never been there myself and to be truthful, I don't want to go. This is where the work's at, buddy."

"Speaking of work, is there any chance of finding some if I come up?" I asked.

"Man, you know Chicago. If you can't find work here, you ain't going to find it anyplace else. Why don't you call me back tomorrow night. I'll talk to the boss. Okay?"

His boss said he'd try me out and that was all I needed to hear. I hit the road. I figured that either way, I'd be better off in Chicago. Even if I had to put a street operation into action it's always better to do it where you know the score, and I knew Chicago a hell of a lot better than I did Oklahoma City. I couldn't trust anybody there. So that's how I ended up with my black ass stumbling down Highway 80 on a dark-assed night.

Now I'll tell you this much, I ain't the kind of Indian that's scared of the dark or anything like that. Being from the country, I do throw some tobacco over my shoulder now and then if I'm walking past a graveyard or something, but generally speaking, I ain't afraid of the dark. I don't worry about animals attacking me—you know, like tigers, bears, or wolves. I know better. Hell, I was raised in the bush up in Canada. I wasn't always the urban fellow people know me as now.

None of this was on my mind at the moment when it happened. I felt something touch my rear end as I heard this disgusting sniffing sound. I'd been in prison for a number of years and so I instinctively reached back to cover my ass, and I touched this wet thing. Man, I let out a scream that surprised even myself. I jumped about ten feet forward and my body snapped into a crouched defensive position: low, arms outstretched, and fists clenched, ready to punch, kick, or deliver a karate chop if I had to. At what? I wasn't sure, but I was ready to put a major hurt on whatever was attached to that cold, wet thing that had been taking a whiff of my butt.

It was a goddamned mutt—a stringy-haired, big-nosed, long-eared mutt. He yelped and scurried out of kicking range. That was about the smartest thing he could have done. As I said, I was raised in Canada, and I had had my share of breaking up dogfights. For a while we had a team of huskies and those dogs would fight. That son-of-a-bitch had scared the hell out of me but only because my head was on other things. I guess I was thinking that as soon as I hit the Windy City I was gonna book on over to the War Bonnet and party. You can guess how quickly that idea disappeared, right?

So after this hound scared me into the next county, he runs a few yards then stops to check me out. Of course it being so dark and all, I can hardly see what he looks like and I'm beginning to wonder if he's really a dog or a coyote. Now at the time, I probably wasn't the most traditional skin you might meet, but the last thing I needed was a coyote messing with my head. You have to remember, the LSD wave hadn't yet subsided. The shit was readily available and my lifestyle being what it was, of course I had taken my share. So I'm actually wondering and hoping that this wasn't some kind of flashback. I'll tell you this much, reality could sometimes get real warped while under the influence of that stuff. But the mutt didn't melt or change form or do anything that drastic, so I figured I must still be straight.

Maybe you don't know it, but there are two things you can count on seeing on any Indian reservation, my friend— kids and dogs. Hell, I was raised with dogs all around me, so I know their ways. This mutt lets out a pathetic little whine and I figure the thing must be kind of hungry. I remember I had some beef jerky in my bag, so I dig out a couple of pieces and toss the flea-bitten son-of-a-bitch a piece of it. He gobbles it down in one swallow. I mean to tell you, that mutt made short work of that jerky. Then he looked up at me to see if I had any more. I knelt down to look at it on its own level and held the other piece in my hand to see if I could lure him to me. It worked. He cautiously edged up to me. Well, I was able to ascertain that it really was a dog under all that dust and funk, so I relaxed, which made him less apprehensive. He even let me pat him, although he shivered at my touch. Oh this mutt was tense, ready to spring away if need be. Someone had been mean to this mutt, that much I could see. When I didn't come up with any more beef jerky the mutt turns and lopes on down the road and out of sight. I figured that was that and turned my attention to finding a place to crash. I knew I wasn't getting no ride in this dark. I was just hoping it wouldn't decide to rain.

In the distance I saw a light—a gas station or something. It looked like it couldn't be more than three quarters of a mile away. As I walked along I could feel fatigue beginning to overwhelm me. I needed to sleep. When you're out on the road like that the worst thing that can happen to you, next to some asshole running you over, is physical or mental exhaustion. Then the thrill of being "out there" is deadened and misery really sets in. You have to maintain a positive attitude because whining sure ain't gonna make things better. I knew it was time for me to stop.

Under normal circumstances, I would have stopped before nightfall, built a fire, and made myself comfortable. I'd spent many a night camped just out of sight of a highway. But what I should have done and what I actually did do were two different things, which is why I was walking along a pitch-dark highway in a state of exhaustion. My mind was working overtime, the way minds do when you're dead tired. That's why what happened next scared the living shit out of me.

So I'm walking along totally spaced when all of a sudden, not more than five feet away, I hear this loud mooing sound. You know what happened! I nearly jumped out of my skin again. After letting out another scream I assumed the karate chop stance again. I don't know about you, but I probably don't scream like that more than two, three times a year. Once I was able to gather my wits about me, I see this herd of cows standing there staring at me, chewing their cud. Now you have to understand, there ain't no cows hanging around the bush where I come from. About the closest I ever got to a cow was at the butcher shop. I freaked and grabbed a big rock and tossed it at them with all my might. I hear this thump and another moo, so I figured I hit the one of them bastards on the head. I guess I expected them to run away or something. They stood staring stupidly, chewing their cud and swishing their tails like they was thinking on what to do with me.

Well, to make a long story short, I snatched up my bag and booked. I didn't want them bastards to stampede. There wasn't anything between them and me but a wire I bet measured less that a hundred and twenty-five thousandths of an inch. I thought about whistling or singing to calm them like they do in cowboy movies, but then I thought, screw them, that son-of-a-bitch just done scared the shit out of me. I don't sing to things that scare me and I don't pay to go to scary movies. I was worried about a stampede because I didn't think that the one-eighth of an inch wire could do much to stop a half a ton of beef on the run. About that time the mangy mutt shows up again but this time he turns out to be a comfort.

What I thought was a gas station turned out to be a storage shed of some kind. I didn't even try to go inside. The wisdom of the road has taught me long ago that you don't trespass in any kind of building. Not even for shelter, unless it's a real emergency of some kind. Those old country boys generally understand that, but they do not hold to anyone busting into their buildings, especially when it's some arrogant bastard from the city. And I'm not so sure I can blame them.

Within a few minutes I had located an ideal campsite behind a clump of bushes in a small gully. I wouldn't be visible from the highway. I built a small fire. As a boy I was always told that fire was an excellent way to chase away evil spirits. It certainly seemed true in this case. I started feeling better right away. I was happy that the mutt was sticking around. I'm sure he felt the same, judging by the way his tail wagged whenever I spoke to him. I gave him the remainder of my beef jerky and rolled out my sleeping bag. The mutt lay next to the small fire and watched me with big, liquid eyes. I noticed his paws were slightly swollen.

"You been out here a while, ain't you Rin Tin Tin?"

He licked at his sore paws.

"Well, I can tell you this much, mutt. When I get me to Chicago, I'm gonna get me a room, find a woman, and get a job. Life ain't worth shit without them three things. I'm getting too old to be running off across the country every time I hear a rumor about some work. I tell you, mutt, being out here is nice, but it ain't what it used to be. People have changed. You know what I think? I think America's gone through a lot of changes. That hippie sense of innocence is leaving. That's it, mutt. America's left the age of innocence— if there ever was such a thing. You think you'd like to come to Chicago with me?"

The mutt's presence was comforting. Our little fire flickered warmly. In a matter of minutes I was fast asleep. I must have slept about six hours. When I woke up the mutt was gone. The grass where he'd laid was still pressed down and the sun was already up in the east. I stoked the fire, warmed some tea, and then hit the road. I was picked up by a construction worker heading east to Highway 55. About ten miles down the road I see the mutt limping along. The guy agrees to stop and give him a ride. I climb in the back of his pickup with the mutt. About ten miles down the road the mutt starts barking and I think he's gonna jump out while the truck's still moving. I pound on the back of the cab to get the guy to stop. He does and I get out with the dog.

The mutt stands there looking at me for a few minutes then he heads back west. He goes about a hundred yards or so then trots back to where I'm standing. He lets me pet him, wags his tail, and takes off again. I sit watching him as he trots down the road. I watch until he is just a speck on the side of the road.

About an hour later I got a ride all the way to downtown Chicago. I often wonder what happened to that mangy mutt that scared the shit out of me, but I'm sure he turned out all right. We both did I guess. He certainly wasn't no Rin Tin Tin, but then, on the other hand, I wasn't no Shakespeare either. We was just two souls out there on the road whose paths crossed for a few hours and that was it.

RUSSELL'S FREEDOM

He may have died happy but none of the people in Sapawe, including fifteen-year-old Russell High-Flying, had any way of knowing. Or he may have been filled with terror, but Russell doubted it, because of that damned smile. There it was, frozen onto his face like the guy had accepted his death as inevitable—or maybe he was grinning because he'd realized too late that he'd messed up by walking out on thin ice. You never know. At fifteen, Russell didn't know much about life and he knew even less about death. He only wished he hadn't been the one to find the guy's body.

Russell shuddered involuntarily as he remembered that day. That face, he thought. I'll never forget that face. The weird expression, and that grin. Never seen nothing like it and hope I never do again, he thought. Who could blame me for being upset? He shook his head to clear the image from his mind and concentrated on paddling the canoe in a straight line toward the opposite shore of Sapawe Lake. This was an emergency and he had to stay focused. It was no time to worry about the past. He had to deal with the here and now. His family was depending on him, and Russell had no intention of letting them down. He took a deep breath and squared his shoulders.

He had found the body in the frozen ice of Sapawe Lake. Now, a year and a half later, he was still trying to deal with his fear when his sister got injured. The accident happened on August 15, just after his fifteenth birthday. That's why he was out on the lake on a chilly and windy evening. Russell's father, a renowned guide, was out with a group of six businessmen from Chicago on a five-day fishing trip. They were after walleyes, and the best place to catch walleyes this late in the season was at the floodwaters where both food and shade from the hot sun were available. Fishing there meant making a base camp at Anderson's Point, more than thirty miles from his family's resort. As he paddled, Russell recalled the conversation he'd had with his dad.

"We should get back about two or three on Friday afternoon. Until then son, you are the man of the house. You know what I mean, don't you?"

"Don't worry dad, I'll take care of things. You know everything will be all right. I'm not a kid anymore," Russell assured his father.

"Yeah, I know you aren't a little boy. You're old enough now. I wrote out a list of things I need you to have done by the time I get back. I have another party coming in next Tuesday. Three photographers and their ladies. They won't be doing much serious fishing. Probably want to water ski and stuff like that." He was quiet for a moment as he packed a bundle of waterproof matches into the survival kit he always wore on his belt, then continued, "Son, I want you to know I'm proud of you."

"I know that Dad."

"Party's waiting," he said as he turned to leave.

Their eyes met—father and son. It was an awkward moment for both of them. Neither said anything. They were both men of few words, quiet men of the north country as his mother called them. Russell's father reached over and toussled the boy's hair.

"You're in charge, son," he said with a grin.

"Good luck, Dad. Be careful."

"You too, son. I'll see you Friday. Don't forget the tarp. We're gonna need it when we go wild rice picking."

"Don't worry, Dad. I'll have it ready for when we go ricing. I'll take care of it," Russell said.

Two days later, Russell sat leaning against the wall of the log cabin. It felt cool and a bit damp. He noted that the purplish shadows had gotten much longer. A slight chill rode the afternoon air. Not that it was uncomfortable, but you could sense that autumn was on its way. There were other indications of fall as well. To Russell they were obvious. A flock of Canada geese circled noisily as they searched for a safe place to spend the night.

"Gonna be a long winter this year," he said to the old black dog curled up in the shade next to Russell. "A cold one too. Geese flocking up like that means bad weather is on the way. Leastways, that's what the old folks say. You gotta pay attention to them because they know what's going on."

Kitchen sounds—the rattle of pots and pans, the hissing of grease, and the chop-chop of his mother cutting up vegetables—caught the young man's attention. His mother and little sister were preparing his all-time favorite dinner: hot, spicy chili with Indian fry bread. The tantalizing aroma of the cooking food teased his nostrils. It mingled with the fresh scent of the pine trees that surrounded their place. His mouth watered in anticipation.

"I'm sure getting hungry, mutt, and you can see why. Just look at all the wood I split today. Enough for a week there. That tarp the old man wanted me to stretch out is taken care of. I can't wait to go ricing. It's the only time I get to see my cousin Richie. They're supposed to be having a big pow-wow. And you know what that means, don't you? It means we'll be partying down."

The dog perked its ears up but otherwise didn't move.

"Well anyway, I'm way ahead on my list of things to do, so I can relax until dinner time." He eyed the pile of wood and smiled to himself. A mature fifteen-year-old, Russell accepted the challenge of responsibility gladly. He watched the dog for a few minutes.

"You got it made. All you do is sleep, eat, and chase bitches in heat. What a life!"

The dog cocked its head at an angle as though he'd understood the boy's words, then laid its head back down and shut its eye again.

"What a life! I sure wish I had your life."

Russell laughed and nudged the dog. He leaned back against the wall and shut his eyes, enjoying the last warming rays of the quickly setting sun. It really is nice to be alive, he thought. Within a few minutes the young man was snoring like an old black bear in the middle of January. He had had a busy day. His small siesta didn't last very long, maybe eight or ten minutes. Suddenly Russell was jerked from his snooze by the piercing scream of his little sister. A split second later his mother's shriek ignited the boy into action. He burst into the kitchen with the agility of a large cat on the hunt.

"Oh God!" his mother yelled, "Leslie Anne's burned herself with hot fry-bread oil. We need Dr. Leishman here right away."

Russell's mother was an even-tempered woman with a soft voice. It took a lot to shake her up, but when it came to her children that was another matter. She reacted like a she-bear when they were threatened. Russell noticed her voice had risen a whole octave. He knew they had a serious matter on their hands.

"We don't dare move her, so you're going to have to cross the lake and call the doctor from Crawford's store. Tell him to hurry because this is a real emergency. Get across the lake as fast as you possibly can. She's burned pretty seriously."

"I was only trying to help Mom cook," Leslie Anne spoke up. I wanted to help make dinner for you because Daddy said you were man of the house. You worked so hard all day. Don't be mad at me, Russell."

"Your brother isn't mad."

"Mom's right, Leslie. I'm not mad at you."

"You promise."

Leslie Anne grimaced as pain shot through her. Russell looked closely at her face. Her brown skin had turned chalky pale. Her eyes were beginning to glaze over and he thought her pupils looked somewhat dilated. She's breathing okay, Russell thought, but she might go into shock. I've got to hurry.

"Don't worry, Mom," he told his mother, who now hovered over the small, scared girl. "I'll hurry as much as I can."

"Please be careful, son. Feels like a storm might come up. Take the big canoe because the little one can't be trusted in the wind. Are you sure you'll be okay? I know how you feel about the lake since you—"

"I'll be okay."

He snatched his rain slicker from its hook by the front door and bounded down the pathway that led to the launching site. In a matter of minutes, he had shoved off from shore in the lightweight canoe. Under his strong and skillful strokes the canoe shot forward. He thought about his sister. The idea of her suffering, the very thought of her pain motivated the boy's every movement. He had to get her a doctor. He prayed silently that the doctor would be in and available.

His mind jumped from one image of his little sister to another. Her playing in the front yard and asking a thousand questions while she skipped around on one leg. He smiled affectionately as he remembered how proud she'd been when she first danced in a pow-wow contest and won. She was so beautiful, he thought, her little braids bouncing with each step. I gotta get across this lake, he said to himself, as he dug deep into the water with each stroke. Gotta concentrate. The rhythmic movement of paddling, however, soon left Russell with time to think about the body frozen in the ice. He tried thinking about other things but to no avail. Fear returned to sit on his chest.

Russell always knew that a day of reckoning would come. He had to get back on an even keel. He wanted so badly to put an end to the crippling effect fear was having on him.

"Well, come on then! Where are you?" he yelled.

It wasn't like it used to be. He would look into the water and there it would be. The image! Sometimes it would be clear and other times it would be hazy. It would come out just like it had been hidden there all the time behind his eyelids. A couple of times it was his own image that stared up at him. That was when dread took control. Well, not today, he thought, a look of determination on his face. He waited but nothing appeared.

He sat in the canoe and looked deep into the water. The only image that came to him was that of his sister and his frightened mother urging him forward.

"Well, come on then!" he yelled again. Nothing. Russell looked out over the water. The moon was beginning to come up. Moonlight danced on the tip of each wave. It looked as if a million small diamonds were dancing on the water. At that moment he knew he was free. His love for his sister had overcome his fear of the water and its image. His fear would turn to caution and so become part of his survival instinct. He wanted to laugh. He felt like standing up in the canoe and yelling in triumph to the Canadian night and the newly risen moon. He felt vital and alive. He thought about his little sister. Oh how he loved her. His arms began to paddle with a force of their own. He knew she'd be okay.

Russell crossed the lake that evening and succeeded in getting the doctor his sister needed. Leslie Anne recovered, taking strength from the knowledge that if they pulled together as a family they could overcome most obstacles. As for young Russell High-Flying, he faced his fear that night and won over it. What he won was a sense of his own freedom.

SAWDUST BANNOCK

"Your dad's gone and he won't be back."

I couldn't believe what I was hearing. I held my breath hoping it would go away, but it didn't. And that's how the summer of 1956 started for me. My mother made her announcement and sat waiting for our reaction. I looked at my little brothers and could see they were afraid. So was I.

We were a poor family, but at eleven years old you don't know from shinola about poverty. You just live life and enjoy it. The summer of '56 was a hot one in Sapawe, Ontario—and I mean that in more ways than one. My parents broke up that summer. Dad left and he never came back—not ever. That summer I started learning about life, and it all started with my mom's announcement.

"What are we gonna do?" I asked. "Where will we get money?"

"I'm going to work. You'll have to help with your little brothers. Deena will be here to baby-sit, but she's going to need help."

"What about her kids?" I questioned.

"We'll all live together." She replied. "I'll be working the day shift and she'll work nights."

"Where?"

"At the sawmill," she said, then added, "Peeling ties."

"No, you can't do that, Mom. That's man's work."

"Don't be silly," she said, giving me an encouraging smile. "It's good money and we do need it. I'm lucky to get that work."

"But Mom, people will laugh at you. They'll talk."

"Let them! At least we'll eat."

"Please, Mom. Can't you work at something else? Peeling ties is hard. You might get yourself hurt."

An intimate silence seemed to fill the room. It was a rough, inexpressible, but powerful moment for all of us. Her eyes watered over. She was quiet for a long time. We all were. My brothers crawled into her lap. I stood there looking at them until she pulled me into the circle and hugged us all.

"I love you boys. You're all I got," she whispered. I buried my head against her shoulder because I could not bear to look into her eyes. I felt shame that he'd left us and my throat burned and my mouth felt dry.

"Why'd he have to go? What did we do?" my little brother sobbed quietly.

The rest of us were hushed, feeling the huge violence and the grinding pain that covered the room. Even though the sun shone brightly outside, in the small cabin we called home a slow, moist, heavy coldness seemed to settle. My mom would have none of it. She kissed us each very gently. We understood her kiss was a pledge, a rhapsodic promise of reassurance. We knew that everything would somehow be all right and felt her strength entering us. The fear in our hearts started to melt away. When she finally spoke, the truth of her soft words roared like thunder on a rainy night.

"It was him. Not us. You boys didn't do nothing wrong. That's how it is sometimes. You're good boys. It was his decision to go."

We sat like that, hugging each other for a long time that afternoon. I can remember that the tea kettle on the wood stove started hissing. In the distance we could hear a logging truck groaning under a heavy load. On the front porch our puppy growled in an imaginary battle with my brother's kitten. A fly buzzed around the room. The sunlight seemed to cast a bluish hue on everything. On the table, the stove, the floor, and even on the pile of laundry Mom was about to do. Everything was blue and so were our moods. I didn't want to cry—not now—but my eyes were stinging. Finally my mother broke the silence again.

"I'm going to have to do it. There is no other choice. That's all there is to that." She then turned toward me. "Can I count on you to be my little man now?"

She had a look of determination in her eyes. It was that look of stubbornness you see in some Indian women's eyes. They set their minds to doing something and will not be changed. All you can do is respect them for it. That was my mom.

"Son," she said, "I know it'll be tough, but we'll do what we have to and we'll be okay. Now look at me boy. Try to understand this: this is not the end of us. Hell no. This is just a new beginning. Remember, it's not an end."

That was that and I knew it. I took a long walk that afternoon with my dog Chum. I wondered why he'd left without saying good-bye. Later on, life would teach me why. That afternoon, I decided Mom was right: it would be tough, but we'd be okay. It was indeed a new beginning. I remembered that old saying, "When the going gets tough the tough get going" and I knew we were a tough family born of a tough woman—a real Anishanaabe lady. We'd do what we had to do. We'd show this town we weren't finished.

Besides working at the mill both Deena and my mother did sewing for other people. Some of the single men who lived in the bunk house would bring their clothes over to have them washed and ironed. At first it was a bit embarrassing, but after being told a few times that they were performing an important service, the sting lessened. Some of the people in the town rallied behind us, helping out in ways that helped us maintain our dignity. Help came from places we'd never have expected—and it was help, not charity. Take old Ed Anderson.

He was this old recluse poet who lived at the south end of Sapawe Lake. He resembled Walt Whitman with his long hair and unshaven face. He'd come to town once a month to pick up supplies and mail out manuscripts or whatever. I never asked. I'd made friends with him the previous winter on one of his trips into town. It was an odd relationship in that he'd rant and rave about things and I'd listen respectfully. Once he came by our place with some sewing he said he needed done. We all knew he could sew as well as most women, but no one said anything. The time he showed up, I was sawing some wood. He looked at me and grinned. Without saying a word he picked up the ax and began splitting logs. We worked like that for maybe ten minutes and finally he spoke.

"I hear tell your old man left."

"You heard right," I answered without looking up.

"Life's like that sometimes, kid."

"I guess it is," I answered. I really wasn't ready to talk about it at that point.

"You guys all right?" he asked.

I nodded.

"Well that's good. You get to feeling like you need to talk, you come by. I'm always there. You understand me?"

I did and so I nodded to him. He smiled. After some small talk he offered us a dozen Canada geese whose wings he had clipped. The only catch was that we had to capture the damned things. We set a date for the following Saturday and the whole bunch of us paddled over to his place. Mom and Deena packed the ingredients for a shore lunch, which consisted of fried potatoes, canned cream corn, and fried fish. Of course, we had to catch the fish. We planned to make a real day of it—and what a day it turned out to be! We had a great time chasing down those honking hissing suckers. The old man fell out of his canoe and we all laughed until our sides hurt. He looked so comical standing there in his soaked clothes. He reminded us of a wet poodle. He looked much thinner and frailer all wet like that. I don't know if any of you ever have tried it, but catching those geese turned out to be the damnedest thing.

Later, as we ate the shore lunch the women had cooked up, old Ed Anderson read us some of his poetry. We could understand it because it was poetry about everyday things we knew about like the weather, the lake, plants, loons and other animals, and the particular quiet of winter. It was a day that would stick in my memory for years to come. A lot of people talked badly about the man because he was different from them, but that summer and into the following winter we found out that the man really cared for people. He spent Christmas with us that year. We ate one of the geese with wild rice and blueberries we'd canned. Ed had built us a great three-man sled we loved. We all wrote little poems for him. He framed them to hang on his walls. Deena gave him a pair of fur gloves she had made. She was renowned for her gloves. She even stitched his intitals on them. My mother did some beadwork on them for him. Real works of art.

Deena was my mom's best friend, and her son Grant, who was only a year older than me, was my best friend. The two of us would always hang out together. Like all boys at that age, we had our moments of war, but for the most part life threw us together and we made the best of it. Both Deena and my mom were strong Indian women. They laughed and teased a lot—maybe too much sometimes. We had good times together so living together sort of made sense. In all there were eight of us kids in a small two-bedroom cabin. It was crowded, but we were having such a good time, nobody cared. Of course there were fights, but everything was settled at the dinner table. Those two women made living together an adventure.

"If you kids play good together all week and don't fight we'll have a big treat this weekend."

They'd bake us a cake or a pie. It was little things like that that made our lives fun. Those two women turned our poverty into a rich experience that served us well our whole lives long. And poverty had a way of making even the essentials luxuries.

"Can we still go to the show in Atikokan on Saturdays?" Grant asked. That was an important question because we had made friends there and even had girls we were "makin' moves on." We always looked forward to going into town on Saturday afternoons.

"You'll have to do something to make your own money because we don't have any extra," his mother told us.

We were going to have to get some kind of business operation going. We tackled that problem with vigor. As our mothers had done, we joined our resources.

"We can run errands or sell pop to the men at work," I suggested.

"Good idea," Grant agreed. "You take the planer mill and I'll take the saw mill. We'll show up at break time. Pop and chips."

"We could cut kindling for people. We could get it from the green chain, haul it home, and split it up real nice. There's lots of things that we could do. You know what? We could get rich doing this stuff." Our boyhood enthusiasm removed the burden of labor.

We ended up with lots of business. We were giving it our all and people saw that. I started picking grass for a Greek woman's rabbits. For some reason she didn't like Grant so she became my private client. She said Grant gave her the creeps. I didn't understand what she meant, so I just shrugged and did her chores by myself. I nicknamed her Ms. Toodley-Ass because I could never say her name. We became good friends, she and I, but only after a labor dispute. That's another story though.

Ms. Toodley-Ass lived alone. In Sapawe that was fodder for speculation. She was a mystery and so she ended up being the target of some mean gossip. She chose to ignore the talk, but I couldn't. One time at the company store I over-heard some women talking about her.

"Did you know she used to be a prostitute?"

"I heard that she married some rich man and he died mysteriously."

"I don't know why she thinks she's better than anybody else. The way she puts her nose up in the air, like she has something we don't, makes me sick."

"And the way she dresses—all in black. It's pretty odd if you ask me."

I wanted so badly to say something in her defense, but what could I do? This was 1956, these were white women, and here I was, a little Indian boy with shaggy hair and raggedy clothes. They would have torn me up. Instead, I accidentally stepped on the toes of this fat woman—the one with the biggest mouth. I couldn't resist. Her fat feet were sticking out of those shoes in such a way that I knew they were already hurting. She let out a screech and I mumbled something about being sorry and left. My ears were ringing as I hurried away. I can just imagine what she was saying about me and my mom.

I mention this incident only to illustrate a point about my buddy Grant. He had unusual knowledge about the world for a boy who was only twelve years old. When I told him about what had happened, he grinned knowingly. He laughed and offered his theory on Ms. Toodley-Ass's situation.

"All the men around here are trying to screw the women. She turns them down."

"What do you mean?" I asked, knowing that I risked some scorn, but at that age a year made a big differences—at least in terms of knowing about women. That summer we were becoming preoccupied with the female gender. Delight-fully mysterious beings.

"You know, get in her pants!" he answered, then con-tinued, "Damm, do I have to teach you everything? Don't you know everything is about sex in this world? She won't go for it, so they talk bad about her."

"So they're all a bunch of liars?" I asked. "She wouldn't do it?"

"That's not what I said. It's a known fact that any women can be had. You just need the right approach. Now if it was me, I'd get up close to her and blow in her left ear. That drives women wild."

"She'd slap you silly. I'm willing to bet on that," I said.

"You're just a little boy. What do you know?" he laughed.

"Yeah? That's what you think. I been around," I said, trying to defend myself.

"Yeah, sure you have. What about Saturday?" he asked.

"We got to figure something out. This is Thursday and we ain't got no money saved. We shouldn't've bought all that pop and candy for the kids. I wanna go to the show."

"Me too," Grand said. "That girl Brenda will be there. Maybe she'll let you kiss her," he teased.

"What about that fat girl? What's her name?"

"You know her name!" He snorted. "Don't be making fun of my girlfriend. Arlene ain't fat, she's just pleasantly plump—well-developed. She got titties," he added with a grin as he puffed his chest out.

"You look like some stupid rooster when you do that."

"You're just jealous," he responded. And I guess I was.

"Well, so does Brenda."

"So does Brenda what?" he said, grinning.

"You know—got some."

"She ain't got nothing. If she does they're so small you gotta use your fingertips to play with them. Like the guys at the saw mill say, 'A woman with big ones is always ready for a good lovin'.' Now I'm the kinda man needs a real hand-ful," he bragged.

As he was talking, he unwrapped a bundle of bannock— Indian bread we always called it—he'd been carrying around wrapped in tin foil. Now you have to understand that cold bannock is a treat for some Native Americans. We both were raised on it and loved it. To an outsider, bannock may not look very appetizing, but many an Indian has survived on it. With strawberry preserves spread on it it's a delicious treat. He broke off a piece and handed it to me.

"Well my dad told me once that more than a mouthful is a waste," I countered. It was a weak effort, but I had to defend the integrity of my woman.

I figured he would come back with some kind of vicious attack on her. Instead he looked off into the distance as he rewrapped the bannock and stuffed it back inside his shirt for later.

"I wonder who the hell they are?" he said, pointing to three figures silhouetted against the sky as they crossed the strip-cut hill where we often played. Some people called it Bald Boy Hill because it looked like a boy's shaven head. Boys traditionally had shaved heads in Sapawe. Just as soon as school was out for the summer we were all sent to see the Italian guy who was the barber of the community. He charged twenty-five cents for shaving a head. That got to be a problem when the Elvis look was big—if you know what I mean.

"Give them the signal! See what they do," I suggested.

Grant let out a shrill yell, our special signal. We waited. Nothing. He let out a second one. The figures stopped. They looked in our direction, then took off running toward the saw mill. We looked at each other, and then it hit.

"Tourists!" I yelled. "Let's go!" The race was on.

Sapawe was mainly a lumbering operation, the last of the company-owned towns in the area. At the time it was booming and the lumber baron would fly in for monthly inspections. Timber supported the town and everyone in it. I remember it as a green, blue, and brown place: forest, sky, water, and sawdust everywhere. A great place for a kid.

Tourists meant money and provided everyone a chance to fatten their otherwise slim purses. So why would it be any different with us kids? First come, first serve! To be first you had to be on your toes and that's why we took off running: we wanted to be first at the boat launch just beyond the sawmill.

We knew we could save precious seconds that could make the difference between success or failure by taking shortcuts. So we took every one we knew—like through the sawmill. Forbidden territory!

The engine room of a big sawmill is no place for kids. We'd been told that a hundred times. For your information we knew every nook and cranny of this engine room. It was dark, gloomy, and ever so fascinating, a daredevil's paradise. It smelled of oil and leather from the big belts that drove the saws. The floor was greasy, slippery, and dangerous. The place roared to boys with an irresistible invitation. There were tools a young boy could play and pretend with and on occasion get hurt with. The sawmill was a dangerous short-cut, but we took it anyway. There were tourists in town and time was of the essence. We needed money so we dashed through the place without a moment's hesitation.

Coming out of that dark engine room into the sun at a run leaves you blinded for just a second. In that brief moment, disaster hit. Grant forgot about the step down and lost his balance. I heard him grunt as he hit oily ground with a thud. I tried to jump over him but as I did so, my left foot hit him in the face. He cried out in pain. I hit the ground with enough force to knock the wind out of me. I moaned as I rolled around in pain.

"What happened?"

"I fell. That's what happened." Grant answered.

"You all right?"

"Not really. But ain't nothin' broken. I can tell that much." He answered.

"Can you wiggle your toes?" I asked.

"I'm all right."

We lay on the ground flat on our backs trying to catch our breath. We said nothing for a few minutes. He rolled over on his side and looked at me. Then he asked me a question I wished he hadn't.

"You ever miss your dad?" he asked.

I wasn't ready for that. After a while I answered him. It took every ounce of courage I could muster. I felt like crying, but the tears had dried up and I only felt a burning in my throat. Our eyes met and in that fleeting moment I cought sight of his fear.

"Yeah, I do. Most every night. What about you?"

It's true that words cut like knives for his next question would slash at both of us for years. Uncertainty and honesty were stripping us both of something we might never be able to identify, much less understand. It was making us into what we were to become—young men capable of survival but destined to taste the salty bitterness of poverty, young men capable of extreme violence, young men who struck out at society until we were able to find our balance.

"What's going to happen when they close the mill in September? Where will our moms work then?"

I couldn't answer him.

"See that cloud?" I said, evading his question.

"That's a nice one."

"It's laughing at us," I said.

"No way!"

I turned and looked at him and said, "You ever hear that saying, 'Haste makes waste'? Well?"

He thought a moment, grinned, and started to get up.

"Well," he said, "I guess the day's not a total waste. We learned something."

"You want to go see anyway. You know, I got this feeling."

"Yeah, you and your feelings. Okay then, let's go," Grant agreed. "But you know they're going to tease."

Grant was referring to the three figures we'd seen on top of the hill. We both knew that it was this boy named Dougie and his friends.

"Screw them, aye."

Three cars were at the launch when we got there. Two of them were fancy rides with fancy boats attached, fancy motors, and two men with even fancier wives. Both couples wore color-coordinated outfits. They had some fancy fishing rods with the best True Blue reels. Those four people looked like money itself.

The third car was a different story altogether. A small economy Nash Rambler with a modest boat and a fifteen-horse Evenrude motor or something—nothing fancy. The owners looked like the original hippie family from somewhere like Milwaukee or Cleveland—back before hippies even existed. The man wore blue jeans and a tee shirt under another oversized shirt. He needed a haircut. The woman wore pedal pushers and a man's shirt with the name John on it. They were dressed modestly, drove a modest car, and had a modest-looking boat. Even their luggage was modest.

The three figures we'd seen running down the hill now ran from car to boat and back again, carrying gear, supplies, and food. It was Dougie and his pals. They were laughing and joking like all get out. A rowdier lot you couldn't find in Sapawe. I groaned in dismay. Of all people to beat us out of this work, it had to be him. Dougie was one mean bastard, especially after his mother had run off with a sweet-talking Swede. She left her three kids with a heavy-drinking, racist father. Dougie was every bit as racist as his old man. If the Ku Klux Klan had been in Sapawe the two of them would have been at the head of it. You didn't have to be a genius to guess what race was the focus of their hate. I was called a nigger before I ever knew what the word meant. He pointed at us and laughed. Of course they started talking their shit.

Now Grant was known as having an extremely short fuse—hell, both of us did. It wouldn't be the first or last time we'd fight with these three guys. They were always game for a good fisticuffs. Dougie was an enemy to be respected: you could never knew what that kid would do. One thing I will say for him, he wasn't afraid of much—and he could fight. It didn't take a lot before Grant was ready to rumble. I held him back and told him to be cool. I did that because the guy who owned the third car sat with his wife on the hillside listening to our bantering.

"Let him talk his shit. Just watch how that lady reacts everytime he puts Indians down."

I made an indecent guesture that the couple couldn't see but that Dougie certainly did. I wanted him to make some more racist remarks because the third couple were frowning disapprovingly. Of course the shithead obliged me.

There was an unspoken understanding between us that whenever tourists came to town the first there to hustle them got all the pickings—unless of course there were mitigating circumstances. When Dougie and his friends finished loading the first two boats, they asked the hippie-looking couple if they needed help.

"No," she said. "We want those boys to help us." The woman pointed to Grant and me.

"But we were here first," Dougie argued.

"I don't care," she replied. "You shouldn't call people names. It's not nice."

Mitigating circumstances! I looked at Dougie with a grin covering my brown Indian face from Indian ear to Indian ear. He was sharp enough to understand but stupid enough to push his luck.

"But they're just Indians."

"They're human beings just like you and me," she lectured him.

Now I'd known Dougie most of my life and I knew he wouldn't stop there. He had a mouth on him and he rarely thought before he opened it. He didn't disappoint me.

"Maybe like you but not like me, lady," he replied.

"And for that we can all be thankful," her husband added. "Why don't you just beat it?"

"Aw hell. Let's leave them to the stinking Indians," Dougie said to his buddies. Turning in our direction, he added, "I hope you choke on your Indian bread. You know they put sawdust in it." His insult served us well.

The three of them had themselves a good laugh and began to leave. When they'd gotten about fifty feet away, Dougie turned around.

"Hey mister," he yelled, grabbing his crotch, "your wife can suck on this, hey."

They ran off laughing. The guy started to give chase and I prayed he would catch them, but his wife yelled at him to forget it.

"What did he mean by Indian bread with sawdust in it?" she asked.

I didn't answer. She repeated her question. I was about to tell her that it was nothing, just Dougie and his teasing, but then Grant stepped forward. He was looking at the ground and was trying to look humble. He even had his broad shoulders hunched up. Oh he looked so pathetic.

"It's true, ma'am," he said very quietly.

"My God, no." She reached out her hand and touched his shoulder. "Why?"

"No fathers. They left. Sometimes we ain't got much food so our moms mix flour with sawdust. Not much really. I don't know how those guys found out."

He turned to me and asked, "Did you tell them?"

Trying not to laugh, I shook my head no.

"It's hard to eat but when you're hungry. . . . You can dunk it in tea, but usually we don't have any . . . " He let his voice trail off. He pulled the bannock from out of his shirt and offered it to the woman. She looked at it with a horrified look. He put it away. As he did so his eyes focused on the ground at his feet.

"I'm sorry, ma'am. It's our problem. Could we help unload your car for a couple of dollars?" He kicked a rock. I gave him an Oscar for acting. They gave us the job of unloading their car.

I don't know where the son-of-a-bitch came up with that story, but it worked. She paid us twenty dollars for hardly anything. We gave our moms one of the two sawbucks. At the matinee that Saturday afternoon, Arlene got popcorn, a pop, and, according to Grant, felt up. As for me, well, Brenda held my hand and I bought her some candy. I ended up with a sore neck from trying to blow in her left ear and peek to see if she had, you know, titties. And that was life in Sapawe in the summer in 1956.

SOJOURNER

Deputy Sheriff George Stillwell's trained eye looked for signs of fear, of guilt. A weapon perhaps. But there was nothing. The hitchhiker looked at him unblinking, an expression of near boredom on his brown face. He's been through this a few times before, thought Stillwell. He seems pretty cool about it. Okay, Cool Hand Luke, let's see how clean you are. The sheriff felt no hostility toward him and the hitchhiker sensed this by the sheriff's demeanor. What there was, however, was a sense of recognition—as though they'd seen each other before. Both men knew better. It was the situation that was familiar.

Roger Ghost Dancer had spied the police car coming at precisely the moment Stillwell spotted him. As the vehicle sped around the bend, Roger glimpsed the emblem on its side door. "Oh shit! Not a damned county mounty." The majority of them were political appointees and could be the biggest assholes: gung ho and very unprofessional. The squad car slid sideways as the tires tried to grasp the hot black tar road. The two men's eyes met, then locked. They were studying each other. This guy's no appointee, thought Roger. He's the real deal. Best be cool.

Stillwell shut off the motor and got out of the car. As he approached the hitchhiker his hand automatically settled on his holster. The leather was smooth and well crafted. The holster had been a gift from his father, the best money could buy. Roger reacted by extending his hands out in front of him, palms showing. Stillwell acknowledged the gesture with a slight nod.

"You got some ID?"

"Yes, sir, I do."

"Let's have a look-see. What are you doing around here anyway?"

"Just passing through, sir." Roger answered.

"The interstate passes through. This road don't."

"Looking for a place to camp the night."

"Where you headed to?" the officer asked.

Roger offered the policeman his wallet.

"Remove your ID and hand it to me, would you, sir?"

Roger did as he was told.

"What's your destination?" Stillwell asked him as he studied his driver's license. "Ghost Dancer. Indian huh?"

Roger nodded. "Chippewa," he said, then continued, "I ain't heading nowhere special. Just traveling. I ain't got no real destination."

"This your home address in Chicago?"

Roger nodded yes.

"You know this here license is expired?"

Again Roger nodded his head yes. Have to be real cool with this guy, Roger thought. This cop ain't the kind to just run you in like that, but if he did, you'd be checked out for a while. Roger knew it instinctively. I was hoping to sleep under the stars tonight, he thought, not on some steel rack.

"No current address, no valid ID, and no destination. Sounds darned near like vagrancy to me. What about you, fellow—does that sound like vagrancy?" The officer shook his head. "Now tell me, Mr. Ghost Dancer, how can that be? Everyone needs to be heading someplace."

"Yeah, well, I'm heading someplace too. I just don't know where. Like that song Merle Haggard sings, 'The highway is my home. . . . Down every highway there's always one more city.' Well, Officer, I'm heading to that city."

Stillwell laughed, a hearty laugh that started deep in his belly. "Ain't no city on this highway, pal. I can assure you of that. There's a gravel pit down about six, seven miles, but there ain't nowhere to camp."

"Well, I guess that's how life is, aye," Roger replied, a big grin on his face. He liked this cop—the way he laughed and the way he asked questions that seemed to get right to the core of things. Roger was glad this was turning out to be a friendly meeting. He would try to keep it that way.

"If I look in your bag will I find any dope?"

Roger shook his head.

"Weapons?"

Again Roger shook his head.

"You sure?" Stillwell asked.

"You can search me and my bag if you want."

"I might do that."

"If you come up with any we'll both be surprised—especially me. I'm telling you the truth."

"Look, Mr. Ghost Dancer, I'm not trying to bust your balls here. One joint ain't gonna hurt nobody, but if you get stopped thirty miles down the road and they find anything on you, dope or weapons, my ass is grass. You understand?"

Roger nodded.

"You don't talk a lot do you?"

Roger shrugged, then said, "I talk."

Stillwell was beginning to relax. The guy ain't hot or nothing, he thought, but I got a job to do. He was interested in the Indian, because he traced his own family tree directly to the Indians in the area. Of course the bloodline had been diluted over the years, but Stillwell knew he was part Indian and was proud of the fact.

"You ever been in any trouble? Any outstanding warrants?"

Roger smiled at the police officer. "Bingo."

"What?"

"Misdemeanors. I got into a few scrapes when I was younger."

"Like what?"

"Illegal trespassing. And a drunk and disorderly."

"How old were you?"

"Just out of high school. I was at a party with a bunch of people and got goofy. I ain't never been able to hold my booze. I was so drunk I could hardly walk. I just wanted a place to lay down before I got too sick. They found me the next morning sleeping in the high school boiler room," he explained.

Roger knew that the small computer in the squad car would supply sketchy information that would confirm what he'd said. As the officer had figured, Roger had been through this routine before—many times, in fact. America's law officers have a tendency to get more than a little curious when they see an American Indian wandering around their territory. Roger Ghost Dancer found that perfectly understandable; it was their job. However, a good number of them suffered from watching too many cowboy movies. There was always an element of hostility when he encountered those types. The young Indian had seen plenty of computer read-outs in the last six months he'd been on the road.

Deputy Sheriff Stillwell reentered the data from Roger's driver's license a second time. He cursed quietly.

"These can be such a pain in the ass. They break down more than they work, he said to himself as he noted the time. It was 4:27 P.M. He would be off duty in a few minutes. As he waited for the computer to respond, the two made small talk.

"You know, I'm part Indian too. Delaware or Huron is what we figure," Stillwell proudly told Roger. He also mentioned he'd served in Viet Nam. He asked Roger what he knew about cleansing ceremonies. He said he had heard that

Native American Viet Nam veterans who had participated in these rituals reported reduced cases of postwar syndrome.

"You know, I think that's mostly because of the way warriors are viewed by society when they return home. In the Indian community to be a warrior is to serve the community. It's one of the highest honors. Veterans are cherished by the community. Smudging and other cleansing rituals just help reinforce that thinking," Roger told the officer. Stillwell started to ask more questions but was cut off by the computer as it began to spit out Roger's information.

"No warrants. No other surprises. I guess you're okay," he told Roger. "So tell me, Mr. Ghost Dancer, what's your plan?"

"I figured to find a lake or creek up this road. Make me a camp and take a bath. I'm getting pretty ripe."

"Don't bother looking up ahead. I can tell you this much, there ain't no good camping sites on this road. The locals are kinda funny too. That's why they live way out here. They don't take too kindly to strangers out here. They defend their privacy. You know what I mean?"

Roger nodded.

"Tell you what I'll do. I'll drop you off by a truck stop over on the interstate. You got a better chance of getting a ride from there. They got showers there too. The owner's a friend of mine. I'll introduce you. What do you say?"

Roger nodded again. Stillwell smiled.

"I gotta search you before I let you in the squad car. Regulations."

It wasn't much of a search, Roger noted. He liked that. They put his backpack in the trunk and got into the car. As he drove, Stillwell chatted with Roger.

"There's been reports of Klan activity around here. Some of these rednecks would just as soon shoot you as look at you. You'll be better off at that truck stop. Out of curiosity, what's your take on the Klan?" Stillwell asked.

"I haven't been exposed to very much of it. Of course I've run into some pretty blatant racism. I would rather have someone straight out tell me if they have a problem with my race. I've run into a few of them but you know what? I find that usually once people deal with their ignorance and fear they tend to get along. At least they ain't at each other's throats. Myself, I say live and let live. I ain't no hippie, but I kinda like some of their ideas—like peace. But I value my privacy too. That's partly why I'm out here on the road. I'm just getting a feel for the country. I hope to write about these experiences. I don't know how the hell a person could live in this beautiful world and be so hateful."

Roger enjoyed the company of this police officer who told funny jokes. He appreciated Stillwell's knowledge of the area. He guessed right when he concluded the man was from this area.

"Hell, Mr. Ghost Dancer, I used to camp all around here. I know it like the back of my hand. You do much fishing? Hunting?"

"No more than I have to," Roger answered.

"Good answer. Hey, are you hungry?"

"Hungrier than a goddamn bear."

"Tell you what, Mr. Ghost Dancer, I'm going to pop you for dinner. You know, I don't get to talk to many Indians. I'd be honored if you'd join me. Do you mind?" he asked Roger.

Roger shook his head and laughed. "Hell, Officer Stillwell, I'm the one should be honored."

At the truck stop, Roger waited in the squad car as Stillwell went in to talk to the owner. A few minutes later he came out smiling. He handed Roger a key on a paddle and pointed toward a building with a sign that said, "Baths! Truckers Only."

"Okay, here's the game plan. My friend Bill says it's okay for you to use the facility. I live just a few minutes away. I'm gonna run home, change, and drop off the squad car. Should take me about a half hour. By that time you'll be ready to eat. I asked them to fry us up a batch of trout. Bill says there's a washing machine in that building too. If you want, you can do some laundry. It's a free service he offers to the truckers. You go on ahead and do your thing. I'll be back in thirty minutes or so."

The trout was excellent. Over dinner the two men talked about everything under the sun—the war, law enforcement, Indian treaties, urban decay, the hippie movement, fishing and hunting, and women. Stillwell informed Roger that when he got home from Viet Nam he had wanted to travel but ended up going straight into the police force. Roger showed the officer some of his poetry and short stories. Stillwell said he never really did enjoy reading poetry but this was different. These poems were about things he could understand and in a language he could relate to. He especially enjoyed a story the Indian had written about a veteran who came home to the reservation. Roger told the deputy he was welcome to keep it if he wanted. Stillwell insisted that Roger sign it for him.

"Hell fire, boy, you're going to be a famous writer someday and I can say I knew you when." They both laughed and Roger was slightly embarrassed at the attention, but secretly he was pleased.

They always say the grass is greener on the other side. In this case, while Stillwell was clearly envious of Roger's freedom, Ghost Dancer in turn coveted the respectability and trust Stillwell seemed to enjoy. He smiled when the waitress flirted with the cop and wished she'd do the same with him. Everyone was nice to him in the restaurant due to his association with the cop. Stillwell introduced Roger to a lot of his friends. He kept making sure, Roger noticed, that everyone knew Roger was a full-blood Indian. They all shook his hand and, strange as it may seem, every single son-of-a-bitch had an Indian grandmother. The two men shared a good laugh about that.

"See, they never really beat us," Roger said. "Not in the sense of wiping us out, and they have continued to admire us so much that some of them even create these stories in their minds so they can be like us. In a way, we have captured their minds." Roger laughed.

"Well, we know they all must like Indian women," Stillwell responded. "Hell, all their grandmothers were Cherokees. Horny Cherokees at that."

"A good idea for a poem there, Stillwell. 'Ode to a Horny Cherokee.'" Roger paused. "Look, I got something I want to give you."

Stillwell ordered another round of beer, looked at Roger with a serious look on his face, and said, "You've already given me enough."

"No, no! This is something you'll really like," he assured the officer as he dug into his backpack to pull out a blue-and-white bone choker.

The lawman's eyes lit up as Roger handed him the choker. He held the piece with a tender hand.

"You know you don't have to do this. Hell, all I did was treat you to a dinner, and let me clue you in to something: It was free. This thing looks very expensive."

"Put it on. It's the real deal. That's real bone. I got it from a Sioux woman I met in St. Paul. She told me I'd meet someone who should have it, and I just did."

Stillwell's eyes misted over slightly as he ceremoniously tied the choker around his sunburned neck. The blue beads and bones seemed to jump out against his skin.

"It looks real good on you, pal. It's yours."

"I don't know if I can accept it. Like I said, this looks expensive. Can I give you ten, twenty bucks for it?"

"In the old Indian way you'd be insulting me if you didn't accept it. Anyway, I ain't giving it to you because you bought me dinner. I want you to have it because of the pleasure of your company. Whenever you wear it, you'll remember me and the ideas that we talked about and how we were able to get past a lot of hurdles by being open with each other. For me, these last few hours have been a real treat."

"It sure has been nice. Too bad you can't stick around longer. You ever get tired of the road, come on back. I bet we could find you some work around here and a place to bunk. Hell, I know we could. Man, we could do us some serious hunting and hanging out. Wouldn't that be something, the two of us? You think about it, Roger Ghost Dancer."

"Thanks. It sounds real tempting, but you know, I got places to go, people to see. There's lots of stories out there and the only way to get them is to be on the move. You know what I mean?" Roger said. Stillwell nodded.

The two men had another couple of beers and talked. The cook sent a bag of sandwiches for Ghost Dancer to take with him on the road. They laughed and said it was the old "bum's rush," although they both knew better.

The deputy used his influence to arrange for Roger to get a ride westbound with a trucker. Roger went to the bathroom and when he returned he was shocked to see Stillwell's hand fishing around in his backpack. He felt a surge of disappointment pass through his whole being. I'll be a son-of-a-bitch. That sneaky shithead. You never can tell about people, Roger thought as he walked around the corner into view. By that time Stillwell had straightened up in the chair.

"Hey, that trucker has just about finished his meal. He says he'll be heading out in about fifteen minutes."

"I don't want to miss him," Roger said, and meant it. He felt angry or maybe disappointed. He was in a bad spot, he thought, because he couldn't say anything to the guy for digging around in his bag. On the other hand, he wanted very badly to say something. It was a macho thing in a way. He just didn't want the guy to think that he was pulling one over him somehow. Screw it, he thought, I still appreciate everything he's done for me, but why the hell would he do that kind of thing? As they walked out of the restaurant the deputy leaned over and said, "I slipped a little something in your bag that I took off of a hippie boy I pulled over. Don't look at it until you get out of my state, okay?"

Roger felt an immediate sense of relief. So the guy wasn't trying to pull one over on him. In fact, it was just the opposite. He felt guilty for having suspected anything different. They stood outside the restaurant smoking while Stillwell talked on and on. Roger didn't say a word. He just nodded and the deputy smiled.

"Well, you take it easy, boy," the deputy said when it came time for Roger to leave. "And when you get to be a famous poet, don't forget to stop by and say hi. Hell's bells, I might just be the sheriff of this whole county by then. I'll be stopping hippies and confiscating like hell then," he laughed. "Wouldn't that be something?"

Roger smiled and said nothing. Stillwell smiled.

"See you later, Ghost Dancer," he said as he got into his pickup truck. Roger watched him speed onto the highway and grinned.

"Who was that masked man anyway?" Roger said out loud to the trucker.

"That be Deputy Sheriff George William Stillwell, Mr. Sojourner." They both laughed.

The trucker woke Roger up to drop him off at the intersection of Highways 80 and 55, just south of Chicago. Roger felt good to be back in the Windy City. And as it turned out, Roger Ghost Dancer ended up staying longer than he intended. He always remembered the deputy sheriff and his kindness. He also enjoyed the gift that Stillwell gave him.

SPIRIT STICKS

"So, will you tell me what the hell spirit sticks are? I'm asking because I don't have a clue and I want to know. You dig?" For the last hour and through half a bottle of Southern Comfort, he'd been saying he had to tell me about these spirit sticks. I figured he was ramming it up my ass anyway. I didn't even know if I believed there was such a thing.

He grinned one of those grins that told me something was up and then he started talking his shit. A bunch of pretty reliable Indians had told me this guy was a good storyteller and I wanted to find out if it was true. They had told me not to expect anything to come out straight. Sometimes he beats around the bush they had told me.

"Is he like a coyote spirit or something?" I had asked.

The old lady grinned at me and her twenty-one-year old son leaned over and said into my ear, "The dude's beyond Coyote. Try Windigo aye."

They told me how to find him after I bought them both two packs of Player's cigarettes. I figured the name Player's was symbolic of something. As you know, smokes ain't cheap up there in Canada and that's where this story takes place. So here I was, sitting in this guy's cabin, in the kitchen area, waiting for him to tell me about spirit sticks.

"Well, you know spirit sticks ain't nothing, just a figment of someone's imagination. But if they work, well, what the hay!" He stopped and lit a cigarette he'd been rolling from a can that said "Black Cats" on the side, then he continued, "Are you with me on this?"

I nodded. He reached across the kitchen table and helped himself to the glass of Southern Comfort I was trying to nurse. I frowned, he grinned. He asked me if I minded, but what could I say? He's my distant uncle or cousin or something, or so he claimed. I was trapped by my culture. I knew damned well that he knew no self-respecting Indian would think of saying no to a relative.

"Now, according to rumor, this Indian guy, Bobby Joe McMillian, a comedian out of Chicago, got himself hired as a guide in the Ontario bush for some man who had a small tourist camp near Sapawe Lake. Like spirit sticks, he isn't real either," he said and then let out this high-pitched laugh.

"Do you get it? They ain't no Indian named that. Leastways not from around here. And this chick, Margo Balledoften, is just like him. She ain't no real broad either, but just let your imagination picture her as this pretty Georgia peach from down in Atlanta. She's a natural-born victim. A sure enough hillbilly dilemma. That's how this story starts. Now remember, it ain't nothin' but a hallucination so don't get uptight about it. It probably ain't politically correct, but what the hell, being born an Indian ain't so politically correct either, hey. Well anyway, this story starts in Georgia with this woman, see? And she's talking to a friend about coming up here. You get the picture?"

I nodded but said nothing, so he continued.

"'I am so looking forward to this trip to Canada,' she says to her friend. 'I'm hoping for a spiritual uplifting. I hear tell that those Indian guides up there are so connected to the earth. They even call it their mother. Ain't that about as spiritual as you can get? I called the lodge and requested that they arrange for one.'"

"That's what she said, that woman from Georgia. You know, the one I called Margo Balledoften. She talked in this real southern accent. The kind with honey and ice dripping off it." He smiled then spit into an empty can that sat by the potbellied stove.

"The guide that was assigned to these five ladies out of Georgia was none other than this unemployed Indian, Bobby Joe McMillian. So what have we got here? We have this Georgia peach who's an accident waiting to happen and this redskinned jokester who likes to make them happen. Ain't that a bite in the ass? They're stuck together for five days out in the bush. As soon as the guy's laid his beady peepers on the broad, he knows her story. Can you picture this now? It's gonna be all hell break loose. I mean to tell ya."

He got up and fetched himself a big old water glass, which he proceeded to fill halfway with my Southern Comfort. I reminded him that it's more than twenty miles to the nearest bootlegger's house, but that didn't phase him and he just winked at me. I'm his long lost relative come from the city to visit family on the rez and so he thinks that makes me a live one. He figures I have money to burn. He's hustling me and I know it, but he tells good stories, so what the hay?

"When they get introduced," he says, picking up the story again, "Bobby Joe hands the woman these two hand-carved sticks, sort of like chopsticks made out of white pine. She's delighted they're spirit sticks, but what exactly are they for, she wants to know. It's natural she'd want to know all about them being as she was already looking for some kind of spiritual experience from whatever Indian that happened to come along. He informs her that spirit sticks are an old Indian charm used by young girls, generally virgins but not necessarily so—especially in this day and age—to ward off evil spirits and hungry bears."

He stopped talking and reached for the tobacco again. I handed him one of my own cigarettes so he wouldn't stop for long. He smiled and commented on how good it was to smoke TMs and started talking again. I interrupted him to ask what TMs meant and he gave me a rather wordy explanation that TMs were factory-rolled, store-bought cigarettes as opposed to handmade ones. Eventually he got back to telling about the spirit sticks.

"Then he tells her they should be used when using the bathroom. Well the clowning bugger can see she's going for it hook, line, and sinker, so he adds a little more detail. He tells her that sometimes they can be used on mosquitoes but that usually wouldn't work unless the woman was a real virgin. Even a finger or two would disqualify her." He started laughing and I smiled at his vulgarity. What I'd been told about him was true: he was a good storyteller.

"To make things more interesting," he continued, "Bobby Joe tells her it was a real bad omen if one of those insects landed on her and didn't bite. Then it was doing that other thing which he couldn't say in mixed company. You see what he was setting up? What a dirty bugger, aye?"

He was looking over at my bottle of Southern Comfort so I grabbed it and took a big swallow. To keep from insulting him, I reached over and poured him a small drink. He looked at me for a minute, then grinned a crooked smile and said it was good of me to share in the Indian way. I agreed but didn't offer him any more. He made a mental note of that and continued with his story.

"Well, the first night out in the bush they made camp and went to bed early because they were dead beat. As he laid on his sleeping bag, McMillian heard someone get up. Soon after he heard a tapping sound in the nearby bush followed by the stream of water. It was that Balledoften woman taking a piss and tapping her spirit sticks. Bobby Joe was picturing her squatted down and trying to maintain her balance while at the same time tapping those sticks and slapping at the occasional mosquito that came near her bare derrière. She didn't want no bad omens."

He stopped talking so I handed him the bottle. He took a healthy swallow, shuttered, and continued.

"Suddenly she lets out this yell and come running back into camp shaking. She looked like someone had been chasing her or something. After they got the poor woman calmed down—and that, my distant cousin, took some doing—she explained what had happened. 'Why, I was relieving myself and when I stood up to pull up my pants I saw it. It was lit up and all I could think of was what Mr. McMillian had refused to say in mixed company. I guess you could say I let my imagination run away with me. I apologize.' Well I tell you, long lost cousin of mine, that Georgia lady freaked out because a lightning bug landed in her pubic hair. Since the son-of-a-bitch wasn't biting her she figured the unmentionable was happening: it was doing the nasty to her and liking it enough to light up. That'd have to be one hot-assed bug if you ask me. It was more than Bobby Joe and the rest of the campers could bear. They all laughed themselves to sleep that night. Miss Balledoften, well, she was getting a little skeptical about Bobby Joe's spirituality. And who the hell could blame her, aye."

I was beginning to wonder what the point of his story was going to be. The way he kept looking over at the Southern Comfort, I was sure he would stretch the story out until the booze was gone. About the Southern Comfort. It was a round one. That means in Indian talk one of those big bottles as opposed to the flat ones, which are half-pints. They're meant to be consumed over a long period of time. Sipping whiskey. I had smuggled the thing across the border with me, and I wasn't even sure that you could get that brand in Canada for less than an arm and a leg. I could see that my yarn-spinning relative—in the Indian way—had himself a plan concerning that bottle: he planned to polish it off. Just to be safe, I poured him another shot so he would continue with the yarn he'd started.

"Well anyway, the story is that they got her calmed down and all went back to bed—laughing themselves silly, of course."

He was starting to slur his words. I was getting a little tight too. I'm not really a heavy drinker and my trying to get my fair share of the Southern Comfort was taking its toll.

"Shortly after midnight the Indian guide/comedian was awakened by screaming and hollering and a loud grunting noise. A bear! A hungry bear! Nothing can wreck a goddamned campsite quicker and they can be dangerous as well. Bobby Joe quickly told the campers to climb a tree. He didn't have to tell them twice. Well, once he'd shimmied up a tree and took stock of the situation, he saw everyone was all right. The bear was a mess. The furry bugger was covered in flour and was shaking it all over the campsite. He destroyed one tent and flung sleeping bags all around. Bobby Joe was actually feeling blessed no one had gotten injured. You understand his concerns, aye."

He reached for another one of my TMs and promised me the best was yet to come. He waited while I poured him another shot, which he swallowed rather quickly, and then he cleared his throat to continue.

"Well, suddenly the bear stopped, stood up on its hind legs, and looked into the tree where Miss Balledoften was perched. If you know bears then you know they can't see for shit and this one had flour in its eyes to boot. Sitting there on a branch, to Bobby Joe's surprise and delight, Miss Balledoften was furiously tapping those sticks together and cussing at the bear in her southern drawl. I personally don't think bears have the longest attention span or any sense of humor, but rumor has it that the darned bear laughed outright and then farted real loud. Miss Balledoften just kept cussing and tapping her sticks. I don't know how true it is but I do know bears will sometimes do the most unexpected things. This one shook its head, blinked his beady red eyes, then dropped to all fours and scrambled into the bush. They never heard from him again. Miss Balledoften just kept tapping and shaking and cussing up a storm."

He stopped talking and smiled. I realized he'd reached the end of his story. What happened to Bobby Joe and the woman, I wanted to know?

This time he just straight out reached for the bottle, took a long swallow, and told me the rest.

"They say she returned to Georgia convinced that spirit sticks do have power in them. Bobby Joe," he continued, after taking another slug, "well, he quit the camping business and went back to Chicago to work as a comedian in a strip joint on Mannheim Road. The bear, he's still somewhere around Sapawe Lake. And the spirit sticks? Well, maybe they're real after all, aye?"

NINETY PERCENT BULLSHIT, TEN PERCENT SKILL

A black mutt, part Labrador Retriever and part English Setter, darted in front of the man and the boy. They made an odd, unlikely, but interesting pair. The man was in his fifties and dressed in a checkered lumberjack shirt, heavy work boots, a grey felt hat, and Mackinaw pants. He smoked a pipe and was followed by an Indian boy, maybe eleven or twelve years old. The kid had long black hair and a slingshot hanging out of his back pocket.

"This tourism business sure is a funny one, son." The old man paused and the boy leaned forward. He knew these pauses always meant some important point was about to be made.

"It's a good business though," the old man added, puffing on his pipe, "but you should know that it's about ninety percent bullshit and about ten percent skill."

"I don't get what you mean," the boy replied.

The old man looked at the boy, smiled, then playfully punched him in the arm. The boy pretended to bob and weave like a boxer and smiled back. He wasn't a large boy. In fact, some people thought him to be undersized for his age, but the old man said that was nothing but nonsense, that he'd be just fine. He was teaching the boy, among other things, how to box and could see the kid had a natural talent and was a quick learner. The old man had been a boxer in his youth, a good one, and now he was a good teacher.

Well, maybe not now you don't, but you will," he told the boy. "You're going to work for me this fall. Time you started learning how to guide. You can start by helping out around the camp."

The old man, C.W., was noted for his bush skills. As a hunting and fishing guide, he was legendary. Sought after by sports enthusiasts throughout the United States and Canada, his shoreline meals, fresh fish, boiled potatoes, baked-in-the-hole beans, creamed corn, and bannock were often referred to as epicurean delights. As storyteller, there was none better. Educated at Wisconsin University he had decided he wanted no part of that society. He moved to Canada where he met and married a local Indian woman. There were some in the community who looked down on that marriage, for two reasons. The first was that the man was white and the woman was a full-blood Indian. Interracial marriages were not looked upon favorably in that area. The second was that the Indian woman's son was illegitimate, and C.W. had readily agreed to adopt him and raise him as his own—an agreement he took very seriously. He could not have cared less what the community people thought.

About a month and a half later, it was time for their first outing. C.W. came to wake the Indian boy early one morning. "Come on son, we have work to do before that party from Chicago gets here. Your mother has breakfast on the stove. She's making your favorite."

"Do you know these people?" he asked the old man as they got dressed.

"Supposed to be two lawyers and a boy around your age. They're from Chicago," he told the boy.

"When are they getting here?"

"Around seven. They'll be late. I want you to stick close to the kid. This is his first trip. I don't want him getting himself hurt or in trouble. Keep an eye on him, you understand?"

He nodded and wondered what the city boy would be like. He was anxious to meet him. He'd never known a city kid before. They finished dressing in silence. When they were together they didn't talk a lot. The boy finished dressing first.

He stood quietly watching the old man. The old man stood up and pointed to his pipe pouch and pipe. The boy nodded and handed them to him. They walked together into the kitchen.

It was warm and cozy and the bacon and eggs smelled delicious. The boy's mouth began to water. He walked over to the stove and took the coffee pot by the wooden handle. He got a cup down and filled it for his elder. The old man smiled and nodded his head. As his mother fussed about them, the two ate quickly and silently.

"You two be careful. Look at that lake. She's mighty rough out there," his mother said. She stood by the stove with a cup of coffee in her hand. The boy thought she was beautiful, but knew she was getting ready to start nagging.

"Did you pack clean socks? What about your blue sweater? It still gets cold at night, and besides, it's going to weather tomorrow or the day after. You're going to need a sweater."

"Everything's packed, Mom."

Turning to C.W., his mother asked, "Are you sure he's old enough for this? Maybe you should wait until next fall." But she knew it was useless to try convince him of anything.

"He's ready. Don't worry your pretty head about it. The kid knows more about the bush than most men do. It's in his blood for Pete's sake."

"I don't know about—" she started to protest but was cut off by the boy.

"Mom, I'll be okay. I know what I'm doing."

The boy watched his mother break into a smile. Her Indian eyes twinkled. He knew she was proud of him on this day, his first working as a guide with the old man.

"Okay," she said to C.W., "but you keep your eye on him. If anything happened to my baby, I don't know what I'd do."

"Mom! I'm not a baby! Would you stop worrying?"

"Oh, don't worry your pretty head about the boy. He'll be just fine."

"It's my job to worry. I'm his mother."

While the boy refilled his coffee cup, C.W. looked out the kitchen window. He could see it was cold. A drizzle blowing in from the northwest made it one of those miserable days, the kind where the ground is damp and soggy and fallen leaves stick to your boots. Perfect, he thought, this is just about perfect.

"Look at that, son," C.W. said, pointing at the lake.

The boy glanced at the lake. His mom was right. The lake waters were choppy. White caps were breaking at the crest of the waves.

"This wind will stop," C.W. said, "and it'll provide perfect weather for hunting. Can you tell your mother why?"

"The air will be heavy and damp. Scent won't carry and the damp ground will absorb the sound," the boy answered. His mother hugged him as he squirmed.

"My little man! Make sure you wear a raincoat when you cross the lake," she warned. "There's going to be a lot of stuff in the boat. She'll ride low."

"Mom, we're on top of this. Don't you worry your pretty head," the boy said.

His mother stood in the middle of the kitchen with her hands on her hips, smiling. Turning to C.W. she said, "Don't worry your pretty head? You know, he's beginning to sound just like you."

"He ought to. We're together at least twelve hours every day."

They were interrupted by the sound of the dog barking as it ran to meet a new station wagon turning into their yard. The three of them watched as the car rolled to a stop. No one got out.

"Go call off that mutt of yours and show them in. Looks like they're kind of timid. You know how that dog gets."

Turning to the woman, he said, "They're going to want coffee and some breakfast."

The boy went outside to greet the tourists. He aimed a swift kick in the dog's direction. It dodged and went to its bed on the front porch. The car doors swung open. The big guy was first to get out. He had a cheerful face, full of energy and sort of red.

"Is C.W. around?" he asked in a booming voice.

"Up at the house. He said to show you in. Coffee's on."

The passenger's door opened slowly. A thin, pale man got out cautiously. He eyed the dog with a look of apprehension. The dog eyed him back. The man turned and glanced at the boy.

"Does that dog bite?"

The boy shook his head.

"Cold goddamned place, if you ask me."

"Come on, John. This is great! Just smell that air."

"I can't, Bob. I swear to God my nose is already frozen."

The big guy ignored him as he reached into the backseat to shake someone.

"Come on, Junior, we're here."

"Let me sleep," a voice whined. "It's barely daylight out."

"Get up now! Dammit, Junior, this should be a big thrill for you. Not everybody gets a chance like this. You have to help get the boat loaded."

"But I thought you said this was a vacation. Why do I have to load the boat?"

An hour later the three tourists were fed and the boat loaded. They pushed off and C.W. headed the boat for the base camp at the western end of the lake. The choppy waters made the going somewhat difficult, but C.W. was skilled at navigating the boat and they crossed without incident. Junior, however, found much to complain about. Upon arriving at the base camp, C.W. and the boy went about getting a blazing fire going and the camp set up. Robert and his friend John pitched their own tent. Junior, however, sat huddled close to the fire, sniffing.

"Junior, get up off your butt and help us with these tents, would you?"

"It looks like those two know what they're doing. That's what we pay them for isn't it? I'm cold. This was a bad idea," he complained to his father.

"What did I just say? Now move it mister or you ain't going to like what happens next."

"What?"

"My boot right in your butt," Robert warned his son. The boy began to help his father with the second tent.

When the campsite was ready and wood for the night gathered, C.W. signaled to the boy that they would leave.

"Me and the boy here are going to go have a look around. A little scouting. You guys relax. Enjoy the campsite."

"I'd like to come with you if I might," Robert said. "Junior's okay by the fire and John wants to take some pictures."

"Photography is my hobby. I enjoy it more than I do hunting with a gun," John stated plainly.

"And a hell of a lot less hassle," C.W. added. "I advise you not to go beyond that point by yourself," he said, indicating an outcropping by the shoreline. "The brush is pretty dense. You might get lost. Well, if you're ready Bob, let's get going."

They walked for about an hour. Suddenly C.W. stopped and looked around.

"This is where they'll be at. They sleep here." He pointed to several spots where the grass had been pressed down. Robert grew excited as he inspected the area. C.W. pointed to where the deer had been nibbling at the tops of some willow trees. He showed the city lawyer where a buck had stripped his antlers. He pointed to several scratch marks on a tree.

"Bear. Good size too."

"You mean there are bear here?" Robert asked.

"And fox," C.W. indicated, pointing toward the opposite side of the large meadow. Robert turned in time to see a red fox slink into the woods. Overhead a whiskey jack scolded them for invading the area. Off to their left Robert spotted a doe standing in high grass, watching them move around. He could hardly contain his excitement.

"Man, this is really nice."

"Look at this." C.W. pointed to a young poplar tree that had been nibbled on. "There must be a big guy around here somewhere."

"Can we find him?" Robert asked, an edge of excitement quickly building in him.

"We sure as hell can and will tomorrow," C.W. assured him.

"Damn, this is nice country. You don't know how lucky you are to live here."

"Oh yes, sir. Yes I do," C.W. answered him. "I've traveled quite a lot in the States when I was younger. I've seen my share of cities. Been to Boston, Cleveland, Chicago, St. Louis—all the way to Los Angeles. Later in life I went with sport shows too. I'm where I want to be, believe me."

The next morning's weather was as C.W. had predicted: damp and no wind. He had them all up and fed well before daybreak. In spite of Junior's steady string of protests everyone seemed to be excited. C.W. took a few minutes to tell them the day's game plan and then they set out for the hunting area.

"If you get a shot off and it's a good hit, fire two shots into the ground. That'll be the signal," C.W. told them. Then, directing his words to Junior, he continued, "You go up on that ridge." He pointed at the boy and added, "He'll go with you."

The drive began. Junior didn't say much as they huddled against a rock cut. The Indian boy said even less. His dark brown eyes scanned the area for signs of movement. He felt Junior watching him. He turned to face him.

"Cold?" the Indian asked.

"Not really," Junior replied. He looked closely at the Indian boy. "I don't like doing this. I'm not the outdoors type. My old man's been planning this trip for six months. I told him I didn't want to come, but he never heard what I was saying. Your dad ever do that to you?"

"I haven't got a dad," the Indian boy answered.

"That may be a blessing. So what's the old man—your grandfather or something?"

"My mother's husband."

"So he's your stepdad?" Junior asked.

"I guess so. No one ever said that. What's it like to live in a city?"

"I live in the suburbs. I don't know what it's like in the city. A lot of poor people. There's gangs and a lot of crime," Junior explained.

The Indian boy leaned back against the rock he was using as a shelter. He studied the white boy. He had on the best of everything. A goose-down jacket made by McGregor, Northland boots, and a beautiful 30/30 Marlin rifle. Junior saw that the Indian boy was looking him over. He shifted his weight.

"You ever get anything with that? It's a real beauty."

Junior shook his head.

"I wish I had one like that," the Indian boy said.

"My dad picked it out for me."

"A good pick too. It's a deer-hunting rifle all right. One, it's got the power to do the job. It's light and that short barrel makes it easy to tote, especially through thick brush like this."

"Jesus Christ, my dad said the same thing. You guys are all alike. You sound like echoes," Junior said.

The Indian boy hesitated, then said, "But it's a good gun." He felt a little embarrassed Junior thought he sounded like his father.

"I guess it is a nice gun, as far as rifles go anyway," Junior answered.

They both turned their attention back to the hunt. They scanned the area looking for movement. Junior saw it first. Like magic, a big buck deer materialized out of nowhere. It looked gigantic at twenty yards away. He let his eyes follow Junior's. The buck nibbled nervously at a branch, totally unaware of the two boys. The young Indian nudged Junior. He reacted by raising the rifle and sighting it.

"It's perfect. You can't miss."

Junior took his eyes from the sight, smiled at the Indian boy, and winked. He didn't move his head, just shifted his eyes. He took aim and waited. The young Indian noticed the beads of sweat on Junior's forehead. The buck was in position for a perfect, clean shot. Such luck, the Indian boy thought. He reached over and tapped the white boy to indicate that it was time to shoot. Still Junior didn't shoot.

"Shoot!" the young Indian whispered.

"I can't do it. I can't kill anything."

"Give me that!" the Indian boy demanded. Junior didn't resist. His face was white as chalk. His hands shook. He looked like he was about to be sick, like he was going to vomit all over the place. The Indian raised the rifle. It felt good in his hands. He could feel the power. He took aim, then squeezed the trigger. Boom!

The buck trembled. It threw back its head as though it were talking to the heavens. It danced to the left. The boys watched transfixed as the buck took three steps back to the right. They watched the deer's muscles tighten. Attempting to bound away, its front legs buckled. The boys watched the deer fall forward to the ground. They both witnessed the frantic look in its eyes as it fell. Breathing heavily, the deer lay on his side, its legs thrashing wildly. Blood was spurting from the bullet hole. The first few spurts were strong, pumped by the heart of the deer. Slowly they grew weaker and weaker. The Indian boy approached the animal slowly and carefully, ready to shoot again. He sensed Junior's presence behind him. He took aim at the writhing animal.

"Don't kill it. Don't kill it. Let it go," Junior pleaded, his voice thick with fear.

"It has to be killed now. Look how it's suffering." He turned and handed Junior his rifle. "You do it. It's your rifle."

"I can't!" Junior whispered, panic choking his words and dancing in his eyes. He took the rifle and handled it gingerly, like he was afraid of it. "I don't want to. I—I can't stand this kind—"

Suddenly the silence was shattered again. A crashing sound erupted to their left. Another larger buck deer bounded into the clearing. The wounded deer raised its head with immense effort. A sound, almost like a whistle, came from its throat. Junior instinctively raised the rifle, but a second later he dropped it and took two steps back. The Indian boy cursed silently. He scooped up the Marlin 30/30, shot from his hip, and swung around to try for the second buck. The white of its tail was all he saw. Silence returned to the bush. Junior clung to a tree, vomited, then looked up shamefaced at the Indian boy.

"I hate this," he said. "I wanna go home."

"Junior! What's happening? Are you all right?" It was Robert's voice piercing the air. The sound of his voice snapped Junior back to reality.

"Oh shit! What am I going to do now?" he whispered loudly to the boy.

"We're gonna dress out your deer. That's what."

"I didn't kill it."

"If you really wanna go home you'd best let your dad think you did," he advised Junior. "Otherwise we'll all be out here until you do." He paused to let his words sink in.

"You'd do that for me?"

The Indian boy's only response was to nod.

Junior's father's voice could be heard knifing its way through the dense underbrush.

"Junior? Did you get one or what? Answer me, boy."

"He sure did. It's a beauty too," the Indian boy hollered, then handed the gun to Junior. "I won't say anything unless you do." Junior looked at the Indian boy with a smile on his face.

"I don't know. Well, we'll see, okay? I don't know if I can face my dad and lie to him like that, but I don't want to disappoint him either. You know?"

C.W. and Junior's father strode across the field of high grass. A few seconds later his friend John crossed the field as well.

"John, look at this. My boy got this one! Come here Junior. John, get a picture of this."

"No, Dad, I don't want my picture taken with it," Junior protested.

"Why not, son? This is a great moment."

"A great moment? This thing was alive and beautiful and free, and now it's dead," Junior said.

Robert turned to his friend. A look of disappointment and frustration was evident on his face.

"What's wrong with him?" he asked John. John only shook his head and replaced the cap on his camera lens. "I don't know Robert. I really don't know."

"Dad, I want to get back to camp. I need to think," Junior told his father. The lawyer said nothing as he went over to the deer. C.W. looked at the Indian boy and with a slight motion of his lip, indicated that he should go with Junior. The boy nodded and followed the other boy. A few hours later a jubilant Robert got his deer. A one-shot kill. John decided not to do any shooting. He returned to camp and spent the afternoon wandering about with his camera at the ready. That evening in camp they celebrated. Robert noticed how melancholy his son was.

"What's wrong boy?" Robert asked his son. "You should be celebrating. You made your first kill today. You've entered a different realm. How many of your buddies at the Academy can say that much?"

"Not many of them. Dad? Can we talk?"

Robert nodded to his son.

"Dad, this hunting stuff isn't for me. I don't get any pleasure from this killing stuff. If that's what it takes to be a man, then I'll pass."

Father and son looked at each other for a long time. John excused himself, got up, and went to their tent to relax. C.W. and the boy walked to the shore of the lake to check on the boat. Junior continued.

"I didn't want to let you down. I know I've been a real pain on this trip, but I really didn't want to come up here in the first place. It would be different if we needed the meat to survive on. If Mom and my sisters were hungry, I'd do it, but we're just playing a game here, that's all. I don't need that, Dad. It just makes me sick. I hope I don't disappoint you too much. I mean, I want you to be proud of me. I want to make you happy. You're my dad and a good one, but I don't like to kill things."

Robert didn't say anything. He leaned forward and warmed his hands by the fire. Junior continued to talk. Finally Robert reached over and pulled his son to him. He hugged the surprised but relieved boy for a long time and then he started to laugh. His laughter could be heard all over the campsite.

"Junior, you know I love you, and hell yes, you made me proud. You made me proud by being man enough to tell me the truth and by doing so, you opened my eyes to some very basic facts. I do this year after year, but to be perfectly honest, I don't enjoy the killing either. Not as much as I enjoy the hunt. What I really enjoy is getting out here in the bush. Communing with nature. I need that," Robert said.

"Well, Dad, why don't we just ride around and admire the view? Let John take some photos. Now that would be fun for me."

"All right. Let's do it!"

That night Junior and his father sat up late into the night. The next morning they were up at dawn and heading back to the cabin and home. As Junior and the Indian boy loaded the last backpack into the station wagon they turned to each other and smiled.

"I really want you to know I appreciate what you did. What can I say?"

"Don't need to say nothing," the Indian boy answered.

"You don't understand. I feel like I owe you something. I want to do something in return. You know what I mean? I could send you something from the city. Is there anything you need?"

"How about sending me some books? It's gonna be a long winter. A couple of comic books too. Now that would be cool."

"You got it. It's a deal," Junior said as he offered his hand. "I'll never forget what you did for me and my dad."

"Hey, it's no big deal."

"I told him the truth," Junior added.

"That's cool."

"Yeah it is. I couldn't live with a lie like that."

"Was he mad?" the Indian boy asked.

"Not even," Junior said with a happy grin.

C.W. and the boy watched the car pull away.

"Like I said, you can never tell about this business, son," C.W. told him. "Robert gave me a hundred-dollar tip." C.W. reached into his pocket and pulled out the roll of bills. He peeled off a ten-dollar bill and handed to the boy.

"You said he gave you a hundred dollars," the boy said as he looked at the money.

"It's your ten percent. Didn't I tell you? You provided the ten percent skill by what you did with the boy and I, on the other hand, provided—"

"Yeah, yeah! I get it. You provided the ninety percent bullshit and still are."

The two laughed. The old man punched the boy play-fully on the arm. The boy bobbed and weaved and pre-tended to throw a left hook. C.W. turned around. He reached into the pile of gear and pulled out the Marlin 30/30 rifle. He handed it slowly to the boy.

"It's yours son. Use it well. Like I said, it's ninety percent bullshit and ten percent skill, but it's a good business, son, with good people involved in it. A guy could do a lot worse. Remember that."

The Indian smiled as he stroked the fine wood stock of his new rifle. He didn't say anything at first. C.W. sat on the boat and lit his pipe.

"You know what? It may be true that this tourist business is ninety percent bullshit like you say but I think it's one hundred percent good. Especially right now." He hesitated a moment, looked out across the lake, then shuffled his feet nervously before continuing. "Is it okay if I call you 'dad'?"

C.W. looked at the boy, puffed on his pipe a couple of times, and grinned.

"I call you 'son.' Hell yeah, it's okay." The shaggy black mutt came running down to the landing site. The boy showed him the gun, and the dog wagged its tail, happy at their return.